The Boy Next Door

Emma Ollin

© Copyright 2022
Emma Ollin

IBSN: 978-1-5136-9908-0

The right of Emma Ollin to be identified as the author of this work has been asserted by her in accordance with the Copyright, Designs and Patents Act 1988.

All Rights Reserved

No reproduction, copy or transmission of this publication may be made without written permission. No paragraph of this publication may be reproduced, copied or transmitted save with written permission or in accordance with the provisions of the Copyright Act 1956 (as amended).

This is a work of fiction. Names, characters, businesses, organizations, places, events, and incidents either are the product of the author's imagination or are used fictitiously. Any resemblance to actual persons, living or dead, occurrences, or locales is entirely coincidental.

Content/Trigger warning: This book mentions self-harm and depression in minor detail and coming-of-age experiences.

For my children – Social media and technology may have wiped the fun and adventure from society, but by writing this story and sharing it with you, I hope to keep the noughties generation alive.

Being considered one of the best decades to grow up in, I only wish you had a childhood like mine.

How an earth we were allowed to roam the street until the street lights came on without phones, I don't know.

Also, to those I got to share my teenage years with, they were unforgettable because of you. You helped build my characters and brought them to life.

Especially the boy next door.

DISK ONE

1. Boulevard of Broken Dreams – Green Day
2. Nobody's Home – Avril Lavigne
3. In the Shadows – The Rasmus
4. You Don't Know My Name – Alicia Keys
5. Jennifer Paige – Crush
6. Breakaway - Kelly Clarkson
7. I Don't Want to Be - Gavin DeGraw
8. Thing's I'll Never Say – Avril Lavigne
9. Get the Party Started – Pink
10. Let Me Be Myself – 3 Doors Down
11. Beautiful – Christina Aguilera
12. Tears and Rain – James Blunt
13. Mad World – Gary Jules
14. Complicated – Avril Lavigne
15. You Said No – Busted
16. Pieces Of Me – Ashlee Simpson
17. Wherever You Will Go – The Calling
18. Everywhere To Me – Michelle Branch

The Boy Next Door

JUNE 2004

From: Sophie
To: Ashley

Name? Ashley Prince
Age? 16
Birthday? June 22nd
Hair colour? Brown
Eye colour? Brown
Best friend? Lauren
Boyfriend? No
Crush? Max
Celebrity crush? Justin Timberlake
Favourite movie? Mean girls
Favourite subject? Science
Favourite song? Anything pop
Favourite artist or band? The pussy cat dolls
Favourite animal? Dolphin
Favourite colour? Pink
Favourite food? Pizza
Favourite tv show? Drake and Josh
Favourite sport? None
Favourite place? My bedroom
Tea or coffee? Tea
Bath or shower? Bath
Hot or cold? Hot
Summer or winter? Winter
Birthday or Christmas? Christmas
Pets? None
Siblings? Sister
Tattoos? No
Ever smoked? No
Ever drank? No
Ever done drugs? No

Ever been in hospital? No
Ever broken a bone? No
First kiss? No one
Had sex? As if
Last thing you ate? Cherry Bakewell
Last person you hugged? Lauren
Last person you kissed? No one
Last person you texted? Sophie
Last person you called? Lauren
Someone you miss? My friends
Something you love? Makeup
Something you hate? Spiders
Something you want? Unlimited phone credit
Biggest fear? The sea
Pet peeve? Slow walkers
Where do you want to be right now? At a party
What do you want to be when you're older? Famous
Five facts about you?
1. I have long hair
2. I love shopping
3. I love my friends
4. I love my life
5. I love school

Sent to: Lauren

CHAPTER ONE

The furry green ball fell back to my hands as gravity pulled it towards me; as I caught it, I securely gripped it before throwing it back up.

I had been lying on my bed doing this for the past hour since arguing with my mum. God, she did grind on me at the best of times. And it had quickly and unexpectedly become the norm. Everyday.

Since my sixteenth birthday was on a lame Thursday, consisting of my last two GCSE exams and a take-out with the parents, I wanted to go out with my friends. But no, she had other ideas of me babysitting my irritating little sister so she and Dad could go and enjoy their Friday night down the pub.

After two weeks of constant revision and back-to-back tests, having to sit in my most hated place on earth, I should be the one letting loose. But no.

What's worse, instead of starting summer early, Mum signed me up for A-level taster classes for the next few weeks. Yeah, that's right, I had no say in the matter.

Sixteen and treated like a six-year-old.

And by my annoyance, you can tell this overbearing, you-can't-have-a-life parental lifestyle choice is a reoccurring, pain-in-the-ass routine.

I didn't know why I expected anything different, even if it was my birthday weekend. It was as if I was being punished for something, being a teenager perhaps. And because of it, I was as lame as a teenager could be.

All my friends stayed out until the street lamps came on. Not me; I'm watching them turn on from my bedroom window. Jealous of the piled bikes on the front lawns.

Katie and Hannah had gone to the cinema and sneaked into the new R-rated film. With their push-up bras, slim figures, and pretty faces, which was something I had not yet been blessed with. I wouldn't have passed for eighteen anyway; I was the opposite.

Puppy fat still hung on my belly and hips, and I was baby-faced compared to the others. Even with maturing earlier than all the other girls, I still hadn't had a boyfriend nor experienced my first kiss.

No boy had ever given me a second glance.

I was a walking teenage body full of innocence, a complete plain Jane waiting for, well, I didn't know what I was waiting for. Anything had to be better than my boring life so far.

My phone pinged. I picked up my Nokia 1100 and read another text message from Sophie. The plans had changed. Instead of going to hers, a group of our friends were heading to a popular boy's house. They were pitching tents in his garden and getting his older brother to buy them alcohol while their parents were away. It was the first time I had received an invite to a house party. Mum wouldn't let me out to Sophie's, let alone a boy's house. I had to admit defeat and miss out on another fun weekend. But I wasn't going to accept it without a fight.

With my parent's strict rules and busy weekends destroying any chance of my social life blooming, Mum couldn't blame me for my frustration and adolescent hormone-filled outbursts.

I cn't come. I ave to babysit my stpd sis agen, soz. I texted Sophie in the most slang form to avoid wasting my credit. Another thing Mum had control of. No weekend job for me meant limited pocket money. I had to make my credit last me as long as possible, but I guess babysitting had some benefits; I'd have more credit tomorrow.

Agen? Ur rents r so lame. Ur nva out @ the wkd. Tht boy u like is going 2. she texted me back.

"Argh. Mum!" I screeched, throwing the ball across the room as I stood and stormed across the hall into hers. "Everyone is going out. All my friends are going to a party and camping in a garden. Please let me go. Call a babysitter."

Mum looked into the mirror back at me and continued putting on her mascara, giving me an irritated sigh. "We have already had this discussion, young lady. You are staying home tonight with your sister," she muttered. "Plus, there is *no* way your dad would let you sleep in someone's garden with god knows who. Especially with no parents around. You're only sixteen."

I shook my head. "Exactly, I'm sixteen, and it was my birthday yesterday. Why can't you loosen the reigns for one weekend so I can celebrate it like a normal teenager?" I growled, stamping my foot.

Mum stopped, slammed down her mascara and looked at me, "It's a no, Ashley."

"Argh, I hate you; all you do is ruin my life," I shouted, punching the air beside me before leaving the room.

"You'll thank me one day," I heard her shout as I slammed my bedroom door.

Muttering to myself, I angrily took my Pink disc case and shoved the CD into my stereo, turning it so loud that it hurt my ears.

Slumped into the chair at my desk, I roughly turned each Smash Hit magazine page. It took around five seconds for me to slam the magazine shut. The skinny, pretty images of Britney and Christina didn't help my mood, not that they ever did.

In hindsight, I hated the magazines and only subscribed because of Lauren and Sophie. They were the ones who liked celebrity fashion and gossip, but I didn't mind the freebies. I got a Yorkie bar with the last one, you know, the ones that aren't for girls. I ate it anyway, and it's no doubt why I'll never be as skinny as those printed on the pages.

My phone didn't stop pinging for fifteen minutes, continuous texts asking if Mum had changed her mind. In the end, I turned my phone off to stop the torture and the niggling in my thumb from having to press the buttons so many times to form a simple word. Not that it helped; I knew the photos uploaded on Myspace later would send me into more of a huff. By nine-thirty a.m., after hearing the kiss and tell stories, jealousy would consume me; it always did.

God, I hated having strict parents; if they had anything to do with it, I'd be in my twenties by the time I experienced my first kiss.

CHAPTER TWO

"Oh my god, it was great, wasn't it, Lauren? You missed so much, Ash," Sophie said with a laugh as the three of us walked down the school hallway. Busy, yet no one appeared to be in the way.

"I know, you keep telling me," I mumbled, rolling my eyes. Despite my efforts to change the subject, Sophie kept bringing it up.

"I can't believe you kissed Max," Sophie said again.

It was only yesterday that I told Lauren I had a crush on him, but clearly, that didn't matter. What could I do? Nothing, absolutely nothing.

It wasn't even lunchtime, and like a CD on repeat, I had heard how Luke got with Sophie, Max kissed Lauren, and Tasha gave Theo a blow job. I was so envious of their weekend.

I had spent mine watching the parent trap with my little auburn-haired sister and playing games on Neopets. And Saturday consisted of being dragged around the shops by Mum and visiting the grandparents on Sunday.

When I heard the camping continued all weekend, I was livid. Green with envy. I lost count of how many photos I looked at, wishing I was there and that it was me who was asleep under a pile of jackets.

Sat around a bonfire, eating marshmallows, and drinking Smirnoff ice is where I dreamt of being. I wasn't asking for a lot, and it was pitiful thinking about it, but it would have made my weekend. I had never even tried alcohol or been to a real party.

The games of truth and dare and spin the bottle were what the weekends were for. So I was told anyway. Not only did they sound fun, but as a teenager born in the noughties, alcopops, flares, glitter, cheesy music, and boys were life. And I was the only one not doing any of it.

I couldn't imagine talking to a boy for longer than ten minutes, let alone sleeping next to one.

It's not that I was shy. I was invisible and had parents who made my social life a living hell. They had made me the dull Ashley no one expected to show up without even doing anything remotely embarrassing. After years of repeated "My parents said no," I'm surprised that they still bothered to invite me. But being best friends with Lauren was the only reason why. And despite being in with the popular crowd, I had always been the outcast. Different.

Lauren was pretty, blue-eyed, blonde, slim, and bright. Every girl wanted to be her, and the boys all wanted to date her.

You might think, why are you complaining if she's your best friend? But our mums being friends and the two of us being together through school since we were five was the only reason I had front-row tickets to Lauren's life.

She never *picked* me. And seeing our differences, I knew I didn't belong with Lauren. But there I was, receiving her morning texts and a part of the gossip. Not that it came without significant effort.

I did everything to fit alongside Lauren and listened to her every critique. I wore shorter skirts, put more makeup on, and dressed in lower-cut tops. I didn't even like that girly fashion and sparkly glitter, and it also didn't like me; I just spent every day of my life doing what Lauren told me to.

Why?

I wanted the boys to say hi to me and to fit in with the crowd. I wanted to be like everybody else, and listening to Lauren was the only way.

Regardless, missing out on every get-together and opportunity to gain teenage experiences took its toll. All I ever was, was the lemon, the third wheel, the one who tagged along.

*

After a morning of lame science and interrupted maths, I earned myself lunchtime detention for laughing at Ben mocking the teacher. I didn't even think I could get detention during the fresher weeks. But it went without saying that school had always been against me, and I was starting to think it always would be. I only had two more years to endure.

I may not have been popular with the boys *that* way, but a few had become accustomed to my company—the troublemakers. Lauren and everybody else often looked down on them, which stupidly even made me jealous, seeing as they were noticed.

"Ash, are you busy after school?" Joe said, leaning back onto the back two legs of his chair, tilting it on my desk. I lifted my head and looked at him, then behind me and back, making sure I heard him correctly.

Tapping my pen on the paper I had been doodling on for the past half hour, I found my words and said, "Erm, no."

"Good. Can I meet you outside the front gates?" Oh my god, the day a boy asked me to hang out had finally come. And so unexpectedly too. Was it because I was now sixteen? Was that the ticket to high school stardom?

Joe's scruffy hair, round face, dark blue eyes, and small frame may not have been as charming as Max or Lewis's, but he was a boy, a popular boy. Being seen with him was what I needed to get on the map.

My lungs pulled in tight as I nodded a nervous yes, and he smiled at me and then turned back around. I watched his chair fall back to the ground, unable to wipe the massive grin from my face. His rasping voice asking a straightforward question lifted my spirits and made the clock move faster, and I couldn't wait to tell Lauren.

*

As the bell rang at three fifteen, I couldn't find my feet quick enough. I piled my stuff into my bag and ran through the school to find her.

"Joe, one of the smokers? I didn't know he liked you," Lauren muttered, hooking her arm through mine as we neared the gates.

I blushed. "We only see each other in detention, but me neither." She shrugged her shoulders with a small smile.

My belly cartwheeled at the thought of him standing outside the school waiting for me. Would he have any friends with him? Was I going to be part of a social gathering out of school hours? Eeeek, I was so excited.

There he was, stamping out a cigarette against the rough bricks. I approached, clinging to Lauren for dear life, trying to keep my cool. My empty hand gripped my bag strap that fell across my chest after I brushed my long chestnut locks behind my pierced ears, hoping I looked all right. I prayed that my eyeliner hadn't rubbed into the corner of my eyes, forming that strange goo and took a deep breath, giving him a little wave. He gave me a nod and walked casually towards us.

"There you are," Joe said, looking at me, then at Lauren. I smiled, my cheeks already glowing.

"Lauren, I wondered if you wanted to hang out in the park for a bit?" The warmth in my face slithered all over my body. No longer nervous but embarrassed. Joe's words pierced my baby skin, burrowed through my chest, and punctured my heart. Erm, what, was what I wanted to shout out loud.

"Err, aren't you going with Ashley?" she tried.

I fought every urge not to seem bothered about how humiliated I was, him having used me to get to her and not having figured it out. He didn't have any classes with her, and she no doubt would have shunned him if he approached her in her usual crowd of sports lads.

"No," he snickered, and my god, it hurt. "I knew you walked home together, that's all." He nodded a minor I'm sorry at me and then acted as if I wasn't there.

"Sorry, Joe, no. I'm walking with Ashley," Lauren started as she looked down at me hesitantly, shuffling her feet into the gravel.

"It's fine, Lauren. You go," I muttered, trying to soften the blow. "I was going into town anyway."

"Are you sure?" Lauren half-heartedly said, twiddling with my straightened hair as the three of us stood in now awkward silence.

"Positive."

"Okay," Lauren nodded. "I'll come with you," she said to Joe, grinning.

I walked down the steep hill from the secondary school with them until we reached the crossing, where they crossed without me towards the park. "See you tomorrow," Lauren said. I reluctantly waved.

My stomach knotted as I watched them walk closely, laughing. Joe lit another cigarette, offered it to Lauren, and she took a drag. Her first by the cough leaving her lungs. I was jealous of another experience she could tick off her bucket list, and I hated the envy I constantly carried.

By the time I reached the bottom of the hill, I wasn't in the mood to go to the shops anymore. I went straight home, walking through the town's busy centre.

A district on the border of two cities and several small villages in the far southeast of England is where I have lived my entire life. It was okay, though it quickly became a vast town filled with snobbery. There was a decent choice of schools, sports facilities, and hordes of shops. As well as an extensive list of supermarkets, country parks and places to eat, I could see why it was upcoming. There was a direct London commute, where I planned to escape this place and live with the thousands of people who resided there. People who didn't know me, a place I could have a fresh start. But first, I had to get sixth form out of the way. That was another matter I kept hiding from.

I thought I would know what I would have wanted to do with my life by sixteen, but I didn't. The idea of another two years within the school's high walls was enough to put me off thinking about it. Bailey High was hell in my eyes.

Once I reached the main stretch home, my feet dragged despite my fast pace, stuck behind dawdling groups and couples of others my age. I was in a solemn mood with no one to talk to, and their slow steps wound me up further. Tears pinched my eyes, but I kept them in, making me sniffle.

Why couldn't I be like everyone else?

All I wanted was to be popular.

I didn't desire to be the most popular to the extent of queen bee Regina George, who all the girls resented, and the boys fancied. I wasn't beautiful, and I hated that my looks determined how high school panned out.

If it were down to me, I would have been skinnier and a little taller, with a bubblier personality making me more likeable, with better grades. But at the end of the day, it was high school and far from a fairy tale with fairy godmothers coming to the rescue. So all I could do was hope that I would miraculously turn from the ugly duckling into a swan during summer before A levels started.

All I wanted was to walk through the halls and have friends say hello to me, not just classmates but actual friends.

CHAPTER THREE

Throwing my bag on the stairs, I entered the kitchen and grabbed the sunny delight from the fridge.

"Hi sweets, how was your first fresher day?" Mum said as she walked into the kitchen. She huffed, grabbing the bottle from my hand. "What have I said about drinking from the bottle."

I wiped my mouth and retorted, "It was shit as always; thanks for asking." Blaming her for giving me an awful start to the day. If she had let me out at the weekend, I wouldn't have felt so sour, and that's all there was to it.

She stopped and scowled, "Ashley, watch your language." I said nothing.

Her big round stare scanned my pissed-off expression as I ruffled through my pocket and met the detention slip in my hand. Mum sighed, "Another one? What for this time? Only you could manage this when you're not actually *in* school." She snatched it from my grasp with a pen at the ready, having become used to the pink letter returning home with me.

"Laughing," I sneered before trailing myself towards the stairs.

Zoe excitedly rushed down the stairs and past me, still dressed in her bright blue chequered uniform. "Mum, Mum, can I go next door and see the new boy? He was in my class today," she squealed, skipping around the kitchen.

"Yes, sweetheart, I spoke to his mum earlier. Just knock on the door and be polite. I'll call you when it's dinner time."

"You must be joking," I let out with a frown.

"What?" Mum said, furrowing her brows.

Oh my f in god, I thought. I had never been around a boy's house. It wasn't only my peers, but my nine-year-old sister had more of a social life than me.

Shaking my head at them, I grabbed my bag and walked up the stairs muttering, "Forget it."

I entered my poster-filled room and went straight to the window, wondering who this new boy was. Observing the street, no one looked to be moving in, and I heard no cluttering. Then Zoe's annoying little voice came from my left, echoing right through me.

Opening the window, I pushed it wide, taking my feet from the floor and gripping the windowsill to look out into the garden that backed onto the side of my front garden. There she was, playing with some blond boy. I watched her for a minute, laughing, screeching and dancing around, wishing I could go back to being that young.

Zoe wasn't going to struggle with her school reputation unless Mum had anything to do with it. And by the looks of things, it was only me who was banned from having any kind of fun.

I leaned on my elbows, fiddling with my earrings, looking on until the patio door slid open. My eyes lifted, and my jaw dropped. My heart was suddenly in my mouth. I felt the pink pigments form in my cheeks and the heat in my chest rise as I gazed at a boy, the most compelling I had ever seen. His hair was dark blond, straight, and messy, with his fringe falling to the right. His skin was tanned, his smile contagious, and I was beaming at him like some foolish, love-sick schoolgirl.

He pushed his brother over jokingly and said hello to my sister as he picked up a football, wiping it on his shirt before dropping it to his foot. Zoe being near him had me dying a little inside, and I wanted to go straight round there to meet him, but I was all sorts of chicken.

I watched him perform an incredible number of kick-ups, not to mention his bronze, toned legs in his baggy football shorts. My eyes didn't leave his Man United kit; the red shade had me drawn to it, and so had he. I wanted to stay and watch, but I needed to tell Lauren, Sophie, Katie, or Hannah. Anyone.

Reaching over to my bag on my bed, I placed it on the windowsill, keeping my eyes on him. Quickly taking out my phone, it fumbled in my hand and knocked a photo frame out of the window.

"Shit," I gasped, peering at the mess and then back to his garden. The boy paused, looked up and scanned my window, making me quickly duck back into my bedroom.

My heart pounded hard in my chest, and my adrenaline ran high. Experiencing the quickest crush I had ever had on the boy next door, a boy I didn't even know. I laughed at how foolish I felt, at how ridiculous I was being.

After composing myself, I crawled away from the window and ran down the stairs, opening the front door to claim my broken photo.

"Holy crap," I said. My new neighbour was standing on the driveway with my possession in his hand.

Oh god, he was beyond gorgeous.

He was perfect.

He had little brown freckles dotting his cheeks and the bridge of his nose. His dark and alluring brown eyes were like a pool of melted chocolate. Nike trainers and a cap added to his charismatic style, and his floating aroma pinged my nostrils so intently I could taste him. Standing before me like a dream, he curiously smiled as I lost my tongue.

"Is this yours?" he asked in a smooth voice, looking at the photo and then at me. He licked his small thin lips as he gazed at me, melting my insides and taking my breath away as I stood flustered.

"Yes. Yes, it is," I stuttered, blushing with an embarrassed laugh, struggling to combine my words. "It fell out of the window."

He passed me the wooden frame with the photo of my dad and me. "Here you go. Do you want me to clear the glass?"

"Thanks," I said, taking it shyly. "No, it's fine; I'll do it."

Nodding, he stepped back. "I'm Olly. I just moved in next door."

"Ashley," I gulped. "My sister is over there. She has made friends with your brother." I tucked my hair behind my ear, realising that this was, by far, the longest conversation I had ever had with a boy, and for once, it was going well.

"Cool, I start school tomorrow. Do you go to Bailey High? My mum has insisted I go to keep me busy over the next few weeks, though it's pointless if you ask me," Olly said, surprising me. He looked older and seemed much more mature than the boys I knew.

"Yeah, I do," I said, looking down at my embroidered polo clinging to my body. "And you're right; it is pointless."

"Well, I'll see you tomorrow then." He smiled, and my heart skipped a beat. Emotions of happiness flew right through me, igniting me in ways I didn't know were possible.

With no words, I just nodded, taking my lower lip between my teeth as he walked to the edge of the driveway. Olly waved before disappearing around the corner. I was stunned and shell-shocked for a long second before my chest relaxed.

It wasn't until I heard his voice again over the fence that I noticed I was still standing on my driveway as if stuck to the tarmac. I shook my thoughts aside with a giggle, went into the garage, grabbed a dush pan and brush, and cleared the glass before going back inside, running straight to my bedroom.

Laying on my double bed, I clung to the photo frame in one hand with my phone in the other. I looked at the screen, about to text Lauren, but then didn't.

I decided not to tell anyone about my new neighbour: a delicious-smelling, gorgeous, sporty boy who, no doubt, by nine a.m., would have forgotten all about me.

CHAPTER FOUR

Since meeting Olly, I couldn't sleep. I couldn't have even if I wanted to. He had my body feeling like jelly and my insides a complete frothing mess. My brain wouldn't switch off and kept replaying our conversation. My ears were ringing with his deep yet tender tone, and all I saw when I closed my eyes was him and his cute smile. I wanted to see him again. And living next door, I knew I *would* see him again. I was just so nervous about how different it would be within those school walls. The walls where once I stepped past them, my invisibility cloak appeared.

Would he treat me like everyone else?

I woke up late and was rushing around like a lunatic. Usually, the mirror would see me at least twenty times before leaving the house. Phone calls back and forth with Lauren and Sophie would have been held, telling me what to wear. At Bailey, your day depended on how good you looked and how popular you were, and since I had no time to do my hair and couldn't find my skirt, I was already doomed.

I couldn't say the same for Olly. Good-looking and sporty, he would undoubtedly be one of the popular boys by lunchtime. In five minutes, he had me hooked, and Lauren and every other girl would be the same.

He was eye candy and would be raking in prom king votes by the end of the day.

I couldn't forget how I felt when his big brown doe eyes locked mine and how his freckles made me want to connect them, to find out what beautiful art they created. Art above art, well, he would be a masterpiece; he already was.

With how he was already sketched in my mind, after a five-minute conversation, I rang stalker alert. I barely knew him but could tell you he smelt how your skin smelled after too long in the sun, combined with fresh laundry powder and a hint of vanilla. He was already my new favourite scent. Imagine how I could describe him if I really got to know him. I could only dream of getting the chance to gain knowledge of the finer details.

I quickly threw my uniform on and ran down the stairs, raking my fingers through my hair, "See you later," I hollered as I opened the door.

"What about your breakfast?" Mum replied from the kitchen.

"I'm not hungry, and I'm going to be late." I had no appetite for the first time in forever, and it wasn't hard to see why with the butterflies swirling in my stomach.

I briskly walked to school, contemplating whether to mention Olly to Lauren and Sophie, changing my mind back and forth with every step. I'd never met a boy they didn't know before, and I wasn't sure how to deal with it. It shouldn't have mattered. It's not like I took a claim on him for meeting him first. That's just how messed up teenage crushes were, and the more I thought about it, the more stupid it made me feel.

I hated that my entire life revolved around boys. Why did it? What had I turned into?

Whatever it was, I hated it. It didn't feel like me. But then, the more I thought about that, I didn't know what being me felt like. Was I being me or playing the role of somebody else? After all this time, was I not being Ashley? Who the hell is Ashley Prince without Lauren and Sophie? What a scary thought. What a horrible idea.

"Ashley," I heard behind me. I turned, and Olly was there, slowly walking toward me. He looked stunning with his gorgeous face hidden under a black cap.

He swept me off my feet, and I nearly fell over and choked on my breath simultaneously. I didn't know what to do next, was I supposed to stop and wait for him, or was he just saying hello? I didn't want to seem rude, so I tinkered with my jacket, took my phone from my pocket, looked busy, and then put it back, frozen to the ground until he caught up with me.

When Olly reached me, he gave a flattering smile, and it had me swooning. Even the way he held onto his backpack strap hanging over one shoulder was faultless. His smooth style and charm intimidated me a little, and it was nothing like I had ever known. He was different to the other boys, and I couldn't figure out why. But I did know how he looked in his uniform was even better than I imagined.

He was wearing his sweatshirt despite the warmth of summer, though the sleeves were pushed back to his elbows, showing me the chord bracelets clinging to his wrists. I wondered what they meant and where they were from. They were enough to take my attention from his toned legs in his black pocketed shorts. Just a little bit, anyway.

I found myself chewing my lip as my eyes took in every detail of him, and when my gaze met his radiant stare, a lump formed in my throat. I was lost for words and looked down at the ground shyly, focusing on his black shoes, which could nearly pass for trainers. If *I* wore them, a pink slip would be instant. I had been on the uniform radar for years and had more detentions than lunch times. I was kissing prom goodbye one more step out of line.

I guess the benefit of sixth form was casual wear, but I was already dreading wearing my own clothes. There wasn't one piece of clothing in my wardrobe I would want to wear to school.

"Can I walk with you?" Olly asked.

"Me? Erm, yeah, okay," I stuttered with a nervous smile.

I moved my feet back in front of the other and walked next to him, waiting for the dream to end, blinking rapidly to ensure I was awake. I tucked my hair behind my ears and played with everything in sight. I pulled at my clothes, my bag straps, and my fingernails. My cheeks flushed, and I didn't want him to see. I panicked and didn't know why; we were only walking to school.

"So, what's Bailey high like?"

For a minute, I thought about it, but there was only one way to explain it, and I went with that. "It's all right if you're popular."

"Are you popular then?" Olly asked, making me laugh out loud. It was evident by looking at me that I was not popular.

My jumper wrapped around my waist, my denim jacket covered my baggy polo shirt, and my black flared trousers hid my chunky black school shoes. My fashion choice didn't come close to the other girls who wore short skirts with their shirts tucked in with colourful bras in clear sight.

"Well, I have popular friends. Yes, maybe, actually, no, just no. I hate school," I mumbled as I became tongue-tied.

"If your friends are popular, then you must be?" His assumption couldn't have been further from the truth. I didn't want to elaborate, so I brushed it off.

"Trust me. You won't have a problem making friends."

"Why? I'm starting school with a few weeks left of the year; there is no point in me even going. It's summer soon." Olly sounded worried, and his wry smile caught me off guard; it stunned me a little. His words were honest and genuine, and I had never heard a boy of our age talk in such a manner. At school, the boys were immature and vulgar. Though he was right, I would have hated starting school so late too.

"Because, well, just because." I blushed. I wanted to tell him it was because he was breathtakingly stunning and sporty, and that's all he needed to be to fit in at Bailey. A stereotypical school with every clique under its umbrella.

"Okay. So if you hate school, tell me, what do you like?"

"Erm." Talking about myself was not the norm; nobody had really asked before, and it took more thought than it should have. "The usual, music, films, magazines," I rolled off. "I'm not that exciting." I shrugged, swallowing hard as Olly glanced at me with curious eyes.

"I don't believe that," he said, tightening his grip on his strap.

"Why?"

"I just don't." The way he looked at me with a Cheshire smile made me feel not quite normal. The interest in his eyes was something of a rarity in my life, and I didn't know whether to trust it.

"Well, what are you into then, Olly?" I asked, using emphasis on his name.

"Oh, the usual," he laughed, making me nervous as I rolled my eyes away with a coy grin. "Nah, I'm massively into sports, all of it, playing, watching, reading, you name it, I do it. I play football a lot and enjoy surfing, though since moving here, I doubt I'll be doing much of that anymore."

"Surfing? Wow. Did you live near a beach then?"

Olly nodded and held out his arm, touching the bands wrapping his wrist. "You see these. These are souvenirs from every surfing competition I have won or participated in. I grew up in Newquay and have spent nearly every day on a beach or in the sea since I can remember."

I didn't know what to say. Olly's life sounded like a dream I would undoubtedly have swapped mine for any day.

"Your childhood must have been amazing, growing up so free," I replied, ignoring how I wanted to ask if it was why he had such bronzed skin and sun-bleached hair. Not mentioning his gorgeous body was the safest bet, seeing how red hot my cheeks already were.

"Yeah, I can't complain." He beamed.

"Well, you will be now you have moved here. It's the furthest away from any beach. If I hate it, you certainly will. Why do such a thing?"

I watched Olly's Adam's apple tighten and then relax as if he was struggling for a reason. It had me reeling with wonder. "We have family up here; my parents fancied a change."

I can't say I was disappointed in the answer; it was a fair enough reason. But even family wouldn't have been a good enough reason for me. Waking up beside the ocean sounded ideal. Even with a fear of open water, I imagined it to be serene and calming, unlike here, where you're surrounded by scaffolding and upcoming housing estates everywhere you look.

"I bet it was hard leaving your life behind."

He glanced at me, and his stare glistened into mine like a starry night. With a smile, Olly said, "It was, but it wasn't. I have no doubt it was a bad decision."

My fists tightened as my nerves started flowing all over the place. I suddenly felt vulnerable. This was the most intense conversation I had ever had, and I didn't know if I was making up the connection I felt between us. Olly was so easy for me to talk to; it was like I already knew him, and I was fascinated by it.

"You can't say that after only one day," I replied. "I would hate my parents if they moved me away from the beach to here."

He clicked his tongue and tightened his lips. "We'll see, but the neighbourhood looks alright so far." He smirked. I bit the inside of my mouth, my hands went clammy, and I couldn't say anything else.

*

"I'll see you around then," Olly said as we walked through the front gate, and my heart sank. The last half-hour was the most pleasant walk since starting Bailey. I enjoyed the conversation and the company. Definitely the company.

During the brief moment when Olly asked me about myself, he made me feel important. He didn't make me feel invisible like everyone else. It was new, different, and I liked it. But with how I struggled to answer simple questions about myself, I kept steering the conversation back to him.

Besides surfing, I listened to him tell me about his passion for football, his brother, Nate, and how they travelled every summer in their camper van.

Olly was not only charmingly handsome, but his personality was refreshing. He was different and relaxed; if I could manage a full-blown conversation with him, that was saying something.

If walking into school with him lifted my spirits, knowing him for the past three years could have made my high school life entirely different. And with school ending soon, it made me sad that I had only just met him.

I watched him walk away and read the signs as we passed the gates. He looked anxious but at ease as he spoke to a group of lads nearby; I knew it wouldn't take him long, yet still, I hoped he would get on okay.

His life at Bailey had started, and when he disappeared out of sight, I already missed him. If my past was anything to go by, our school friendship was now over.

"There she is," Lauren shouted, hurtling towards me with Sophie. They gave me their usual exaggerated morning hug and toyed with my hair. "Where have you been? We haven't heard from you all morning, and what are you wearing? Where is your skirt?"

I looked at them both, pulled at my bag and grounded my feet so harshly into the floor that my sole hurt. "I woke up late."

"Oops, well, we can sort you out," Lauren said as I nodded warily. She pulled a hairbrush out of her shoulder bag and started raking it through my hair.

"Tell her," Sophie nudged Lauren, giggling.

"Tell me what?" I said, wincing as she made her way through the knots.

I knew Sophie and Lauren were closer to each other than I was with them. They were so much similar to each other. They gossiped daily about boys they had chatted to all night, and I didn't. But for once, I did, yet I didn't feel like giving them the pleasure of gossiping about the new boy. It's not that I wanted to keep him to myself; I had grown tired of their little secrets. And with the way Lauren stood there looking like she wasn't going to tell me anyway, the bell saved me from being the third wheel for a second longer. I brushed Lauren off me and said nothing.

They walked off together, arm in arm, chatting, and left me behind. I walked straight to an English taster class, sat in the corner window seat on my own, and buried my head in a book.

CHAPTER FIVE

"So tell me what it was like?" Ben said to Joe, sitting at the table in front of me.

"I'm not going to kiss and tell," he hinted with a nudge of the elbow.

Even after the humiliation, I had somehow forgotten all about Joe and Lauren leaving together. It now made sense to what Sophie was excited about earlier and why Lauren acted so apprehensive about telling me.

Leaning my head on my crossed arms on the table, I tried to ignore their conversation, though, through Joe's constant bragging, which took five seconds to crack, I heard every detail. So much for not kissing and telling. And by the time detention was up, I had concluded that Lauren was an easy hook-up. Their get-together was the first time she had spoken to Joe, and she was off kissing him already, but I guessed that was my jealousy talking.

"Right, you're free to go," Mrs Bond said, placing her book down and looking at the three of us. Ben and Joe fled as fast as they could. "Miss Prince, let's not see you again, please."

"Believe me, the feeling is mutual," I frowned as I stood.

"Then stop upsetting the staff. You are much brighter than this. These fresher classes are meant to be fun and helpful. I think you broke the record by getting detention during them." She shook her head at me as she packed her books away.

"I don't do anything, and what about Ben and Joe? They are always in here. I'm not the only one."

"Their attendance is none of your concern. Just promise I shall see you less during sixth form."

Anger was bubbling in my chest, my stomach was churning, and I suddenly wanted to shout at her. I had felt off all day, more so since yesterday. I was fed up with everyone's attitudes toward me, and it wasn't like being nice was getting me anywhere. Trying to be perfect was a waste of time. Out of nowhere, it felt more natural to lash out than to suck it up.

"Right, Miss, then perhaps if I stopped getting the blame for everything and everyone got off my back, I wouldn't be here."

Mrs Bond stopped in her tracks and widened her eyes as I stood tapping my foot with my arms crossed tightly, staring right at her. "Ashley, leave before you get yourself banned from prom."

"Miss, I didn't set them books on fire; the boy next to me did. He did a runner."

"Oh, what does it matter? I get the impression you would rather be in here than in the cafeteria anyway."

My shoulders dropped slightly. "What is that supposed to mean?"

She approached me and placed her hand on my arm. "Between you and me, those friends of yours, they do nothing for you. You could do much better. Perhaps find some new ones over the summer, people who will let you be you." She smiled and then walked towards the door.

My throat was tight, and I could no longer feel my feet. I wanted to follow, but I couldn't. I was frozen. Put in my place.

"Ashley, come on, it's time to go." She grabbed the handle and waited as tears pinched the back of my eyes.

I swallowed harshly, reclaimed my composure, and stepped towards the door. As I met Mrs Bond, I looked at her and said, "Is it that obvious?"

"To those who care, yes. There are many peers you have a lot more in common with. I could tell you where they spend lunchtime if you like?"

I shook my head, "No, Miss, it's fine; I can figure it out for myself."

"Have a nice evening, Ashley." I agreed and left.

Detention after school had me walking the empty streets towards home, giving me more time to myself. And after that conversation, I wasn't keen on my thoughts coming out to play.

How could she talk to me like that? Was that even allowed? I knew it was all true, but still, what the hell? Was it that obvious I didn't belong? It had only been the past few days since *I* had realised it, and she had kept it until now to bring up the matter.

Could I make new friends and start fresh after summer? Was that even possible? Sure it was, but if this morning's conversation with Olly taught me anything, I think I had to come to terms with being *my* friend first. I needed to find out who Ashley Prince was. It wasn't until I couldn't tell him what I liked rather than what Lauren and Sophie liked that I realised I had lost my identity. If I had ever had one, that was.

*

"Ashley, this is becoming too regular. Do you actually want to get into university? This on your report won't look great," Mum muttered.

Taking my slip, she signed it and handed it back, where I shoved it in my bag and said, "I didn't do anything wrong. Everyone at Bailey is a jerk, the kids and the teachers. When are you going to listen? I wish you would believe me."

"You must do something. I never hear of Lauren getting detention."

"Oh well, you wouldn't, would you? Lauren's perfect, isn't she," I retorted, rolling my eyes as I stormed out and went upstairs.

*

When mum called me for dinner, I had finished all the taster class's optional tasks and was just getting ready for football training. Yes, you heard me, football training.

To lose weight and look like the others, I chose to study P.E as a GCSE and joined the local girl football team. I wasn't wow fantastic, but I did okay and met some pretty cool girls.

But the way the kit made me look chunky and uncomfortable was enough to put me off wanting to eat anything or leave the house. The material clung to my jelly belly, and my thighs looked thick.

I stood looking in the mirror and lowered my shorts as far as possible, hanging them on my hips, trying to hide my thunder thighs. I fought with the girl staring back at me as she brought me no confidence no matter what I did. And when I eventually made it downstairs for dinner, I only took a few bites before climbing from the table.

"Mum... Ashley's throwing her dinner in the bin," Zoe shrieked in her high-pitched, annoying voice.

"Shut up, you little snitch," I snorted, glaring at her.

"I'm not hungry," I told Mum, placing the plate into the dishwasher.

Mum approached me, felt my forehead, and stroked my pigtails, "Ashley, you didn't have breakfast. I doubt you ate much for lunch, and now you're saying you're not hungry. This isn't like you. Is something the matter?"

"No, I'm fine. I'm just not hungry."

"Okay, if you say so. You will need your energy for training, though. Take a snack bar or something," she said as I went to my dad in the living room.

I turned off the television that no one was watching. "Dad, are you ready?"

It was either the gardening channel, MTV, or nickelodeon in our house. I could tell you what music video went with what song. I was that obsessed with music.

Dad looked up at me, away from his newspaper and got up. He wasn't a big talker; he worked all hours, came home, gardened or decorated, and would fall asleep watching TV. I loved him more than I could put into words. He was quiet but much easier to talk to about things that troubled me than Mum; she was too opinionated.

When we pulled up at training, I could see more teams than during my first session last week. The season must have fully started, and since the girls welcomed me with open arms, I wasn't as nervous. I enjoyed it more than I thought I would and was looking forward to getting into it. It got me out of the house, was exercise, and I believed Dad also liked having something non-girly to talk to me about.

"Have fun. Are you walking home, or do you want a lift?"

"I'll text you," I said with a smile, climbing out of the car.

*

"Well done, Ashley. Keep going," the coach shouted as I ran around a player and passed the ball to Sammy.

We had done a warm-up and drills by the time I was ready to give in, and when the coach said we were finishing with a game, I about died. I was working harder than I ever had during P.E lessons, and my clothes were sticking to me more than they originally were. I was exhausted, but in a way, I was more relaxed and couldn't wait to go to bed.

My stomach panged. Visions of my favourite treat appeared in my mind, the biscuits and cherry bake wells, which I enjoyed too many of most evenings alongside a hot chocolate before bed. I felt like a greedy pig as I saw the shiny cherry glistening upon the white icing in my vision. I discreetly rubbed my stomach, feeling the disgusting rolls I was hiding. It was enough to tell me things needed to change. I didn't want to feel like this anymore and desperately wanted it to stop.

Shaking the image away from my mind, I shouted "no" at myself and used my growing frustration as my last bit of energy. I ran as fast as my aching body could as Alex passed the ball across the pitch to me. I stopped it, glanced up and took a shot. The ball soared through the air and bypassed the goalkeeper.

"Oh my god!" I shouted as my teammates ran at me, cheering. I had scored the winning goal, my first-ever goal, and I couldn't believe it. I was ecstatic, jumping up and down with my new friends.

"Well done, Ashley," I heard roaring from the crowd, making me stop and glance across at the group of spectators.

The boy's team had already finished and was watching our game. At the front was my handsome next-door neighbour yelling my name. His mere presence knocked me back, and my every emotion spiralled, slapping me in the face. I was suddenly out of sorts, losing concentration, and my foot slid a little. Instinctively I gripped Alex beside me and prepared myself to hit the floor, but she grabbed me just in time, "Woah, Ashley, are you okay?"

"Yeah," I laughed, "Thanks."

I firmly regripped my studded boots into the mud beneath me and looked back to Olly, but he had already gone. How embarrassing, although it could have been worse, I told myself.

Standing with my team catching my breath, I removed my shin pads. My legs were killing me, needing to get used to them.

"Ashley, we're having a sleepover at the weekend. Do you fancy coming?" Alex asked, smiling at me and then at the others. A giant grin sketched over my scarlet, sweaty face, and I nodded as I took a swig of water.

"I would love to, but I'll have to ask my mum."

"Cool, let me know next week then," Alex said, "See you soon."

I waved goodbye to them and walked towards my bag on the edge of the pitch. Picking up my bag, I took out my phone, about to call Dad for a lift home.

"Ashley," I heard, turning to find Olly walking toward me. He didn't look half as sweaty as me, and it mortified me that he was seeing me in such a state. If I knew he would be here, I wouldn't have come.

"You're better at football than I expected."

"Because I'm fat?" I involuntarily blurted out. I didn't even process the words.

Olly closed his eyes, his expression changed, and silence suddenly stood between us. I felt uncomfortable, wishing I could reclaim my thoughts about myself, but it was too late. I had ruined whatever opinion he had of me by saying something horrid and stupid.

I was twiddling my fingers and scraping my toe across the gravel path, unsure of what to say next as his intense eyes looked into mine. It was time to leave, and as I went to say something, he exhaled profoundly, raised his hand to my cheek and brushed my messy hair aside from my face. I was shocked, and it made me retreat a little.

"Don't ever say that again; you're not fat," he said, glaring down at me, startling me a little with his tone, but I managed a smile at the first pleasant thing a boy had ever said. He was not only stunning but the friendliest boy I knew. Olly nodded to the exit of the pitch. "Come on. I'll walk home with you." I agreed in silence, mute from disbelief and walked next to him, quickly texting my dad on the way.

It was getting dark, and the roads were quiet, and considering I was with a boy I barely knew, I was at ease. It was as if I'd known him all my life, and I had never felt safer.

"How come you're here?" I asked.

"Lewis, at school, told me to come along for a trial session for a kickabout. I wasn't going to pass it up, seeing as I have no other means of playing proper football yet."

"Cool. So you made friends with the most popular boy in school on your first day?"

"What is it with you and popularity?" Olly retorted, and I looked at him, picking at the label on my bottle.

"Nothing," I said, shaking my head. I let out a deep breath and looked out into the darkness. "It's nothing."

"Well, just so you know, being popular isn't important to me, and it shouldn't be to you either. Perhaps you should stop watching all those films you told me you watch. You would be much happier if you just be yourself."

"How can you say that? You don't know me. You have known me five minutes," I said, attempting to brush off his entirely correct judgment of me.

"I didn't mean anything by it, Ashley. It's how you come across, that's all," he paused. "Sorry."

I said nothing. I didn't know what to say. It wasn't the first time I had heard it, and I didn't want Olly to think of me like that. I wished he didn't.

"But, why did you call yourself fat?" Olly continued.

My throat dried, my stomach churned, and my palms started to sweat. I swallowed hard and tried to find the right words to end the conversation quickly, but my mind was blank.

"Ash."

"Don't call me Ash. I don't like it."

"You don't? Then why does everyone call you it?" he asked, burning his eyes right into me as if to read me without asking. My gaze caught his stare, and for a moment, I held it, feeling something I had never experienced.

His aroma lingered within the wind, enhanced by his sweet-smelling sweat. It was hypnotising, and it made me feel alive. Strangely he felt familiar, which was weirdly comforting. It made me want to be nothing but honest with him. "No one has ever asked, and I have never told them," I paused. "No one cares about what I think or how I feel."

"Why do you say that? That's not true."

"It doesn't matter," I shrugged.

"But it does. You can talk to me, Ashley. I won't tell anyone."

I looked at him; his smile captivated me, and my worries disappeared.

When we reached our road, he stopped, which I mimicked. My house was in sight, and despite our conversation being more personal than I would have liked, I didn't want to go in yet.

"Why did you say that you are fat?" he repeated, making me wish I had never let the damn word burst out my mouth as it seemed he wasn't going to let it go. If this conversation were with anybody else, it would be around the school by the first lesson, and I would be the newly labelled eating disorder. Still, I was naïve, and he seemed trusting.

"I, I'm just not happy with the way I look. It's a girl thing, trust me, it meant nothing; I shouldn't have said it," I tried.

"I like the way you look. You're beautiful and far from fat," he said with a twinkle in his eye. His words were overwhelming. The fluttering of nerves that suddenly hooked my stomach told me that this boy was something special.

I hid my embarrassment and looked to the floor. I should have said thank you, I wanted to, but flattery wasn't something I was accustomed to. Olly had stolen every sense from me to respond, and since stopping, I had come over all tired. My feet were burning, my legs ached, and my stomach rumbled. My foot was tapping rapidly against the floor, and I was wringing my wrists, not knowing what to say in return.

When I found the courage, I raised my head and looked at him as we stood under the amber street light to see him curiously smiling at me. The darkness brightened his amorous glance, and his lips shimmered as he sipped his water. His expression was warm and compelling me by the second. Visions of us together flashed in my mind. We walked into school holding hands; my friends were green with envy. We went to prom together and then to college. We were married with children, and he earned millions being a professional football player. I was a writer of hopeless romance novels. We lived happily ever after.

My mind wandered until it was interrupted by a loud noise. I shook my head and widened my eyes, glancing behind Olly, and seeing Dad locking the garage door before going back inside.

"Thank you," I eventually said. If I had been brave, I would have told Olly that he was the first boy to call me beautiful. "Thanks for walking me home."

"I didn't walk you home. I walked myself home. But you're welcome," Olly joked, breaking the awkwardness floating around us.

"Bye then," I gulped.

Olly then took me by surprise again when he leaned towards me and planted a kiss so softly on my cheek that I barely felt it. He stepped back and ran his hand down my arm, squeezing my hand gently before walking off without looking back.

My hand raised to my kissed cheek as if touched by magic, and tiny sparks of static quickly danced over my skin, causing me to shiver as my mouth altered into a gleaming smile.

When my world stopped spinning, I ran inside and straight upstairs, throwing my bag on the floor and myself on the bed. I squealed into my pillow, kicking my legs like an excited little girl. I refused to let the moment end and didn't want him to leave my mind.

Climbing from my bed, I opened my window, peering into his bedroom, and like a dream, he was there, looking right back at me. As our eyes locked, he bewitched me. The moment felt intense and unreal, as stuff like this only happened in fairy tales, but it was happening to me, and it felt so right. But then the villain entered, his mum made him turn from me, and his curtains closed, bringing our moment to an end.

CHAPTER SIX

"Thanks for the lift, Mum," I said as I grabbed my bag and clambered out of the car into the pouring rain.

"Have a good day, sweetie. No detention slips today, please." She crossed her fingers with a hesitant smile.

I stretched out my jacket and used it to cover my hair. "Don't get your hopes up," I mumbled. "But I'll try." I shut the door and ran inside the school building.

Lauren, Sophie, Katie, and Hannah sat at our usual table in the hall. They were all looking towards the sports lads blushing and joking as they waved at them—their table in clear view as Lauren picked it back in the first year. It had just stuck after that, and we spent every morning, break, lunch and free period at it.

We enjoyed cheese and bean toasties or spaghetti hoops and waffles and played cards or squares at it. I had gotten relatively good at Cheat and Rummy over the years; sometimes, I was lucky to play against the boys. Give me a GCSE in card games, and I'd ace it.

My actual GCSEs, well, I'd be happy with my predicted C grades, and I probably didn't do much better with how the exams went.

"Morning," I said, joining them, shaking the rain off my jacket before hanging it over my chair.

"Hi, Ash," Lauren said as I sat down, joining my hands in front of me on the table.

"What are we all laughing at?" I asked.

"Have you seen the new boy?" Katie and Hannah gushed, turning to me with beaming smiles.

"He is so cute," Louise butted in. "I went over and said hello."

I giggled along with them, tucking my hair behind my ears, trying not to fluster. I hadn't quite figured out how I would tell them after keeping the secret for the past few days. How they would take the news that Olly was, in fact, my next-door neighbour, I didn't know.

The lads were rolling a football back and forth over the cafeteria table. Olly looked striking; his cap was sat backwards on his head with his hair brushed up inside. His whole face was on a show, and his laugh was infectious. But he hadn't looked at our table since I arrived; none of them had. The fun and games were over, and my stomach was in knots over the thought that Olly was part of their social group.

Just as my gut had told me, I would be invisible to him during school hours, exactly like the others, even with the chemistry between us. The unspoken connection I was suddenly questioning I was imagining.

The bell rang, and everyone disbanded, jumping from the chairs and off the tables. I stood and grabbed my bag, slipping on the puddle below me, and before I knew it, I was flat on my back with my backpack on top of me.

Laughter rang through my ears as I looked up at the ceiling stroking the back of my head. I sighed, mortified, wishing the floor would swallow me whole and take me to wonderland to save me from getting up and seeing everyone staring at me.

I put my palms out onto the floor and sat up, peering into the faces of the jokers around me. None of my friends came over to help me; they were chuckling, pointing and imitating me.

The walls felt like they were closing in as everyone around grew bigger, and I became smaller. It was like being in a scary funhouse of clowns, seeing my pathetic reflection in their amused stares. But just as I lost all hope in regaining any sort of reputation I had, something astonishing happened.

Olly was standing above me, offering me his hand. His expression was troubled as he looked down at me while I didn't move. I couldn't. Oh my god, that was all I could think.

With a gulp and a heavy exhale, I managed a small smile and took his hand, gripping it tightly and stood up, embracing my first touch of his smooth, gentle grasp. I brushed myself off as he picked up my bag and handed it to me. He then raised his hand towards my face brushing my hair behind my ear. My cheeks were hot and rosy instantly.

"Thank you," I stuttered, and Olly swallowed harshly with a wry smile.

"You're welcome," he said.

Every time I saw him, something hit me, something extraordinary. His smile was as if invisible arms hugged me tightly, telling me everything would be okay, and right then, I believed him. For that moment, time stood still, and pure bliss wrapped around me. And it wasn't until he walked away that I realised everyone was watching, and I had Lauren and Sophie surrounding me.

"Are you okay, Ash?" Sophie asked.

"Do you know Olly?" Lauren said, looking outside the window at him, then back at me.

"I have spoken to him once or twice," I told them, shrugging my shoulders as I put my bag on my shoulder. "Thanks for the help, by the way," I said before heading to class.

*

"Tell us how you know Olly," Lauren repeated as she pouted in her compact mirror.

I swallowed my sip of Dr Pepper. "Why does it matter so much? It's no big deal." I sighed, refusing my lunch. "He only helped me up."

Hearing my peers sniggering across the room was enough to take my appetite even if I was hungry. I hadn't managed one lesson without being mocked, and the ache in my head was still pounding, reminding me of it. Instead of being invisible, I was the joke, and I couldn't decide which one was worse.

I hated high school.

Lauren shut her mirror with a slam and scorned, "It looked like you know him more than that from where I was standing."

I gazed across and stared right at her. Her bitchy scowl confronted me. Truth be told, it was getting on my nerves. "So what if I know him? I don't have to tell you everything."

"Well, yeah, you do. That's kind of what we do, isn't it?" Sophie added.

I flared my nostrils and puffed out my chest. "Um, I don't think it is. Since when do I ever have a say in anything? I just listen to you two all day."

Lauren leaned over and placed her hand on my arm. "Oh, Ash, it's not like you ever have anything interesting to say. We don't want to hear about your boring weekends at home, you understand that, but when you have juicy boy gossip, you're supposed to tell us."

I uncrossed my legs and sat up straight, brushing her hand away. "I don't consider Olly as gossip."

Sophie let out a gasp, holding her chest. "Any boy is gossip, or do you need reminding of the rules within our friendship group."

"Sophie, shut it a minute," Lauren cut in. For a moment, she stopped playing whatever game she was playing and said, "You didn't tell us because you like him, don't you?" She cackled. Sophie then joined.

"You knew you would have no chance once he met us," Sophie said. My throat was as dry as sandpaper. I didn't know how to escape the humiliation. I closed my eyes and remembered what Mrs Bond and Olly had said.

Taking a deep breath, I stood up, aggressively pushing my chair away. "So what if I know Olly. So what if I didn't tell you, he's my next-door neighbour, and there is nothing you can do to change that. Perhaps he's just a nice person, unlike you two," I snapped, clenching my teeth. "All of you are a bunch of selfish jerks. To hell with you."

I grabbed my bag, stormed out of the dining hall, and spent the remainder of the day ignoring snide comments and being blanked by my so-called friends.

When the bell rang, I was relieved that the day was over and it was now the weekend. Two days away from the nightmare of a place was what I counted down for every day of the week. Even if it consisted of staying in my bedroom, it was better than Bailey.

Not once had I had a reasonably good week at school. Not once.

CHAPTER SEVEN

"Mum, where are you?" I shouted as I entered the house.

"Upstairs, Ashley."

I threw my bag down and ran upstairs, and as soon as I saw her, my eyes welled up, and the tears started to fall.

All day I had pretended to be strong. To be okay. But that was far from what I was. I had just become incredibly good at being something I wasn't. And the more time alone I had, and the truths I faced, the more I realised my entire life had been a lie.

A big fat game of being someone else.

I wasn't Lauren, Sophie, or any of the others. And I sure as hell wasn't cut out for the glitter, the pop music and the skimpy skirts that came along with them. But at the same time, I wasn't Ashley. I had become this stupid plastic wannabe, Ash.

I don't know why I thought I could get away with it.

If I were a Matryoshka doll, even the smallest one would be a form of someone else; that's as bad as my identity was. No Ashley was there; if she were, she was clinging on by a thread screaming inside a locked box to let her out. To let her breathe. To let her be free.

"What's happened?" Mum said, concerned, putting the pile of washing down on her bed before wrapping her arms around me.

I cried into her shoulder before I managed any words, embracing her hug, which didn't often happen. I never really confided in her much, not like I should have, but she never asked and was always too busy nagging at me.

"My friends are shit," I mumbled. "I slipped over this morning and became the joke of the day. Lauren, Katie, Hannah, and Sophie all stood there, laughing at me with everyone else."

Her arms tightened, and her hand slid up and down my hair. "Oh, sweetie, I have told you numerous times you should make better friends. You have never really fitted in with them."

"I know." I sniffled. "But I don't have anyone else."

Mum tutted, stepped back, kept her grip on my arms and looked at me. "You have the new football girls, and they seem nice. You can put today behind you and enjoy your sleepover with them; that's something new and exciting."

When I asked Mum and Dad about Alex's sleepover, I didn't think they would let me go, and when they said yes, I didn't know whether to believe them or slap myself around the face to make sure I wasn't dreaming. I couldn't remember the last time I was allowed out socially. It had been years, and I didn't ask why the sudden change in heart or risk them changing their minds.

"I guess so," I muttered.

"Before you know it, high school will be over. You have the prom to look forward to and then the summer away from them," Mum said, reassuring me as she tucked my hair behind my ears.

"I'm not going to prom. I told you that." There was no way I was going. For one, I wouldn't have a date, and no one would ask me. Two, I would look horrid in a dress, and three, I had no reason to celebrate my years at high school.

"Oh, well, there is always time to change your mind," she tried. "Anyway, have you met the boy next door yet? His mum said she had got him in for some activity days before summer."

"Erm, why?" I said, wiping my eyes dry.

"Well, your dad and I are going out tonight with his parents."

"Oh, Mum, not more babysitting," I huffed. "I'm not in the mood."

"This time will be different," she paused as I furrowed my eyebrows. "Olly is coming round with his younger brother Nate so he can play with Zoe."

"Oh, god, no," I blurted out, horrified.

"What? We thought you could babysit together."

"I doubt that's how Olly would want to spend his Friday night; he has a life," I said.

"Well, his mum said he was okay with it."

I swallowed my surprise discreetly and peered out the window to his house. "It doesn't sound like I have much say in the matter," I said, mulling over ways the evening could go in my head. "I suppose it won't be too bad. Olly is alright."

"So you have met him?"

I looked up at Mum with a small smile and said, "Yes, I have," then left the room, leaving her pondering.

Despite Mum's constant efforts to rid me of social life and banish my chance of ever having a boyfriend, I was to spend the night with Olly. If she knew how the boy next door had me utterly smitten, she might have been more cautious about the idea. But since I had a non-existent love life, I think Dad was the only one who worried about that, and with the way my body trembled around Olly, he had every right.

I walked straight to my window and peered into his garden, where he often practised his football skills, but he wasn't there. I didn't know if he knew how much I stood watching, but if he did, he had never said anything about it, so I wasn't going to stop. He had become my new favourite programme, and I could watch him all day. He was that addictive.

My eyes roamed to his bedroom window, and there he was. My heart burst and my face warmed. "No way," I gasped, planting my hand on my mouth as I watched him strip his shirt off before glancing away. My body, however, had the opposite idea as my stare drew right back to him. My glance widened, and I was suddenly the new curtain twitcher of the street, unable to break away from the perfect image of the boy next door just a few yards away.

The sight of a semi-naked boy was something I had never seen before. His trim, athletic, sun-kissed body took my breath away and had my knees weakening beneath me.

Olly was perfect, even much more so than I imagined, and there were no words better to describe him.

CHAPTER EIGHT

Mum shouted to me from downstairs. In an instant, I was on my feet, switching off my mp3 player and checking myself in the mirror. I brushed the creases from my red vest top and straightened my flared jeans, trying my hardest not to get nervous about Olly being downstairs.

I stood hovering on the bottom step as they all looked at me. My grip tightened on the railing as Olly stood there with his assessing gaze. We hadn't spoken since he helped me up, nor did I plan to mention it. But with the tension vibrating off me, I knew I was in for a long night.

"Right, we will be back at eleven. Get Zoe into bed at nine, no later and don't let them play on the screen for too long," Mum said.

"Same goes for you, Olly. Get Nate ready for bed here, then go back next door when Zoe is in bed; his PJs are in his bag," his mum added.

I rolled my eyes at my parents, fighting the urge not to say anything that would make me sound like a brat. It was awkward already, and being told what to do in front of Olly was humiliating. Still, embarrassment seemed to be my most used emotion in front of him.

"Got it. It's not like I haven't babysat before," I let slip, catching Olly's grin, "Just go already."

"Ashley, behave and be nice," Dad grunted, looking back at me as he edged closer to the door and opened it. Mum waved, as did his parents, and once the door shut, we stood in the hallway in silence.

*

Olly had suggested a game, and as he seemed pretty into it, I couldn't complain. I didn't know if he was showing his cocky sportsmanship or was simply massively competitive. But his smile grew every time he said, "You owe me two hundred pounds," and he had said it plenty.

I was the banker, and I had always been rubbish at it. Monopoly was my least favourite, and we had been playing for over an hour, draining every ounce of my brain cells. Although when playing with such a distracting person, no one could blame me for forgetting how to count.

We had barely had a conversation, which had thrown me from our previous connection. I was relieved the mention of this morning hadn't risen, but it did confirm how things had already changed and that school had affected how Olly treated me. No doubt he now saw me like the others. The sad, lonely outcast who clung to the tiniest opportunity of popularity.

Regardless of his opinion, the way he had my heart pounding was only becoming more intense by the second.

When I handed him the colourful money, my fingers brushed over his causing me to blush a little more. The butterflies in my stomach were swirling so fast that I was nauseous. He had me feeling things I had never experienced before. Making me want to do the things I never had. Until him, I wanted to do them coming-of-age things; now, I *needed* to.

I rolled the dice, moved twelve spaces, and landed on his hotel. Scanning the few notes I had left, I could finally say the words I had longed to say, "I'm bankrupt." I laughed and knocked over my little metal dog. "I have never won this game."

"I'll be banker next time, maybe slip you a few notes here and there," Olly joked as he stood up from the cross-legged position he had been in for an hour and a half. I wanted to do the same, but I had pins and needles running through my feet. I knew I'd fall over if I did, and I wasn't doing that in front of him again.

"No, next time, I pick."

Olly turned the bands on his wrist. "Can I grab a drink?"

"Yes, of course, I'll get you one," I said as I shook my legs. I gripped the sofa and pulled myself up, tapping my feet against the floor as I waited for the fizzy feeling to subside.

"Are you okay?" he said, waiting as he eyed my mum's small DVD and VHS collection.

"I have pins and needles," I laughed.

"Oh," he muttered. "I hate that."

I nodded and stepped forward on my heavy feet. They felt normal again once I made it to the kitchen.

Grabbing two glasses and the orange juice from the fridge, I poured us a drink and handed one to him. Leaning against the counter, I sipped mine, watching him fixate on the photos of Zoe and me. I was mortified, wishing my mum had a wall of lovely photos rather than silly ones.

"Where is your room?" he asked, making me choke as knots formed in the pit of my stomach. Until that moment, the idea of showing him my bedroom hadn't even occurred.

A boy had never been in my bedroom; not many people had. It was a kept secret, my safe haven.

"Upstairs," I said, putting the juice bottle back in the fridge.

"Wow, really? I wouldn't have guessed," Olly teased. "Can I see it?"

"Erm," I stuttered as I closed the refrigerator, reluctant, but he had already walked out of the kitchen and was halfway up the stairs. "Erm, yes, okay." I briskly caught him up. "What if I had said no?" I asked, hanging my thumbs in my jeans pockets.

"You wouldn't have," he said, and his certainty intimidated me. Suddenly he relaxed, and with that, I became more anxious.

Olly popped his head into Zoe's room, had a nosey and said, "Are you two okay in here?"

"Go away," Nate replied, sticking his tongue. Zoe just hummed and nodded without facing us, busy building Lego.

"Jerk," Olly muttered under his breath, looking back at me as I tried not to laugh.

"Your house is identical to mine." Walking across the landing, he opened my door. "I didn't get so lucky having this room, though, I would love an ensuite, but my mum insists it's our guest room. Not that we ever have any."

I didn't tell him which room was mine; it was evident with the stickered door, plus with how we met, he was clever enough to have figured it out.

"Yeah, it does come in handy, I guess." I smiled and walked behind him into my room as he glanced around it.

He flicked through my pile of CDs and ran his fingers along the bindings of my book collection. I watched him peer through all my stuff as I was too nice to say otherwise.

"You're not like the other girls, are you?" Olly asked. His words were harsh but true, and they saddened me, but apparently, it was more evident than I was aware.

Behind closed doors, I wasn't the typical girly girl whose interests were pop music and anything pink and glittery. Anything black and red was my favourite. I didn't own cheesy pop CDs but preferred Avril Lavigne, Pink and Blink 182. I didn't enjoy reading celebrity gossip or glossy magazines. I only bought them for the new fashion trends because Lauren insisted that Sophie and I read the same as her every week. Instead, I liked to read books where every story had a twist and a happy conclusion, sometimes thrillers. And don't get me started on the clothes. Short denim pleated skirts and knee-high pointy boots made me want to heave; I didn't know how I had let them sit in my wardrobe without burning them for so long. Dark flares, chords, fishnet and mesh tops are what I want. That is what Ashley liked.

If you hadn't caught on by now, I had to like the usual teenage girl things to be accepted, even if I didn't like it. I tolerated it; that's what I did. And I did anything and everything to have friends.

I fumbled with my fingers, looked down at my feet and leaned against my desk. "Is it that noticeable?" I muttered shyly, feeling a lump forming in my throat.

Olly continued roaming around my bedroom. "It's not a bad thing. The girls at Bailey always try to get my attention, and you don't. That's why I like you." He pointed at my Avril poster and smirked. "She's hot." I laughed and bit my bottom lip.

"Those girls are much prettier than me; why would you like me?"

"They have ugly personalities, and you don't."

"You barely know me."

"I don't need to; I trust my gut," Olly said as he shut the door, which made my insides stir.

I stood in silence, looking at him as he stared at me with alluring eyes. "How is your head?" he asked, stepping towards me, brushing his palm against the bruise on the back of it. His touch was electric, quivering my nerves and sending shivers down my spine.

"It hurts a little, but it's okay," I muttered near whispering as my breathing became shallow.

"Your friends are bitches for being like that earlier; you shouldn't let them treat you like that."

"There isn't much I can do when they are my only friends. It's always been that way."

"I can see why you feel the way you do. You deserve better."

His words were calm and relaxed me. "Feel like what?" I asked.

"Well, seeing your choice in music and posters, you act like them to fit in. I don't see Britney on your wall, I see Avril, and she's no Britney. I doubt you have ever worn this either," he said, picking up a pink beret off my shelf and brushing off the dust. "You know, you will never love yourself if you pretend to be someone else."

"You're wrong," I tried, feeling my chest tighten.

Olly leaned his head to the side and stepped closer, fiddling with my hair, "No, I'm not, and you know it."

I wish I'd had the confidence to let my guard down and tell him he had me all figured out. But who I was, I had pretended to be for a long time, and I was worried about being unable to figure out my true identity. He was right; I didn't love myself, not this girl, Ash. I wanted to be Ashley but didn't know who she was or where to begin.

As silence wrapped around us in a double bow, I gazed everywhere apart from him. I was nervous, jittery, and trying to be perfect. But putting aside my continual desire for someone to make me feel like this, I was out of sorts. Truthfully, I feared such an unfamiliar feeling.

Olly gently touched my chin and raised it until my eyes were on his. Quietly he said, "I want to kiss you."

I gulped. My voice trembled as I said, "Why?" The moment I had been waiting for was so close, and the notion alone was surreal.

"Why not?" he replied, tapping his heels one after the other.

Olly, a boy I barely knew, was in my bedroom. Not only that, he had witnessed me be the laughing stock of the day and had heard my troubling opinions, yet he still wanted to kiss me.

I had always expected my first kiss to be at a party with someone I didn't know in an intoxicated state. Not with a boy who knocked me into oblivion every time I saw him. He had to be a figment of my imagination; it was all too fairy-tale-like and the only explanation.

"So, can I?" he asked, and I said nothing. It was so quiet I'm sure he could hear the rapid beat of my heart as I failed to respond. "You haven't kissed a boy before, have you?"

I licked my dry lips. "No, never."

"Why?" He moved his hands to mine. They were gripping the edge of my desk tightly, hanging on for dear life. He fumbled with my fingers and loosened my grasp as my eyes dived into his mysterious dark stare. I was melting inside and still questioning if this was really happening.

"Because I'm invisible."

"Not to me, you're not."

Olly didn't ask again and instead inched closer to me. His warm breath ran over my face and down my neck. The tiny hairs all over my body stood, and fear took hold of my stomach. My toes scrunched up into the carpet, and I closed my eyes. The second his gentle lips touched mine, I was way out of my comfort zone and pulled back.

I didn't know what to do.

He looked at me again and smiled shyly. "Relax," he said as he cupped my face and slowly guided my lips to his.

I watched his beautiful tempting eyes move closer to me, then shut them tightly.

His lips were back on mine as I allowed him to take control. He started gently, then pushed closer against me as I sighed at the strange feeling rising in my body. My hands felt silly, like they were hanging there, so I touched his arm lightly. When he poked his tongue into my mouth, I found it strange, but his fruity, moreish taste filled my senses and had me stroking mine against it. My chest warmed, and my face glowed. His palm touched my back, and my hand moved to the crease of his neck. It felt like we kissed for ages before he pulled back and blushed at me.

"That wasn't so bad, was it?" he asked, leaning his forehead against mine before letting go.

"No," I shyly grinned, swiping my hair away from my face, moving from my desk, and sitting on the bed.

My heart was pounding so hard in my chest that it ached. My whole body felt like it wasn't my own.

"It was nice," I said, looking up at Olly and placing my lip between my teeth as it quivered. The guard I held up dropped, and my fear dissolved. "Have you kissed girls before? Done other things with girls?" His chest rose as he exhaled deeply, looking into my wondering eyes.

He sat next to me, straightened my heart-shaped earrings and leaned in, "Not so much." He kissed me again. His touch was more intense, as if he had been careful the first time. I struggled to contain myself as I wouldn't allow my hands to stray too far.

He was a fantastic kisser. Surely, he had kissed girls before. Why wouldn't he have? There was no way he hadn't had the opportunity, but I didn't care about that; Olly had claimed my first kiss. I just hoped it wouldn't be the only one I shared with him.

When the moment ended, I was disappointed. More so when the clock on my wall told him he had to leave.

I didn't want him to go.

I wanted him to stay forever.

Babysitting wouldn't be so bad as long as Olly was around.

CHAPTER NINE

I climbed over the others as I made my way to my sleeping bag on the floor of Alex's bedroom. I'd had a great day with them all, the best day in forever.

We had walked down the town, had a mooch around blockbuster and explored every clothes aisle in Tammy Girl, Morgan's, Etam and Littlewoods. I didn't buy anything besides a new CD from Woolworths but still enjoyed watching them all try on clothes. And when Morgan put a cap on my head, she only went and took my mind straight back to Olly, who I couldn't stop thinking about. Even when the girls and I played football down the park, he was in my mind. Football was his thing, and he was always clinging to one.

Nothing, absolutely nothing, had taken my mind off him since we met, and I didn't think anything could.

Sammy had insisted we had a girly pamper, spa kind of sleepover, which wasn't as bad as I expected. We had a Chinese take-out, did our nails and wore facemasks while watching a chick flick. It was all right, a bit cheesy, but it made me laugh, and for as long as I could remember, I felt like I belonged, and my shoulders were looser because of it. I had never realised how tense I was, but it wasn't easy putting on an act all the time; I was no A-grade drama student.

Unlike Lauren and Sophie, me and the girls had similar interests, and I didn't feel the need to impress them. I hated that they went to Oakley Prep and not Bailey.

Morgan sat behind me, brushing my hair as we sipped on hot chocolates and ate marshmallows. I took a handful of toffee popcorn and relaxed, enjoying my head massage.

I loved hair care; there was always something about someone playing with your hair that made everything seem better.

"Ashley, have you ever kissed anybody?" Alex asked, and I smiled. It was a question I had usually avoided, but since I could say yes, I was more than eager to reply. I knew the night was turning into a real girly sleepover, the kind I had seen on TV, and I suddenly came over all nervous. Excited nervous.

I reminisced about my kiss with Olly, and it made me gush and go all gooey inside. I hadn't seen him since and didn't even have his phone number. I didn't know what to think about our friendship, but I knew I liked him. I liked him a lot. Though with the doubt in my mind about him treating me differently at school still hovering, I tried not to overthink it.

"I have," I giggled.

"Really?" The others all gathered around me with their snacks, waiting for details.

I blushed, picking up my pillow and hugging it, keeping my head back as Morgan continued. "It happened just yesterday."

"Tell us what it was like. Who was it? That cute boy from football? Please say it was him," Sammy probed, kicking her legs wildly as she lay on her front.

I glanced at my new friends. They were all in cosy pyjamas, staring at me with wide eyes. Interested, happy and enjoying my company. If this wasn't what true friendship felt like, I don't know what did.

Alex sat beside me; her long blonde hair was French plaited, hanging over one shoulder, and her polished black fingernails were twiddling. She was bubbly and born to be a leader.

Morgan was behind me; her hair was short, I had crimped it, and it had gone puffy and wild. She was a little clumsy and laughed a lot. Her contagious laugh had us all in stitches every time she looked in the mirror.

Emily, who sat on the other side of me, had thick brunette hair, and Alex had curled it. It looked pretty, but my god, it took forever. She's clever, loves to read and was the tallest of us.

And then there was Sammy. She had a blonde bob, which we all put into tiny plaits. It was going to take her ages to get them out; they were that small. She was petite and the girliest out of us all. The rest were more tomboyish, whilst I still hadn't embraced my love for the type of fashion I truly loved for anyone to see.

"Yeah, it was Olly," I giggled.

"Yes," Sammy squealed, and we high-fived. "He is so dreamy. How was it? Good, it was good, wasn't it."

"Jeez, Sam, let her breathe," Alex said, nudging her into silence.

I took a bite of popcorn and cleared my throat. "Well, it was awkward at first. Olly asked me out of the blue."

Alex clicked her tongue. "He asked you as in point blank asked you?"

"Yeah, he said he wanted to kiss me, then asked if he could."

Sammy glanced at Morgan with a bashful smile.

"I've not heard boys being like that before," Emily added. I couldn't agree more. The only kiss-and-tell stories I had heard were about people fumbling around when they were drunk.

"Oo, get to the juicy part," Sammy probed, toying with her hair.

"I was too shy to answer, so he did it anyway. He was gentle, and it was weird and wet." I laughed, covering my face as it burnt.

"What about the tongue, was there tongue?" Alex wondered, and I lifted my head, giving her a Cheshire grin. Sammy couldn't hold her laughter in any longer, and once she started, I joined. Then the others did.

"Oh, I dunno how to explain it. It was just the perfect first kiss. I couldn't have imagined it being any better," I finished.

We laughed, cringed, and talked about boys.

There was no competition or group leader with Morgan, Alex, Sammy, and Emily. And when I was with them, I didn't care about being popular anymore. Not until they mentioned their school anyway, which quickly reminded me of Bailey and how I stormed out of the dining hall on Friday.

I hadn't heard from Lauren or Sophie, and seeing as they didn't care about me, I had started to think I should listen to Olly. He was right; they were a bunch of stuck-up bitches, and I didn't deserve the way they treated me, and they didn't deserve me as a friend.

As we lay in the dark, the conversations started to fade as they fell asleep; I was yet to feel sleepy, buzzing after such a fun-filled day.

"Ashley, can I ask you something?" Alex then said, turning on her front to look at me, shining her torch on her face. She looked a little wry.

"What is it?" I asked.

"How did you get that boy to kiss you?"

"What do you mean?"

"Like, how did you get him to like you?"

"Erm, I don't know. It just happened. Boys don't normally take any interest in me, but Olly seems different. He's genuinely nice," I said, shrugging my shoulders. "It helps that he is my neighbour and his parents had us babysitting together last night. We got talking. Not just general chit-chat but more personal questions. Then he asked if he could kiss me." The story sounded a little bizarre, even as I said it aloud.

"Can you show me?" she asked, knocking me back a tad.

"Show you what?"

"How you kissed him?"

Alex's words made me shy, but I wasn't horrified by the idea. I knew some girls at school experimented with each other.

"There's a boy I like, and I want to kiss him at prom, but I don't want to do it wrong," she explained. I fully understood her predicament.

I sat up and faced her. "Okay, come on then."

"What? Really?" she said, suddenly nervous.

"Really," I nodded. "I wish I had the confidence to have asked one of my friends, so why not."

"Was your first kiss that bad?"

"God, I hope not," I laughed. "Olly kinda showed me the way."

I edged closer to Alex, took her torch from her, and placed it on my lap. She looked at me anxiously, then closed her eyes. I inhaled deeply and leaned in.

"This is so weird," Alex muttered, keeping her eyes closed, trying not to laugh.

"Ssh," I said, and she zipped her mouth with a chortle.

When my lips touched hers, I kissed her as Olly kissed me. At first, just on the lips, then with a bit of tongue, and it didn't compare in the slightest. The butterflies weren't flying around my stomach, and my heart wasn't racing, but I knew that was because it wasn't him. It was Olly who flustered me, not the kissing.

As I released her lips from mine, we watched each other and burst into laughter; my belly ached from how hard I giggled.

"I like the taste of your lip balm," Alex said, making me snort.

"Stop it; you'll wake the others," I giggled.

"Oh my god, we should wake them; you could show them too."

"No. No, we shouldn't."

"Why? We could all do with the practice."

"Maybe next time," I smirked.

"Spoilsport," she said, playfully throwing some popcorn at me before laying back down.

I got back in my sleeping bag and made myself comfy, "Thanks for inviting me," I said with a yawn.

"Don't mention it; you're one of us now, and you're going to have so much fun. You wait until the parties begin," Alex replied, and it made my heart triple in size.

I finally had the group of friends I had always wanted and a boy in my life, and I tried not to let the pessimist part of me win and question if it was too good to be true. Instead, I shook my worries aside and talked to Alex until one of us fell asleep. She asked me about prom and if I had a dress. I hadn't planned on going, but someone had changed my mind; I just hadn't found the courage to tell Mum or him yet.

CHAPTER TEN

Mum turned to me in the car. "How come you have changed your mind? I thought you hated the idea of the prom?"

I fiddled with my fingers, looking down at them. "I do hate the idea. I just don't think I want to miss such a special event."

"Okay, well, we can go shopping now if you like?" she said.

My head lifted, catching her beaming smile. "Now? Like right now?"

"Yes, why not, we have all day, and I doubt you will want to wait until next weekend when all the dresses will be gone. You have left it late as it is." She changed direction and headed towards the bigger shopping outlet.

Mum looked excited. I had never seen her face so bright. It must have been the sleepover that had me in high spirits, but I didn't want to burst her bubble for once. I got the impression through all the nagging and mentioning that all she wanted was the mother-daughter prom dress trip, and I had stripped her from it. I never thought about her once, and I felt selfish for never asking if it was okay if I didn't go. I knew she loved her prom and preparing for it with my granny; it was all she ever went on about once I first mentioned it.

"It wouldn't have anything to do with the boy next door, would it?" Mum cautiously said. My cheeks flushed as I thought about him, and I hid my smirk, looking out the window.

Of course, it was to do with him.

"No, why would it be?" I shrugged.

"Oh, no reason," she mumbled, drumming her fingers against the steering wheel to Bon Jovi.

A few seconds passed. My heart was pounding, and my feet were tapping aggressively against the floor. "Fine, it is," I let out.

Mum looked straight at me. "What? Really?"

As I glanced over, her cheeks were rosy. We never had personal conversations. The only one I remember was when I wanted my first bra and asked to get the pill to reduce the heaviness of my periods.

I wasn't sure what had happened to our relationship over the years – possibly my terrible choice of friends and the impossibility of fitting in. Or the constant mood I was in from the struggle of teenage life. We used to be close, but it had become resentment. I did always long for that close mother-daughter relationship, and to be frank, I knew I would be jealous if she had it with Zoe and not me. I knew I needed to be more myself and let her back in. If I let everything fall into place instead of forcing it any other way, I might be much happier. We would be happier in each other's company.

"Yes, really. Olly is nice and nothing like any other boys I know."

"He is very charming, I must admit."

"He is, that day, I fell over, and everyone laughed at me. Olly helped me up."

"That was kind of him."

"Kind? It was incredible; *he* is incredible," I gushed, blushing as my words fell out.

"Incredible, hey?"

"Not that it matters. Olly doesn't like me like that, and he won't ask me to prom; no one will," I said. My tone swiftly changed as I spoke, nearly enough to make me change my mind about the idea. Miraculously my deep thoughts beat my wanted feelings every time.

"Wow, Ashley, where is this sudden anger erupting from? You are gorgeous," Mum replied, trying to calm me as my body language stiffened.

"You would say that. You're my mum," I mumbled, looking away from her as tears pinched the back of my eyes.

"What? No. You *are* gorgeous. Why do you think otherwise? Is it them friends of yours? Is this why you aren't eating as much lately? You're worried about how you look?" Her voice trembled as I wiped the falling tears from my cheek.

"Mum, isn't it obvious? I don't fit in with Lauren, Sophie or anyone. I need to be skinnier and prettier to be popular like them—more sociable, which you don't allow. Because I don't go out at the weekends, I'm a loner. A complete loser with no life."

I confessed how I felt. My lip quivered the entire time as I tried to hold it together, but eventually, I let go and broke down, silencing Mum. She pulled into the car park and said nothing until we stopped; she unbuckled her seat belt and leaned over to hug me.

Moving my hair and hands away from my eyes, Mum cupped my face and said, "Ashley, listen to me. You are beautiful exactly the way you are. You are intelligent, funny, and kind. Please don't try to be like them. Your friends don't deserve you, and you don't deserve the amount of pressure they put on you. I love you the way you are, and so do your dad and Zoe," she paused as I nodded, pulling my lip between my teeth as my lungs tightened.

"You're sixteen. You think you need to be like all these stereotypical celebrities to be seen by boys and be popular but take it from me; your loyal friends will come when you just be yourself. Look at Alex and the other girls; you barely know them, and they like you, and you don't dress up for them. And what about Olly?

He hardly knows you and sees something your friends you have known since you were five don't even see. Maybe it's time for a complete makeover, clothes, hair, and friends. Let's go all out today, get rid of this false, insecure Ashley, and get the real one back. The one I know is in here." She pointed to my heart and then wiped my tears with her thumb.

"Thanks, Mum. I needed that."

"You're welcome, sweetheart. Now let's go shopping." She opened the car door. "Oh, and Ashley, we don't intentionally keep you at home to damage your reputation. It's those friends of yours. I hear what Lauren is like, and it's our way of keeping from doing things I know you will only regret. Perhaps we would let you if you chose to go out with your new friends."

I had never thought of her strict rules like that, and once Mum had said it, I felt a little less anger towards her. If she let me out with Alex and the others, my summer holidays wouldn't be as bad as expected.

*

I caught Mum with glossy eyes whenever I started a war with the mirror when trying dresses on. It was clear she had been oblivious to how I felt about myself. But after trying on at least thirty dresses and experiencing every emotion about myself, I finally found the perfect one. It made my bust look good, my eyes pop, and my waist looked slim. My usual size hung on me, so I managed to go down a size, which boosted my mood by itself alongside her million compliments.

That's when the real tears came.

She bought me a matching clutch bag, shoes, and a pashmina and treated me to a hand massage while she got her nails done. I had my hair trimmed, and chunky red highlights added, which I had wanted for a while though my friends had put me off.

I loved it; it enhanced the darkness of my eyes, and I looked more like myself. The Ashley I wanted to be. The Ashley I was meant to be.

Once the makeover was over, I told Mum I wanted new makeup and clothes, hoping it would help bring out my true colours.

While Mum shopped for Zoe, I ventured into the area of the clothes shops I had never dared go to. And I didn't let those with piercings and tattoos intimidate me as I looked lost and out of place.

I bought a range of dark blue and black flared jeans, some cargo pants, and chords. As well as designer tops, red, black, and brown vest tops, fishnet and mesh tops, some chunky black boots, and a new leather jacket.

I had never felt comfortable in the clothes I had worn over the past few years. Lauren told me to wear the mini skirts, the pink, and the below-knee boots, regardless of never having the figure for them. I don't know why I ever listened.

After talking to Mum, I was calmer and happier, but I didn't know how long it would last. The next challenge I faced was returning to school and facing the backlash of doing things my way.

CHAPTER ELEVEN

"So, is it any good?" Mum said as she sat beside me at the kitchen table, sipping her cup of tea as I finished a blended fruit smoothie.

I wiped my mouth. "It was all right; I think I'll prefer the strawberry flavour to the spinach and kale."

"But," Mum tried, and I cut her off.

"But at least I've not skipped breakfast; I know, Mum, I know," I finished, and she gave me a hesitant smile.

Having discussed with Mum about my weight worry, we finished our girl's day doing a food shop in Kwik Save. We bought more fruit, vegetables, soups, and fewer sugary snacks. I even refused to put the Cherry Bakewells in the trolley. Mum fully supported my decision, providing I didn't skip meals or starve myself.

I think she enjoyed our day together as much as I had. There was a much more relaxed vibe coming off her. And when I woke up, I found smoothie recipes on my desk, which she had asked Jeeves for, printed and neatly filed in a folder.

"Are you sure you're going to be okay today?" she asked, taking my hand into hers, and before things got serious all over again, a knock at the door saved me.

I rose to my feet and tightened my jumper knot around my waist. Looking down at Mum, I put my hand on her shoulder. "I'll be fine," I said with a reassuring smile, picking up my bag and heading to the front door.

"Bye," I shouted.

"Morning, Olly," Mum bellowed as I slammed the door on her embarrassing screech.

"Morning," he only just got in.

"Wow, Ashley, you look…different," Olly paused, adjusting his collar as he swallowed. "Did you get your hair done?"

"You could say that," I beamed, a little nervous about the sudden pink pigments in his cheeks. I hoped I looked okay. Was it a good difference or a bad difference? I should have asked.

I had spent all morning staring at my new reflection, worried about the comments I was bound to receive. My ponytail was high and straight, showing its length and fresh colour. I had replaced my heart-shaped studs with small silver hoop earrings, a choker decorated my throat, and my black nail polish shimmered. My eyes were powered with a slight metallic colouring and laced with a line of eyeliner and the most discreet flick of mascara. I wore a high-waisted black knee-length skirt instead of my usual baggy clothes. My polo shirt was tucked in, and my jumper wrapped around my waist. My new bra pushed up my bust more than usual, and completing my outfit was my new leather jacket. I liked how I looked for the first time in forever and felt terrific, but I knew it would come with consequences. And detention was the least of my worries.

I knew I was wearing more black than Lauren would like, and she would disapprove of my curves. Still, after hearing wisdom from Olly, Mum and even Mrs Bond, I thought I would try being brave.

"After listening to what you said, you know, about being myself, I thought I would give it a go," I said, running my fingers through my ponytail. "I got my hair done and new clothes. No more pink, skimpy outfits for me."

"And that pink beret?"

I laughed. "Oh, that's long gone."

"Well, you look great," Olly said. "It suits you."

"Thank you," I blushed.

He looked at me, his feet, and back at me, toying with his tongue. "How was the sleepover?"

I loved how Olly made small talk on the way to school; it was the highlight of my day.

"It was great. I had the best time, and we're having another one in the summer."

"Sounds good," he wavered. "What are you going to do about Lauren and Sophie? Do you think they will accept this new Ashley?"

I glanced at him, biting the inside of my mouth as my stomach flipped. "No, not at all, and when they don't, I have no idea who I will hang around with."

Olly altered his bag strap. "You can sit with me."

"What? No. No way."

"Wow, thanks, Ashley," he retorted with a puff of his chest.

"No, I didn't mean it like that, I mean, you wouldn't want a girl at your table, and neither would your friends."

"Umm, you're wrong. But seriously, come and sit with me."

"Okay, I'll keep it in mind, thanks," I said, twiddling my fingers, unable to take the beaming smile plastered on my face.

"What else did you get up to?" he asked, bouncing his football as we walked.

"I got a prom dress."

"Prom?" he said, surprised. "I thought you weren't going."

"I changed my mind."

"Oh, good. I'm glad."

I furrowed my brows. "You are?"

"Yes, you would regret not going. It's a special occasion."

"Oh yeah," I muttered, "I guess so." And with nothing more coming from the mention of prom, I knew the question I wanted him to ask me would never come. I asked about his weekend instead of prolonging the inevitable.

As we neared the park, I could see the school gate at the top of the hill. Crowds had started to form, and the usual knot was in my stomach. I slowed, suddenly panicking, and wanted to go home and change into my regular uniform.

I hated Mondays.

I hated being back at school, performing the same charade of fitting in with my so-called friends and competing with my weekend activities. And with the upcoming facing of remarks I had prepared myself for all morning about my style change, I knew I was in for a bad start to the day.

"Olly," Lewis shouted, waving his hand up. I watched his expression alter as he saw me walking up the hill with him. The other sports lads and Lauren standing nearby also did. I watched her nudge Sophie's arm, pointing my way, making her glance over.

"Olly, this was a bad idea. I need to go and change," I muttered, barely opening my mouth.

Olly gripped my arm as I went to turn around. "No, you don't." I carried on walking with him.

My chest tightened, and my throat dried as we grew closer. I felt like a model on a catwalk, except I was no model, and this was more like a walk of shame than anything glamorous.

"Blimey Ash, what's going on here? You look great," Lewis said as we reached them. "Alright, Ol, did you catch the game last night?"

"Nah, I haven't watched any since Portugal beat us on penalties; my dad's still moping around about it. I'd get grounded just for saying Euro at the moment," Olly said, nudging me as I nervously fiddled with my bag, looking to the floor, saying nothing.

"Correct him," he mumbled, and I agreed, inhaling and exhaling deeply, searching for my courage.

I lifted my head and looked at Lewis. With a small smile, I muttered, "It's Ashley, and thank you."

"Lauren, you have some competition with your bestie today," Lewis laughed as my shoulders lifted. The mere presence of her crawled under my skin and set me alight.

Competition? I disagreed. I didn't say anything or feel smug like I should have. Still, her mortified expression was worth the compliment and something I would sleep soundly over.

"Right," is all that Lauren replied as I watched her cheeks flush pink for the first time in our entire friendship.

"I'll see you later, Ashley," Olly said, nodding at me before walking towards the football pitch with his friends. I heard them say my name and look back at me—something I was used to, so I didn't let it bother me.

"Ash, want to explain?" Lauren scorned as she hooked her arm with Sophie's. They were both looking up and down at me, and it pissed me off instead of making me feel small.

"Explain what?" I said, crossing my arms.

"This," she replied, gesturing at my new appearance.

"I dyed my hair and bought new clothes, so what?"

"You didn't tell us you were having a makeover. It's rather emo, isn't it?" And there it was, one of the words I had prepared myself to hear.

Emo, goth, grunge, punk, and even skater, if you were into any of that, Lauren had something to say. I didn't know why, but she hated it, and over the years, she made it abundantly clear. She ghosted anyone who wore it, spoke it, listened to it, or resembled it.

On the first day of school, I remember Lauren telling some skater boys where to go when they tried to sit at the table next to ours. I don't even know where they went. It's like she used her evil sorcery to make them all disappear. I was already tangled too far in her web to stand up for them, so I stayed quiet, even if I did disagree.

"You're just missing the nose piercing, lip ring, and the tramp stamp on your back," she said, smirking at Sophie.

Usually, her words would have offended me, but not while Olly's and Mum's words were in my head. I wasn't going to let her beat me down.

I tightened my grip on my bag straps, stood tall and let my words fall. "Lauren cut the bull shit; I've had enough of it."

Her eyes widened, and her mouth fell open, as did Sophie's. My toes curled into my shoes so hard, and my stomach felt like it was in my ass, but I carried on. "Firstly, my name is Ashley, not Ash, so don't call me that; I hate it. Secondly, I don't have to ask your permission to change my style, and thirdly, this is me, and if it means we're not friends anymore, then fine. If you were my real friend, you would accept me as I have you. I have done what you said for years, and I have never felt so uncomfortable in my own skin. You have treated me like shit for so long, and I'm sick of it. From now on, I will be who I am supposed to be," I finished, catching my breath.

I thought I had the confidence to stand up to her, but the trembling in my hands and knees told me otherwise. My throat was like sandpaper, my palms were clammy, and sweat dripped down my spine as I waited for her response.

Damn, why did I open my big mouth?

Lauren was stunned, eerily silent, and I hated every prolonged second of it. Sophie, Hannah, and Katie had surrounded her, all looking down at me as I stood alone.

She glanced at them, then around and back to me, scowling. "Ashley, stop kidding yourself. You have never been one of us; without me, you will have no friends," Lauren bit back. "Who would want to sit with a chubby loser like you." She laughed an evil laugh, and the others joined. "Do you think we will miss you being around? I don't think so."

Her words were cruel and caused every emotion of mine to escalate. I thought I was strong enough to ignore her comments, but the mention of my weight got me every time. I was vulnerable, especially when what she said was true. I had no friends.

I was kidding myself, thinking this could have played out any other way. Thanks to my stupid decision to try and be myself, I had undoubtedly lost my social status for the last few weeks of school. Why didn't I wait until summer?

"Arr, what's wrong, cake got your tongue?" she said mockingly as I stood mute. "See, Ashley, you know I'm right. I don't know why I let you hang around with us for so long; you're a loser. No one cares about you. You might as well not be here."

Her final words hit hard and caused my first tear to roll down my cheek, taking my mascara with it. Before I knew it, I had walked back out of the gates and down the hill. I left my best friend of eleven years behind for good. Her words were unforgivable, and she had again succeeded in making me believe I was worthless.

I had no one calling behind me and didn't have the phone number of the one person I trusted.

Instead of going home, I walked to the park and sat on the swing, slinging my bag down as tears streamed down my face questioning what I had ever done wrong.

CHAPTER TWELVE

As the clouds turned black and the rain started to pour, I stayed on the rubberized tire, clinging to the metal chains. I was numb, as if the rain was avoiding me, and why shouldn't it? Why should it waste its precious tiny droplets on me, the waste of space I was? No matter how much I wanted people to see me, my efforts were pointless. No one cared where I was. I could disappear, and no one would notice. I could scream from the top of my voice and still stay unheard.

For so many years, I'd had all this pressure to be someone I'm not, and what for? Regardless, I was still sitting in an isolated park alone, becoming a smear of tears and rain. I wished I could go back to the start and change every path I had chosen and every friend I had made. I knew who I needed to avoid now, yet it was too late.

I had scarred my reputation, and one word from Lauren about it would surely destroy any hope I had for prom, a good summer, and a fresh start in sixth form. I could only hope she didn't know half as many people as she made out, as I was bound to go to university with at least one of them.

The only idea I had was to run. To run and turn my back on everyone I loved. To choose between being alone or being miserable. Where would I go? Would Mum, Dad, and Zoe miss me? Would Lauren be sorry for saying such damaging words, words she couldn't take back, and what about Olly? Would he take her to prom? That's what she wanted and why she was so mad at me. She was jealous, her biggest trigger to becoming the bitch she could be.

I shivered as the rain soaked me. My hands were cold, and puddles filled my shoes. I didn't know what time it was or how long I had sat there. But I did know that I wanted to see Olly, and without him, I felt hollow.

Since meeting him, I confronted my feelings and experienced things I never had. My heart ached heavily like never before, and I thought about him when I wasn't with him. When Olly walked away, I watched him until he was out of sight, hoping he would return, yet he didn't see how much I needed him, and I wasn't aware either. I missed him, and he was the only one who could make everything okay. How could this have happened? I didn't know him, yet I felt like I couldn't live without him. If only I knew he thought the same, but he didn't; he was way out of my league. The truth brought me to the conclusion I needed; I might as well not be here.

After struggling to loosen my grip from the cold bars in which the rust had stained my palms, I slowly swung towards my school bag, picked it up onto my lap, and opened the zip. I took out the packet of sleeping pills and opened the child lock. The sound of Lauren saying, "You might as well not be here," repeated in my mind as I apprehensively tipped the entire contents into my palm.

Bringing it towards my lips, I put them in my mouth, crunched down on them, and then reopened my bag to reveal a bottle of vodka I had sneaked from my dad's cabinet. Opening the cap, I sniffed the liquid, which I hoped didn't taste as bad as I expected. As my hands shook uncontrollably, I then tipped it towards my mouth.

The first sip was the first swig of alcohol I had ever tasted, and instead of being at a party with my friends, I was praying it would send me to sleep. I wanted to escape from the nightmare of being a teenager, the struggles of being bullied by my best friend, and being invisible to everyone else.

The liquor burned my throat as I took larger sips, gagging on the tablets as they made their way into my empty stomach. Tears streamed down my face as my reckless decision took control of me. Every hateful word I had experienced intruded on my broken mind. The more alcohol I consumed, the drowsier I felt; I was now warm despite the rain covering me. My tired body swayed on the swing as it became light, and my vision blurred. The next minute I felt my head hit the floor.

CHAPTER THIRTEEN

"Urgh," I muttered as my eyes flickered, slowly opening as they altered to the light and the white walls surrounding me. I was no longer at the park; that much was clear.

The ache in my head was intense, and I couldn't move it from its position. As I lifted my arm to touch the discomfort, the sight of tubes inserted in my hand flipped my stomach and made me heave. The sudden movement pained my chest, abdomen, and throat all at once, bringing me back to the reality of my earlier choices.

The monitor next to me took my attention as the noise echoed through my aching face, heightening my scenes. I listened to the beeps and watched the wavy lines shift across the black screen, swallowing hard as they mesmerised me; it hurt, so I looked away.

Over on the chair were my clothes neatly folded along with my bag. I looked down, pulling at the chequered gown draping me. Crossing my arms, I rubbed my hands up and down my goose-pimpled skin. It felt tight and itchy, yet numb. My entire body was groggy, and my memories were disorientated.

I needed to know what had happened and how I came to be lying in a hospital bed.

Struggling, I sat up slightly, trying not to move too suddenly. When I managed to stroke my fingers where the pain was, I was horrified to find something parting my hair. My fingers gently moved down what felt like stitches, even though I didn't recollect hurting myself. My chest tightened at the thought of my missing memories, my breathing fell out of sync, and my eyes welled. I was panicking, but then the door opened, distracting me.

"Mum, Dad," I tried, but my voice didn't come out. I cupped my throat, gulping to soothe the dryness, but the pain was excruciating. Yet the worry on my parent's faces didn't compare to the guilt I carried.

Weak and ashamed, I burst into tears, hiding my eyes.

"Oh, Ashley," Mum cried. She hugged me so tightly that it felt more like punishment than comfort. I knew what I had done, and as I looked toward Dad, he confirmed it. His expression was sad, and his eyes creased as he tried not to weep.

The tears I watched trying to form in my dad's glossy eyes were rare. My mum bawling over my shoulder was heartbreaking. I instantly wished I could turn back time and have stayed at home like I wanted to. Instead, after reading articles about depressed teenagers, I put vodka and pills in my bag as a last resort. I never thought I would use them, and I couldn't believe I did. Why would I have since I enjoyed my shopping trip with Mum and felt so optimistic on the way to school?

But with the hollow pain in my chest and the still atmosphere in the room, I was fully aware of how foolish I had been. I had been selfish and caused those I love pain rather than talking to them.

"Mum, Dad, I'm so sorry, so so sorry," I said, forcing my rasping voice out, crying as I let go of her.

"I know...We know," Mum sobbed, wiping my cheeks with her trembling thumbs. "We're just relieved you are okay. But sweetheart, what were you thinking? You could have killed yourself."

"I wasn't thinking. I don't know what came over me. I just..." I paused as my throat clenched. I couldn't breathe. "Lauren was so horrible to me this morning. She told me I might as well not be here." I broke down as sadness washed over me, covering my red, swollen eyes with my hands. Humiliation and regret beat me for letting Lauren's hurtful words win.

"Lauren is fully aware of what her actions have caused. She won't be back in school until the next school term, thanks to them taking immediate disciplinary action. Let's hope you being here is enough for her to change her attitude towards her friends," Mum said with a sigh. She brushed my hair behind my ears before looking back at Dad.

"How did I get here?" I asked, rubbing the droplets from my face as I calmed myself.

Dad sat down on the edge of the bed and took my hand as Mum moved back, placing her hand on his shoulder. He said, "A boy found you unconscious in the park, and he rang an ambulance. You passed out and banged your head on the floor. You have six stitches."

With a harsh swallow, I watched his Adams apple quiver.

"We didn't know how much you had consumed, but with the empty bottle and packet, the doctors decided to pump your stomach, which will explain the pain in your throat and why you feel rotten. Your vitals have stabilised since you have been on the iv drip, so hopefully, you can go home in a few days," he finished. Then for the first time in my life, I witnessed Dad cry. It ripped my heart out.

"Oh, god, I'm sorry. I've been so stupid. I will never forgive myself for this and what I have put you through."

"No, Ashley, we are sorry we didn't notice the signs sooner. You have been so distant lately," Mum said. "I should have asked more questions yesterday after your episode in the car. Just promise that you will talk to us if something is troubling you from now on."

"I will, I promise." I leaned my head against the pillow, raising the bed to a better position. "I'm sorry for disappointing you both."

"It's okay, kiddo. Your friends have a lot to answer for; put it that way. You scared the hell out of us, and nothing had prepared us for it," Dad muttered as he stood and kissed me on the forehead before hugging me.

"I love you so much," I mumbled, holding him tightly. "Where is Zoe?"

"She is with Nate and his parents," Mum said. "Which reminds me, Olly seemed rather upset with the news, so I gave his mum your mobile number to pass on. I hope you don't mind that I gave it to him."

"Oh, okay, yeah, that's fine," I said with a small smile as my delicate stomach swirled and cheeks flushed.

"Right, I will get the doctor and tell them you are awake." I nodded, and Mum left the room as Dad sat on the chair and opened the newspaper.

I slowly picked up the plastic cup of water from the unit beside me and took a sip. A sound tried to escape my bruised throat, but instead, I breathed through the pain as the liquid sliding down was like drinking razor blades, and the pain didn't stop until it hit my empty stomach.

"Are you okay?" Dad asked, looking up as I winced. I slowly nodded, put the cup back down, and closed my eyes.

*

"Night, Ashley," Zoe said, crawling over the bed and sprawling the UNO cards everywhere. The game we had been playing since she saw them in the gift shop. I didn't mind, it limited the questions, and I beat her every time.

"Night, Squidge," I said, cuddling her, embracing how close she was and how I had people who loved me surrounding me. The thought of losing them was tormenting, having nearly lost them forever. I had put them through too much, and I was sure it would take an eternity to make up for it.

"I love you all," I said, blowing them a kiss as they left the room.

Shuffling, I attempted to make myself comfy in the typically hard hospital bed I had been in all day. I did try to go for a walk, but I only made it to the door. My stomach churned and made me sick, which the doctor told me would pass once I ate. I'd waited all day for the flapjack and a box of grapes beside me to look appetising, but it never happened.

As silence filled the room, I picked up the colouring book Zoe picked, fiddled with the pencils, and started to colour. I let my creativity kick in and allowed my mind to relax.

Lauren's harsh words, the event in the park, reliving my missing memories with Mum, and discussing with the doctor if I was depressed and suicidal soon floated away.

I denied the accusation.

Seeing the look on my family's faces was enough to clear the fog in my mind. I was loved and didn't need to be popular.

Having been absorbed into believing that boys and social statuses were the most critical thing in teenage life, I now knew it was far from true. As long as I had Mum, Dad, and Zoe around me, I would be okay, and I didn't need to feel sorry for myself anymore. What I chose to do during a moment of weakness and stupidity could have been the worst way I could have discovered it. Still, I had a chance to start fresh, to be me, the real me, away from Lauren and Sophie.

I was far from feeling sad about it all. I was more comforted than anything.

CHAPTER FOURTEEN

"Ashley, dinner is on the table," Mum warily said as she opened my bedroom door. I listened to her sigh. I was wrapped under my duvet on my bedroom floor, surrounded by my magazines, with tears rolling down my face and Avril's CD on repeat.

"I'm not hungry," I mumbled, my voice croaky and sore.

"Sweetheart, you need to eat; it's been four days since you came home. I know you're fragile, but I'm worried about you. Maybe you should go and talk to someone?" she insisted again. Since the doctor mentioned it, I knew she wouldn't drop it until I did.

"Mum, I'm okay," I huffed. "Stop worrying. I'm not going to do anything stupid. Don't you think I have learnt my lesson already?"

"Ashley."

"Mum, don't. I'm fine," I grumbled, pulling my cover down.

"Okay. I'll leave it in the oven."

I nodded, refusing to look at her for too long so she couldn't see my red-raw eyes, which burnt when they opened, and teardrops fell from when they closed.

I had done nothing but cried from the moment I returned home. I thought I was okay; I told the doctor I was okay, but I started to think owerwise as every message that filled my phone closed the walls a little further in on me.

I was getting a text from everybody. People I didn't even know somehow had my number. But the one text I was waiting for was still to arrive.

When Mum said Olly was upset, I thought she meant because I was in the hospital, but his silence told me he was upset with me for being so idiotic.

I climbed onto my bed and pulled the duvet over my head, "Thanks, Mum, but I don't want it."

Mum exhaled profoundly and closed the door behind her as I continued to lock everyone out. I let my thoughts take over, and my cries fall. This behaviour was what I promised myself I would change. But, admittedly, I was struggling to change my perception of life. Perhaps Mum was right, and I did need to talk to someone as everything I was doing wasn't normal.

Why didn't I want to speak to someone?

That's obvious, isn't it? I was sixteen, stubborn and uninterested in anyone's opinion. I was so afraid about being judged, despite it being something I had been for so long, which was now no secret as far as my whole school was concerned.

*

The door opening brought me around from the sleep I had fallen into. "Mum, I told you to leave me alone," I groaned.

I listened to the door shut. "It's not your mum," he softly spoke.

"Olly," I whispered, flinging the duvet straight from me.

"Ashley," he hesitantly said. His tone was stiff, and his expression was still. When he stepped closer and the light from the window hit his face, I gasped, standing up so abruptly it pulled my aching muscles.

"What happened to your face?" I said. He had a bruised eye, cut cheek, and split lip. Uncrossing my arms, I moved my touch to his jaw, but he moved away. I dropped my hand and perched on the edge of the bed.

"Olly?" My voice quivered.

He moved his gaze from my bruised arms and hands to my pale face and injured head. His dark, mysterious eyes fixed on my sorrowful state, looking like he had a lot to say.

I had prepared myself for the lecture and the stupidity he would bring up, knowing he couldn't keep his opinions to himself. But him looking like he had been in a street brawl was now my biggest concern.

"Olly, talk to me. What happened to you?" I said sternly, tightening my fists so tightly my nails dug into my palms.

"Ashley, don't, it doesn't matter. You are what matters."

I let out a sarcastic laugh. "Not when you look like that, I don't. Who did that to you?"

Olly huffed and pulled at his bracelets. "There was a fight at Bailey. I was in the wrong place at the wrong time. Now can we drop it?" I saw anger in his eyes or regret; I couldn't tell. Either way, it had taken four days for him to come and see me, and I was ruining it.

I nodded and swallowed my curiosity as he sat beside me, handing me a McDonald's bag. Its aroma had filled my room and panged my rumbling tummy.

"Your mum told me you need to eat," he insisted, sipping his large coke.

"I do," I said, being too polite to turn down the food he had brought, even when I didn't want it.

I crossed my legs, facing him and unravelled the chicken burger, tipping the chips into the opposite side of the box. Picking up a salted chip, I took it slowly to my mouth and licked my lips. Taking little, tiny bites, I chewed slowly, attempting to avoid worsening the pain in my bruised throat, sipping water with every mouthful. My body loosened instantly, thanking me for finally feeding its starving state.

"I was going to text you, but I didn't know what to say," Olly muttered, watching me intently.

"It's okay. I don't blame you after what I did," I mumbled, avoiding Olly's sad eyes.

I hated that I couldn't confess what I did. I couldn't say the words without feeling ashamed, and rightly so. I should feel ashamed. I hated myself for doing it and upsetting so many people.

He twiddled with his straw before reopening his paper bag, putting the cup in and pulling out a Mcflurry. It made me smile. "My mum has something to do with this, doesn't she."

"Of course." He smiled, handing it to me. "She told me it was your favourite." And with how it slid down my aching throat like someone was smoothing out the bumps in it, I couldn't be more thankful to her.

"Thank you," I said as I held the spoon in my mouth, sucking it clean and ditching the chips and burger.

"No problem."

Olly's glossy eyes wandered my room, noticeably avoiding me the more silence filled the gaps. "Ashley," he paused, swallowing harshly. "You scared me."

"I know," I muttered, "I'm sorry."

"You don't know, though, do you? Otherwise, you wouldn't have done it. You would have come to find me like I told you to."

I moved my gaze to him; it was the least he deserved. "I don't know what?"

"See. Why do you act so ignorantly of how I feel about you," Olly said with an exasperated sigh.

"What do you mean, how you feel about me?" I tentatively stuttered.

"I need to protect you," he said in a tone much sharper than I expected. "You should have come to me instead of being alone and doing something so stupid."

Olly's words were far from what I imagined and wanted to hear. What did he mean by that? Protect me?

"I'm sorry, I thought we were just neighbours. We only met two weeks ago," I replied cautiously, one, not to hurt my voice and two, arguing with Olly was the last thing I wanted.

"I know, but...." he stopped, raking his hand through his hair.

"But what, Olly?"

"You have been my closest friend since moving here, and I nearly lost you by your careless decision." His words choked me. I was gasping for air, fighting back the tears forming again. His lyrics puzzled me, and I was too shy and out of sorts to ask if he liked me the way I liked him. Why couldn't I say what I wanted to? I wanted to scream it out for him, to show him how sorry I was.

"You can cry. I won't think any less of you," Olly said, reaching his hand to my shoulder and pulling me closer. His arms wrapped around me, and I returned the gesture, hugging him so tightly that I didn't want to let go. It was amazing, and his musky, vanilla scent only made it more perfect.

As I leaned my head against his neck, his warm breath reached my back and shivered my spine, awakening my body. It was as if he was bursting the life back into me. My thoughts went into overdrive. I wanted to kiss him; I so desperately wanted to kiss him, but I didn't know what we were. Protecting me wasn't exactly boyfriend, and I didn't want to ruin the moment.

Okay, I was too much of a wuss to think I could just assume I was allowed to kiss him.

"Please don't do anything stupid again," Olly whispered. He stroked my hair, gliding his fingers slowly over my healing stitches.

"I won't. I promise," I mumbled, and my tears fell. There were so many words I wanted to say to make it right, but I couldn't; I knew someday I would, but just not then.

Olly's shirt caught every one of my sorrowful cries as I chose not to hide anymore, and with every drop, the truth set me free from the girl I'd been pretending to be a little more.

With every swallow, agony flowed down my throat and into my aching chest, but being wrapped in Olly's arms made me glad I could feel the pain. The warmth of my tears warmed my cheeks and burnt my sore eyes. They reminded me that I was alive and that he was not just a figment of my imagination. I was being who he wanted me to be, and that was myself, my fragile broken self.

CHAPTER FIFTEEN

"It was nice of Olly to come round last night," Mum said as she placed a cup of tea and slices of toast in front of me on the kitchen table. "What time did he leave?"

Raking my hand through my knotted hair, I gave a little shrug. "I don't know. I fell asleep. He was gone when I woke up."

"Oh," is all Mum replied.

I furrowed my brows, "Oh?"

Mum placed a glass of water with fizzing aspirin on the table beside my tea and gave a small smile. "I'm not used to you having a boy in your bedroom, and he's been here every day." Her cheeks flushed a little.

"It's not like that, Mum. I wish it were, though," I joked, and her reaction pulled a quiet and painful laugh from me. "We talk all night, that's all. You wanted me to confide in someone, and he is that someone. Besides, he was only here because of you."

"What? Me? No, no, I never," she tried.

"He told me," I said with a bit of a giggle.

"Oh, well, he's crap at keeping secrets," she grinned. "Drink up; it will help with the pain."

I looked at the now settled cloudy water and heaved, "You know I hate it."

"Just drink it, please." And I did, gagging on every mouthful.

"Thank you," she said, taking the glass. I quickly washed its vile sour flavour with my tea, grimacing at how they didn't combine well together.

Mum sat beside me, brushed her hand down the back of my hair, and sighed deeply.

"What is it now?" I warily asked.

She rested her hand on her fist. "This isn't the end of the school year I had expected for you, no prom, no friends, no goodbye. It doesn't seem like you have had any closure."

Breaking the toast into smaller pieces, I fiddled with it. "I know, and that's why I'm going to go to school today."

Her posture straightened, and her anxieties sketched over her face, "You are? Are you sure that's a good idea?"

"I am. As you said, it's the last day. I need to put it behind me by facing it head-on and not running from it like I have for the past week and a half." I rose to my feet, binned my remaining breakfast and put my plate in the dishwasher.

Stepping back toward Mum, whose eyes hadn't left me, I placed my hand on her shoulder and smiled. "I'll be fine, Mum. I love you. Stop worrying about me."

"That's easier said than done," she muttered as I walked out of the kitchen.

A knock at the front door came as I approached the stairs. I could see Olly's perfectly shaped silhouette through the frosted glass and his scarlet top beamed across the carpet as the sun caught it.

I lowered the handle and beamed as my gaze fell on him. "Morning, Olly, I won't be a minute. Come in." He stepped in the doorway, placing his bag down before saying hello to my mum and Zoe.

"Hi, Olly," Mum said, flashing a quick smile, "Make yourself at home. Ashley, go and get dressed."

"I'll be back," I said before going up the stairs.

*

I ran a brush through my hair, thankful it was naturally straight and that the length covered my stitches. Being the last day of term, it was dress as you please, so I could keep my hair down and wear what I wanted—no more unflattering uniform.

Opening the sliding doors of my wardrobe, the image of clothes I had forgotten I had brought greeted me. I hadn't gotten dressed all week and was used to lounging around in my pyjamas. I was a little nervous about stepping into any of it after the last time I wore an outfit of my choosing.

I pulled my new pair of navy flared jeans from the hanger and shoved them on. They hung looser on me than before and needed a belt. Seeing as I had wanted to lose weight, I was now worried I looked ill; I couldn't win either way.

I covered my bra with a new black vest and my leather jacket. My ensemble was comfy and how I wanted it to be, as I didn't wish to stand out. I slipped my feet into my new black converse and skipped down the stairs.

Grabbing my bag, I took out my sunglasses and sat them on my head. "Olly, I'm ready," I hollered, and he appeared from the living room with Mum.

"You look nice," Mum said.

"She does," Olly added, making me blush. He picked up his bag and opened the door.

"Ashley, can I check your bag, please?" Mum then muttered, making me turn back to her with a frown.

"Mum," I groaned, and she gestured her hand. "Fine," I said, opening it and letting her see inside.

There was nothing in it other than my purse, a bottle of water, and an old school T-shirt, which, when the time came, I'd ask my friends for a scribble. It would undoubtedly only have Olly on it by the end of the day, so it felt pointless.

"Thank you," she muttered, running her hand up and down my arm. "If you want to come home, please do."

"I will, Mum; please stop worrying."

She rolled her eyes at Olly. "Make sure she eats something."

He nodded and straightened his cap. "I will."

"Jeez, I don't need babysitting. Can we please go?" I snapped, leaving the hallway and stepping into the first bit of fresh air since coming home.

The sky was a gorgeous shade of blue, the smell of fresh grass filled my senses, and my body immediately relaxed. Summer had always been my favourite season, and I was glad I could put my sunglasses on to hide the tiredness in my eyes.

"Your mum is only worried about you," Olly said as we left the driveway.

"I know; she can just be smothering at times."

"And rightly so."

I rolled my eyes. "Okay, can we drop it now?"

"Sorry," he stuttered. My mood placed silence between us as we walked side by side towards the school for the last time, and I said nothing more.

I was nervous, my stomach was churning, and my legs felt heavy. I could feel my palms shaking as I clung to the straps of my bag, denying the gravity trying to pull me back home. Still, I knew I couldn't hide in my room forever. If I wanted some closure, I needed to say goodbye to the hell hole of a place that made me the miserable, self-conscious girl I had become.

*

"Are you okay?" Olly cautiously asked as he noticed me start to slow and freeze to a statue-like position once we reached the park.

Over the last week, I had cried uncontrollably, felt alone, and thought I couldn't take any more. But there I was, having managed to get up today, with food in my system, wearing a new outfit and standing beside my one friend who was honest and genuine.

"Ashley?" he probed, bringing me from the thoughts.

"Huh?" I quietly stammered, breaking my gaze from the swing.

"Are you okay?"

"Yes, I'm fine."

"We can go home if you want?" he said as I shifted my eyes to him.

His deep brunette stare was concerned, and when his hand reached out to mine, my reaction was to pull away, but his hand reached further. He entwined my fingers with his and said, "You can do this. I'm here with you."

Olly tugged me up the path, and I exhaled profoundly as my feet started to move. My heart sank. I didn't look back at the park as we left and prepared myself to face my problems head-on.

I could see Olly's friends at the gates, and we were heading towards them. His hand was still holding onto mine, and his grip was getting tighter as people around us started to stare. I suddenly couldn't breathe and unknitted my fingers from his. I checked my hair was covering my head injury, trying to compose myself.

"Hey, Ashley, are you all right, feeling better?" Lewis asked first, taking the group's attention to me.

I had envisioned everyone pointing, shouting mocking words about trying to hurt myself. And as all their eyes interrogated me, I didn't know what to say to get it over quickly.

I found no response escaping my mouth as Lewis stood looking at me, waiting. I already needed rescuing, and it had only been five minutes; how would I manage another six hours?

"You are doing okay, aren't you, Ashley," Olly said, and I looked at him and nodded hesitantly.

"Considering what you have been through, you look great," another lad added, bringing a small smile and altering my worried expression.

"Thank you. I'm fine," is all I managed.

"Good, at least you are okay, and something good came from it. Girls can be so bitchy, and at least Lauren is finally getting punished for bullying so many girls. I still can't believe you were one of them. She was supposed to be your best friend. She didn't deserve to win prom queen anyway," Lewis finished. I narrowed my brows and glanced at Olly, who was warily looking at his feet shuffling on the ground.

"What do you mean, something good?" I queried.

"Have you not told her?" Lewis said, rolling his football up and down his torso.

Olly stepped a few inches away from me, and his presence no longer kept me safe. I put my hands into my pockets and waited. "No, I haven't. I wanted her to see it for herself."

"See what? What's going on?" My stomach knotted, and my throat tightened. "Olly, what's Lewis on about?"

"Ashley," Sophie shouted from behind me, making my body sweat more than it was. Her voice went straight through me as I turned, finding Katie and Hannah linked to her as if she was the new Lauren.

"Now I want to go home," I muttered to myself.

I wasn't ready for what she had to say to me.

"Wow, look at you. You look great," Sophie smiled, hugging me tightly, though I failed to respond, nor did I have time to dodge her.

She stepped back from me, letting me go. I crossed my arms tightly over my body as their three sets of eyes swept me up and down.

What was wrong with my outfit? Was my hair too long or the wrong colour? Was my makeup terrible? Did I look fat? I panicked.

She hadn't even said anything horrible, and my worries had risen rapidly. I couldn't control them. I retreated, digging my feet firmly into the ground.

"Ashley," Olly said, stepping closer, as did Lewis.

"Sorry, I'm fine, I'm okay," I muttered, watching Sophie question what was wrong. It was evident she had no idea how I felt about her.

"Sophie, leave Ashley alone, please," Olly said, standing in front of me.

"Ashley, what's going on? We're friends, right?" she tried as she moved toward me.

My lungs caught and then relaxed as I cast my tears aside, looking at Olly for focus. When I found my bearings, I moved Olly and locked my gaze with hers.

"Sophie, we're not friends anymore, not after what you and Lauren have done to me for the last few years." I licked my dry lips and swallowed harshly.

"It was never anything; it was a joke. You were always one of us. We have known each other since we were five. You can't say we're not friends anymore," she said as her pretty blue eyes glossed over.

I shook my head. "A joke? If you had been me and experienced what I have, you wouldn't be calling it a joke." I clenched my fists tightly. "Sophie, I nearly died. I wanted to kill myself because of the toxic things you and Lauren said and put into my head. I don't need friends like that, like you, not anymore," I managed before the words choked me, and tears started running down my face. And with that, I turned away, nodded to Olly, and walked through the gates with him and Lewis, not looking back at her, knowing she was also crying.

I was heartbroken, but a huge weight lifted with every word, and I meant every one of them.

Sophie wasn't as mean as Lauren, I could consider her as one of her followers, just as I were, but she never backed me up when the time called for it. Together they had both made me feel worthless, and it wasn't in me to treat them differently. It was time to move on from them, regardless of how hurt I felt.

"Are you okay?" Olly muttered, holding the door open for me, and it wasn't until I entered the halls that I saw what Lewis was on about as posters and banners filled my eye line.

"Holy shit. What the," I blurted out, horrified, covering my wide-open mouth.

My photo was all over the place, plastering every sheet pinned to the walls and panic flowed through me as I had no idea why.

Olly ripped one off the wall and handed it to me. "Here," he said.

I clutched onto the brightly coloured poster and read the words.

Beat the Bullies
You are never alone
It is not difficult to be kind
Let's raise awareness and vote Ashley prom queen

"Over the past week, the school has been holding bake sales, raffles, sports activities, stuff like that to raise money for bullying awareness," Olly explained. "I know you won't believe how many people care about you, but they do. The school has raised over fifteen hundred pounds."

My grip tightened, and the paper crumpled in my hand. I flared my nostril and puffed my chest. "*This* has been going on, and you didn't think to tell me. I'm not the laughing stock but instead am the face of what happens to the unfortunate victims of bullies, which by the way, doesn't feel much better," I retorted.

"Ashley, calm down. It's not like that," Olly tried, reaching out to me, but I brushed his hand away.

"No, Olly, you could have prepared me for this, knowing I wouldn't like it. You have had all last week and this to tell me." I threw the sheet to the floor and yanked at my hair. "And the prom thing, *me* as prom queen, that's a notion I may have liked, but it is completely and utterly ridiculous."

"Ash," he said, and I cut him off.

"I'm not going anyway, so what's the point? It's a stupid idea. Prom queen is the last thing I want. Jeez," I huffed, rolling my eyes.

"Is it? I thought you wanted to be popular?" he asked more sternly.

"No, Olly," I shouted. "Being prom queen for being the sob story is never what I wanted. And I don't want to be noticed, not anymore. I always thought I did, but I want to be like everyone else, confident, happy, and ordinary. Just myself," I paused, breathing as my heart started to beat rapidly. "I want people to say hello to me as I walk down the hallway and not be invisible. All I have ever wanted was to be worth something and important to someone. Argh!" I punched the air beside me. "Oh, it doesn't matter; you wouldn't understand. You *are* one of the popular ones."

"Ashley, stop it," Olly yelled. My breathing was out of whack, uncontrollable, hyperventilating almost.

"This is all so so stupid. It's worse than I imagined," I said, pacing up and down the hall, not knowing what to do, think or say; I was losing it.

"Stop," Olly ordered me, grabbing my arm. He placed his hands on my arms and rubbed them up and down. "Take a deep breath, in and out slowly," he said, performing them with me as I copied.

I puffed my chest out and sucked it in, staring into his eyes, which had irritated and compelled me to the spot simultaneously.

"Everything is going to be okay. *You* are going to be okay; I promise." His words soothed me and worked quickly, and I didn't doubt that I needed him by my side for the remainder of the school day. "Can we get one thing straight?"

"What?"

"I care about you. Stop saying no one does. I have been here without you, seeing what everyone's been doing to raise awareness. I'm the one people have come to ask how you are, and talking about it every day hasn't been easy. You need to stop thinking everyone is against you; they aren't, especially me."

As I watched him talk, my gaze fell to his luscious thin lips, which I could see were frustrated as the tension in his jaw was prominent. I couldn't take my eyes off him as his words became distant, and I zoned out of the room. I recalled when he kissed me and how much I would love it to happen again. But, as he kept telling me he cared about me, I knew he meant as a friend, and I forgot how infatuated I was with him with everything that had been going on. I wanted to feel his lips on mine to stop me from feeling numb. I wished I had the confidence to make the first move.

"Is that a yes?" he said, clearing his throat.

"Is what a yes?" I questioned, shaking my thoughts away.

"Were you even listening to me?"

"Sorry, I zoned out."

"I asked you to come to the prom with me?"

WHAT THE FRACK.

"Me? Really? What?" I stuttered.

"Yes, you." He smiled.

"I'm not going," is what mumbled out of my mouth, altering Olly's expression. He was annoyed, and I knew I had ruined the moment with three words.

"Are you for real?" He frowned. "I got the impression you would come if I asked you."

I sighed and said, "I wanted you to ask me, but that was before. I don't want to go anymore; I honestly don't."

"Okay. Well. Thank you," Olly said curtly before walking off and outside, slamming the door behind him.

Bloody hell, why did I just do that?

CHAPTER SIXTEEN

The lame fresher classes were over, exams were done, and the last day had arrived, a few weeks earlier than the other years. They had sports day, and we had activities all over the place, so the school was more crowded than I would have preferred. But seeing as I could do what I wanted with my time, I could keep away from those I didn't want to see.

The media department showed films; the cooking department made cookies; the drama had a show. You get the gist. It was a free choice and meant to be fun, not that I would call walking around alone fun.

Since Olly left in a huff, I was left in my own company, but it was nothing new. Except for a change, I enjoyed the peace and planned to use it to mull over how I would fix things with him. I didn't get very far when some girls approached me. At first, my butt fell into my mouth as I panicked, but they were genuinely friendly and kept me company.

Where had they been the entire time? I questioned. I should have asked them, seeing as I had never noticed anyone other than my social group. It was then I realised how oblivious I had become. I was wrapped up in my world of wanting to be popular and utterly obsessed with wanting to be like Lauren.

I spent the remainder of the day with these girls. I enjoyed playing badminton in the sports hall, playing music on the keyboards, and making heart-shaped cookies. And despite seeing Sophie's eyes scolding me in the cafeteria, I was happily surrounded by like-minded girls. I didn't look at her or speak to her again.

I was sitting watching the last fifteen minutes of the football game before school finished, hoping Olly had spotted me from across the field. I still wanted to walk home with him and hoped he did me.

Something hit my back, taking my attention from the match. Mila put her hand on the skateboard that had knocked me and pushed it back across the concrete.

I watched it roll over to a group of lads surrounded by sets of wheels, a cloud of smoke and a glorious array of black and red clothes.

When a foot stopped the white, chipped board, my gaze rose, halting on the face staring right back at me. My jaw dropped, my throat was as dry as sandpaper, and my stomach flipped. Never had I seen an expression so evocative, so mesmerising. What was more taunting was that it looked familiar. *He* looked familiar. Freshly sculptured by heaven yet dressed for hell. But he couldn't be. I had no idea who he was or where he and his crowd came from. But I did know that group looked more my style than Lauren ever did.

"He is so dreamy, isn't he?" Mila said, pulling my gaze back to her.

"Huh, who?" I said, clearing my throat.

"Er, Olly, who else?"

I glanced back behind me, and the group was gone. My heart fell back into its rightful place, and my smile returned to Mila, then to Olly.

Mila was kind and pretty, and I liked her denim skirt and vest top style. She was no skinnier than me, wore little makeup with shiny lip gloss, and her hair was in high bunches. I could only hope I would feel as confident as her one day. She was the kind of friend I could have done with all along. It was disappointing that I had only just met her, but I was glad I'd had the chance too, and we swapped numbers to get together in the summer.

"He keeps looking at you," she said as Olly caught my eye before running back for the ball.

I bowed my head, pulling a daisy out of the grass. "We argued earlier, and we haven't spoken since."

"Why? What happened?"

"He asked me to the prom, and I told him I wasn't going."

"Are you fricking kidding me? Why would you say no to him? Are you insane?"

"I know. I don't know what happened," I sighed. "All I have done is dream about going to the prom with him."

"So why aren't you?"

"I don't want to go, not after everything."

"Oh, well, that's understandable. I'm sure Olly knows how you feel; he was probably just embarrassed after putting himself out there."

I thought for a moment about how this morning went down. "Oh crap, you're right. I hadn't even considered that," I said, rolling the daisy stem between my thumb and forefinger. Mila shrugged her shoulders with a small smile.

"Do you have a date for the prom?" I asked, and the whistle blew, and the sports coach hollered.

"Oh, oh," Mila said. "Looks like the skaters are trying to crash their game.

I stood up, brushed the cut grass from me and frowned as I watched Lewis square up to a guy. And as I squinted, it was the boy from behind me. He was shouting at Olly, with Lewis intervening. My first instinct was to go over.

I took a step, and Mila gripped my arm, "No, Ashley, don't. Don't you know who that is? He isn't worth getting involved with."

I furrowed my brows, mouth gaping, palms sweaty. "But Olly could get hurt."

"And what are you going to do?" My shoulders relaxed, letting a large breath out. She was right.

I froze beside her and watched a display of shouting and pushing before the teacher got involved. The guy then looked in our direction, as did Olly. I didn't know what to do or what to think.

Olly then stepped closer to him, tensed his jaw and muttered something before wiping his beautifully smelling sweat from his forehead and picking up his bag.

"Do you know what's happening?" Mila said, picking up the long cardigan she had been sitting on and shaking it.

"Not a clue," I muttered, biting the inside of my mouth.

"Oh, he's on the way over. He looks pissed, and I don't like confrontation, so I'm going to bail. Sorry, I hope to see you soon."

"Enjoy the prom," I shouted as she crossed the field.

I watched Olly saunter towards me. His gaze was fierce, and it had me flustering as it did every time. He looked as tense as I felt. Behind him, I could see the skaters watching, that guy with his skateboard firmly behind his head on his shoulder, staring.

As he drew closer, my heart rate rose as my nerves got the better of me. When he was in earshot, I said, "Olly, what's going on? Who was that guy? How do you know him?" but he cut me off.

He chucked his bag on the floor and grabbed me into his arms, planting his lips onto mine, stealing my breath and every other sense. His hand was firmly on my quivering spine and the other within the crease on my neck. His lips and his kiss were unbearably fragile. There were no words, just a smooth sensation beautifully awakening me, so tender I felt powerless and was suddenly stoned.

The atmosphere between us was hot and thick, and I was fully aware our classmates were around us. I didn't let it embarrass me and responded naturally to him. Gently cupping his face, I fell hopelessly into his arms, embracing the exquisite taste of his kiss.

When he let go, he leaned his forehead against mine and grinned. His arms stayed tightly wrapped around me, protecting me and making me feel safer than I ever had.

"Forget about him," he whispered, and when I scanned the field, he was there, punching someone else.

"Erm, I'm so confused," I swallowed.

Olly cupped my face and guided my gaze to his. "About this morning, it doesn't matter if you don't want to go to the prom. I won't go either. Come round mine instead."

Smitten, I didn't falter to question whether my parents would agree. I just nodded, smiled and kissed him again. It was so dreamlike that I forgot about everything else. The moment couldn't have gone any better if I had planned it myself.

*

"I'll see you later," Olly said, letting go of my hand as we reached my front door. He kissed my cheek and walked towards his house, glancing back before disappearing.

As he left my sight, I let out the breath I hadn't realised I had been holding, giddy and infatuated. I shook off the goose pimples dancing over my body and opened the front door, ready for the thousands of questions I knew Mum and Dad would have for me.

Before the door shut, Zoe screeched my name and ran towards me, wrapping her tiny arms around my waist. It made my smile beam, considering that nothing could make me feel happier than I already did, and I cuddled her back.

"I missed you today, Ashley," she said, snuggling into me.

"I missed you too, squidge."

"Ahh, my goodness, what is going on here? Let me in," Mum laughed, approaching from the living room and wrapping her arms around us. "How was your day?" she questioned, squeezing us so hard I could barely breathe.

"It was great, probably the best day I have had since starting," I managed through broken breaths.

"Oh honey, I am so pleased. I've been worrying about you all day," she said as she released us, and Zoe ran back off.

We walked into the kitchen, and I took a glass out of the cupboard. I filled it with cold water from the tap and sipped it.

"So, tell me about your day. Did Olly look after you?" Mum said whilst making herself look busy. Although it was clear I didn't need to say anything, she could see the glow on my face as I grinned at the mention of his name. "Ashley?" she pried as I swigged back the rest of my water, refilling it, only running the tap longer until it was freezing.

"Did you know the school had been raising money for bullying awareness? And that I have votes for prom queen?"

"Wow," she gasped. "I'm glad the school is doing something about the ongoing issue of bullying. And prom queen, that's fantastic."

"Is it, though? I'm not so sure. I don't want to be prom queen for being the sob story of the year, and I don't want to go."

"You don't have to go, Ashley, do what you feel is right. Why not end it on a high if you had a good day?"

I hesitated, then sat down on the chair beside her, mulling over what she said. "But Olly asked me to go with him."

"He did? Oh my goodness, how cute is he," she squealed, wildly clapping her hands.

"Yes, and when I told him I wasn't going, it upset him a little," I said as I ran my finger along the rim of my glass.

"But I thought you wanted to go with Olly? You like him, don't you?"

"I do like him; I like him a lot, but like you said, going to the prom may ruin my day, and I can't be doing with the pressure and risking another panic attack."

"Panic attack? When? Why? What happened?" she worried, straightening her posture and grabbing my hand.

"Oh, it was nothing. When I saw Sophie and the posters plastered on the walls with me all over them, I lost it a little."

"Sweetie, maybe we need to go to the GP about these panic attacks," Mum gently said. "Sophie wasn't horrible, was she?"

"No, Mum, she wasn't. Seeing her was enough. Olly told her to leave me alone."

"See, he does care about you, and you thought he didn't."

"It seems that way." I smiled.

"Umm, what's that beaming grin for?"

"He kissed me at school," I paused, "And he asked me to go round his tonight, and I really want to go."

"Olly kissed you!" she gushed, nearly falling off her chair as I witnessed a mortifying display of excitement.

"Mum, you're so embarrassing. It was only a kiss." A great kiss with a perfect boy, not that I would elaborate on the details with my mother. Nor would I tell her it wasn't my first kiss.

"Sorry, I just know you have been waiting for so long. You wait until I tell your dad."

"Erm, no, please no," I said, hiding my face in my hands.

"You can go round his later," she then said, and I was the one nearly falling off my chair.

I instantly dropped my hands and widened my eyes at her. "What? Really? I didn't think it was even worth mentioning."

"Ashley, I'm not that bad. Although going round a boy's house on prom night will require a conversation with me and your father."

"Ew, cringe, Mum. I don't need that chat; trust me," I said, trying not to laugh or fluster at the idea of having anything remotely physical happen with Olly. "We had that embarrassment years ago, remember."

"I know, but I want you to be safe. It may seem like you just met Olly, and nothing will happen, but one thing can lead to another, and the next, you're pregnant at seventeen."

"Is that why you have been so hard on me all these years, you're worried I will get pregnant in school and never go to college or university like you did? I hate to remind you, but I'm no social butterfly, and I'm obviously a virgin."

"Just be careful," Mum said.

"I will. That is when the time comes." I smiled, rose from the table, and left, eager to escape the conversation sparking butterflies in my stomach.

I hadn't thought about anything happening with Olly, but the more I thought about it, the more it crossed my mind. The way he made me feel was intense. What if something did come of it? What if he wanted to take it further? Holy hell, I panicked.

I was suddenly unsure of what to do. Should I text Olly and cancel or prepare myself for the occasion? But then he texted me, and it said.

Wear ur dress. C u @ 7.
XxxX

My heart jumped out of my mouth and burst right in front of me. Don't overthink, Ashley. Breathe, just breathe. I'm sure he just wants to make sure I wear my dress, I told myself. It was expensive, after all.

And that's what I did; I prepared myself for the occasion. I showered and shaved my legs and bikini line, making myself look as good as possible. I worked with what I had, perked my boobs up in my new bra, and tried to look slimmer in tight pants. Although I had lost over a stone in the past month, I didn't need them in the end, I didn't look as frumpy as I used to, and I couldn't breathe in them anyway.

"Mum, can you come here, please," I yelled down the stairs from the landing and then went back into my room.

I spent over an hour moisturising, straightening my hair, and experimenting with makeup before wiping it off and going for my everyday look. Subtle with a stroke of eyeliner and lip gloss before eventually stepping into my prom dress.

Even with not going to prom, I was as excited as I could imagine I should feel. Although, a night around Olly's would be better, even if my nerves were shot at the idea.

"Wow! You look gorgeous," Mum gasped as I stood in front of my full-length mirror in my prom dress, holding it up.

"Thank you. Can you do it up for me?" I turned my back to her as I moved my hair over my shoulder, watching her in the mirror. "You haven't asked why I'm wearing it?" I said, and she grinned.

"What?" I warily muttered.

"I think Olly is a true romantic."

"Oh, god, no. Why? What do you know? What are you guys up to?" I flustered.

"You'll be fine, don't worry," she said as she pulled my zip up and took my hair, brushing it down my back.

I stood looking in the mirror. My dress was silk, a dark purple shade with a slight ruffle on the belly area; it had small straps and reached the floor. It fit perfectly, not too tight and not too baggy. My reflection didn't argue back, and I looked quite pretty.

"You look beautiful," Dad said as he entered my room.

"Doesn't she just," Mum beamed, wiping a tear as she became the embarrassing scene I feared. Thank god Olly wasn't there to witness it.

"You think he will like it?" I then worried as I rubbed down the creases over my waistline.

"Of course he will; there is nothing not to like."

"Hopefully not too much," Dad added, making me blush and cringe simultaneously.

"Dad!"

"What? It's prom night. Dad's worry about these things. Anyway, I'll let you continue getting ready. Olly will be expecting you in ten minutes," he said, kissing my forehead. "Oh, and Ashley, I know I don't tell you enough, but I am so proud of you; I hope you know that. And tell Olly I know where he lives."

"Dad!" I laughed again, and he grinned, then left the room.

"Ignore him," Mum giggled. "He knows we had a little chat earlier; I think it freaked him out."

"Oh, Mum, you didn't."

"Your dad is best to be prepared rather than finding out after."

"Mum, nothing is going to happen," I insisted.

She smiled at me and tucked my hair behind my ear. "I hope you have a great night; it's the least you deserve. Let's go downstairs and take lots of photos before you go."

I took one last glance at my reflection and exhaled deeply, preparing myself for what would come next.

CHAPTER SEVENTEEN

I nervously walked up to Olly's driveway. My hands were trembling, and my legs felt weak, hidden, and shaking under my dress.

When I knocked on the front door, he opened it promptly, standing there dressed in a black suit, white shirt, and purple tie. I instantly flushed and bit my lower lip, and my chest puffed, falling short of words.

My high school crush was standing in his prom suit, looking incredible with his hair brushed to the side and deep brown eyes sparkling at me.

As he released his first word, his welcoming lips performed the perfect o, "Wow, you look beautiful," he softly said.

"Thank you. So do you," I shyly responded with a gulp.

"Come in." He took my hand, and with one touch, the hairs on my neck stood up.

Olly constantly kept me on edge. I had slowly become addicted to how he made me feel. I was strung and couldn't think of anywhere I would rather be as he stood before me looking the way he did, like a dream.

He guided me inside his house, which looked identical to mine yet smelt like him, fruity, warm, and morish. I scanned the photos on the wall and saw him age within the pictures, which ached my chest. If he could see through me, I was sure he would see my beating heart glowing brightly for him as everything new I learned made him all the more perfect.

"My mum cooked us dinner before she went out. If you're hungry," he blushed, seeming nervous as he walked me into his dining room. I had never seen him nervous before, and it relaxed me slightly.

"Your parents aren't here?" I mumbled. The idea of us being alone was even more daunting, yet the swirling in my stomach stopped me from wanting to leave.

"No, it's just us. Is that okay?" I nodded and smiled at him, trying to keep my composure.

In the dining room, he had the table set out for us both, with the effort of a simple tea light candle sitting on the table and dimmed lighting. "This is sweet," I said timidly.

Olly took out my chair and sat beside me. We enjoyed a delicious meal whilst discussing anything and everything that came to mind. But even though the night was even more perfect than I could have imagined, the guilt I felt about him missing his prom night denied me to loosen entirely. I didn't want to be the girl who made him miss out on his high school prom and for him to have to reminisce about an evening with me instead, someday in the future.

"What's the matter?" he asked as he sensed my distance.

I shook my head a little in an attempt to avoid ruining the night with my usual negativity, "It's nothing."

"It can't be nothing. Something is bothering you," Olly muttered. "I can tell."

I sighed, looking toward him. "I feel guilty you are not at the prom."

Olly rolled his eyes, placing his fork down, "Ashley, why do you do this?" He used tone toward me, and his expression and body language changed instantly. I knew I had pissed him off. We may not have known each other for long, but he knew I was one for ruining the moment by being my own worst enemy.

I dropped my fork and pushed my plate aside, suddenly losing my appetite, "Do what?" I asked, and he looked away, clenching his strong jaw as he grunted a little.

I stood up, knowing it was my cue to leave; I knew prom night of any sort would be a disaster for me.

"Where are you going?" he snapped, standing up. The sadness in his eyes guilt-tripped me for wasting his efforts. A girl who was like him and could make him happy deserved this treatment, not some loser like me.

"Home. I shouldn't have come round, and you shouldn't have asked me to. You should have gone to prom with someone who deserves to be with you. I hate that I have become some girl you need to look after. I would have been fine being home tonight. You should be having fun with your friends."

"What is wrong with you, Ashley," he said, stepping closer to me. "I asked you to the prom not because I felt sorry for you or because I had to. I asked you because I wanted to. And because you said no, I didn't want to go without you. I like you. Why else do you think I would be here?" he paused. "Stop this. Stop making out that everyone is out to get you, especially me. Put all the high school drama behind you; it's over. You are not at prom competing with the girls. You are here with me at my house, where I want you to be," Olly finished, exhaling as his glare intently burned into mine.

I was silent.

Olly shouting at me was not what I wanted, but his honesty had put me in my place.

I hated that he thought I assumed he was like Lauren and pretending to be my friend. But was he right? Did I? I had never trusted anyone, but I thought I had let my guard down around Olly.

I looked at him; he was upset and wringing his wrists, avoiding me, and I couldn't blame him. Him baring his soul had ruined the night, and I caused it. I somehow needed to save it to revive the few hours we had left together, and if my romance novels had told me anything, there was only one way I knew how.

I stepped towards him as he looked down to the ground, hiding his frustration. When I took his hand, he raised his head. "I'm sorry," I said, hoping that was enough to rewind to half an hour ago when we were laughing.

He stepped back a little and released his hand from mine, and it was like a knife had stabbed me in the chest. The last thing I wanted to do was hurt him. "Just trust me," he quietly said.

I took a small, discreet breath and moved towards him, planting a kiss on his lips. Without pause, he reacted flawlessly, taking me into his arms. His hand reached behind my neck and pulled me closer. I cupped his face with my palm, stroking my fingers on his silky-smooth skin as our tongues entwined, and we relished the moment.

The minute I tasted him, the world stopped spinning, and the unspoken thing between us prepared to erupt. It was perfect, and I didn't want it to end; I wanted to be in this moment forever and for him never to let me go. It seemed like I had finally had my prince charming rescue me. But, being a devoted reader, I knew it was too early for this to be my happily ever after, so I made the most of it for as long as possible.

"Come with me," Olly whispered. He pushed play on the CD player, took my hand, guided me to the patio door, and slid it open.

I remembered the first time I saw him walk through those doors, and now I was walking through them with him, which only seemed realistic in my dreams.

As we stepped outside, my eyes filled with sparkly lights draped all over his garden, a beautiful sight enhancing the darkness of the night. "Would you like to dance?"

I pulled my bottom lip between my teeth and shyly shook my head.

"Oh, come on, you'll be fine. I've got you." Olly took the tips of my fingers in between his.

I gripped his hand tighter as he spun me to face him. I giggled, looking into his compelling stare. A stare that could get me to do anything he wanted to without asking. It quite literally had my heart running away with him.

He wrapped his arms loosely around my waist as mine rested behind his neck, nervously stroking his hairline as his eyes dove down into my very core.

"I'm glad I didn't wear heels now, or you would have been witnessing me fall through the gaps in this decking."

"You're not that bad of a dancer," he said as we swayed to the lyrics of classic love songs, which only went and clenched my heart further as I fell for him even more.

The lyrics of The Calling Wherever You Will Go filled my ears, and my body melted against his. I leaned my head against his chest, and he held me tightly. Closing my eyes, I held on for dear life even though I was beginning to believe he wouldn't let me fall.

If it weren't for his voice singing the chorus so impeccably gently, I would have considered the entire night nothing but a beautiful dream. He gave me hope, and I couldn't help but think he was singing it to me.

During the moments of pure bliss, dancing to god knows how many love songs, fireworks exploded in my stomach and the clouds cleared from my foggy mind. The cloudless sky finally allowed me to see Olly standing close. He really was real and more than a silly high school crush. It was more, so much more, and it was petrifying.

The thought of being without him, separated from him, was overwhelming. It was frightening how he was a stranger only weeks ago, and now, I was utterly infatuated with him. Being around him made me feel like I had never lived before, and everything I doubted now seemed possible.

I was young, which made me seem foolish and naïve, but there was no denying it; I loved him more than anything. The worst part about it was that it was so easy to do; admitting to him would be harder.

It wasn't until the playlist of perfect songs finished that I looked at him. He kissed me, melting my soul and compelling me to the ground.

He entwined his fingers into my hand and led me inside, where he said nothing to me as we slowly walked upstairs. Opening his bedroom door, I nervously followed.

Football and music posters covered his walls, and a double bed sat alongside a desk in the middle of the room. CDs, films, and books stacked shelves, and on his bed was a beige velvet box with my name written. He picked it up and handed it to me, "This is for you," he smiled, opening it, revealing a sparkly diamanté tiara. "Every prom queen deserves to wear a tiara," he said, biting his lips shyly as he took it from the box and placed it lightly into my hair.

I touched the tiara, fiddling with the band as I began to question where it had come from, hoping he hadn't spent any money on it.

"Stay there," he said.

Grabbing his Nikon camera from his desk, he stood behind me and stretched his arms on either side. We both filled the small screen as the diamond glistened in the darkness of the lamplit room. I felt his chest leaning on my back closely, and his breathing sent shivers down my spine as the pace captivated me. "Smile then," he joked, making me laugh, and with a few clicks, I watched the camera save the first photo of him and me together. A picture of me with a boy wearing a prom dress completed with a tiara, a souvenir I never thought I would have and will never want to lose.

As he moved away from me, I sat on the edge of his bed, watching him put the camera down and plug it into his computer. He fiddled with it for a minute as I looked around his room before we drew our attention back to one another.

He guided me back to my feet and placed one hand on my waist, the other stroking the tiara and my hair before taking my chin into his fingers and kissing me. His breathing increased as we enjoyed the flavour of each other, and for the first time, he strayed away from my mouth.

His warm breath trembled behind my ear as he softly kissed my skin, slowly settling down my neck. His petal-soft kisses were intoxicating, and I was under his spell. My eyelids fluttered as my head tilted back, offering him my throat as his fingers entwined with my long hair like torn silk. As my body quivered, sudden panic cascaded me, knowing I was heading into dangerous territory, unchartered waters.

My grip tightened on his arm, and it stopped him, taking his eyes back to mine. "Are you okay?" he asked, and I shyly nodded. "I'm only going to kiss you if that's okay." I smiled.

I was relieved, not because I didn't want to do more, but because I was inexperienced. I didn't want to look stupid in front of him. Olly said he was too, but something kept telling me that couldn't be true; he was too good at it.

I responded by kissing his delicious-tasting lips as I caught my breath. His sweet kisses pecked my cheeks, lips, ear, and throat before I found the courage to remove his jacket with my shaking hands.

 He moved me, pushing me against his bed, slowly guiding me down onto his pillow, and laid beside me as our kiss became intimate.

As he flicked off his shoes, so did I, bravely pulling him closer as I laid back and let him kiss me. We giggled and fooled around with each other without drifting too far. The nauseous feeling in my stomach told me how nervous he made me, and the trembling in my whole body warned me of how caught up I was. The emotions were intense but not enough to stop me from kissing his neck and nibbling his ear lobe as he breathed rhythmically into my ear.

An hour must have passed before we heard his front door shut, bringing us back to reality. Olly beamed, looking down at me as I giggled shyly, gliding my fingers through his thick hair and styling it back into place. He then did up his top few shirt buttons and rose from the bed, offering me his hands. I took them and stood up, brushing the creases from my silk dress, sorting my hair out, and putting the tiara back on, "I best go," I said.

"I wish you didn't have to."

"Me too." My face shone, and my heart clenched.

"Can I walk you?" he said, putting his trainers on before handing me my shoes. Taking my hand, we walked down the stairs.

"Mum, Dad," he said.

"In the living room," Olly's dad replied. I gulped as I now had to meet them properly. Something I was prepared for earlier, but not now, not since spending the last few hours fumbling with their son.

"Darling, how was your night?" his mum said, rising from the sofa. She hugged him tightly as his hand still hung onto mine. The next minute, she hugged me, and I gave her an awkward one in return.

"It was great," he said, smiling at me, then at them.

"You look beautiful, look at your dress, and that tiara looks lovely on you," his mum slurred, touching my hair as his dad gleamed at me.

"Right, thanks, Mum, Dad. I'm going to walk Ashley home," Olly said, hiding his embarrassment as he tugged me out of the room.

"Nice to meet you properly, Ashley," his mum shouted back from the living room.

"You too, Miss Carrick," I muttered, trying not to laugh.

"It's Marie; call me Marie."

"They are drunk. Ignore them," Olly said as we stepped into the warm air of a summer evening.

We slowly walked around the corner and down the short path to my house. Before approaching my drive, he stopped and kissed me goodnight before stroking his thumb down my cheek. "I know you don't believe me, but I have never kissed anyone else but you."

"Really?" I looked into his mesmerising glare. "It's just…you're so good at it." I blushed.

"Honest. I don't know how to explain it, but with you, everything feels like déjà vu."

I smiled, leaning my cheek in his palm, "I know what you mean; I feel like I've known you all my life. You seem so familiar to me; it's a little strange."

"Evening," my dad's voice cracked, startling us both.

Olly dropped his arm, and I took a step back. Dad was leaning against the door frame with his arms crossed, trying to be the intimidating father he wanted to be in front of Olly. All it did was make me laugh, and Olly didn't falter.

"Evening, Sir. I was just walking your daughter home."

"Right, thank you, Oliver,"

"Olly, his name is Olly, Dad," I added.

"Night, Oliver." Dad waved, leaving the door open for me as he went inside.

My brows knitted together as I fell curious, "Is your name Oliver?"

"Yes, it is, not that anyone calls me that," Olly said. "I'll see you tomorrow then?"

"You will." I nodded, beaming at him before letting go of his hand. I stood still, and he reluctantly backed off the driveway and waved me goodnight.

"Sweet dreams, Ashley," is the last thing he said. I eventually shut the door and melted against it, catching every breath he had stolen from me during the evening.

After a minute of collecting my thoughts and regaining my senses, I found my feet, walked straight upstairs to my room, and sat on my bed. Mum soon entered.

"How was your night?" she asked, waiting eagerly for my response. I looked at her, and my bright smile told her what she wanted to know.

"It was more than perfect," is all I said, keeping the details to myself other than showing her my tiara before she left the room.

*

Comfy in my pyjamas, wrapped in a blanket, I sat in the dining room, swivelling in the chair, waiting for the dialling tone to stop so I could log onto Myspace. I hadn't been online for a while and wanted to earlier, but I had to wait for Mum to finish her phone call with my nan. She was eager to tell her all about my prom night.

The computer repeatedly pinged with notifications, quickly gaining my attention and stopping me from swivelling. I rolled the seat closer and scrolled down with the mouse, "What the," I muttered.

You look gorgeous, Ashley.

So glad you won.

You two look so cute together.

Have a great summer, queen Ashley.

I scrolled through the comments, all fifty-three of them, finding them all saying similar things. I couldn't stop staring at the photo of me and Olly, which he must have uploaded earlier. Alongside it was titled, **Here is the beautiful prom queen, Ashley.**

I couldn't believe it; I was in a photo among all the other prom photos. For once, I was part of the school's movement.

It was the last day of school, but hey, better late than never.

When I read the bottom comment, it had tears swelling in my eyes and a lump forming in my throat.

Ashley, I'm sorry I haven't apologised until now. I didn't know what to say. What I did was cruel, uncalled for, and wrong. I hope you forgive me for being a bitch and such a shitty friend. I am glad you are okay. You look incredible. You look happy and deserve that tiara. I hope you have a good summer. Lauren.

Being Lauren, I knew an apology wouldn't have come easily, especially doing it for everyone to see. Putting aside that she had been my longest friend, we will never be what we once were. I didn't want to be. But now, having gained the closure I needed to move on, there were only three words I had to say to her.

I forgive you.

CHAPTER EIGHTEEN

I was finishing my bowl of Cheerios at the kitchen table when Dad walked in. He was stretching out his back, yawning, and wearing last night's clothes.

"Good night then?" I mumbled before taking my bowl to my mouth to finish the milk.

He flicked on the kettle, grabbed a mug, and popped two aspirin in a glass before filling it with water. "Yeah, you could say that, don't let your mum talk me into going into town again."

I laughed, nearly slamming my bowl down, "You went into town; I thought it was just the usual drink in the Cherry?"

Dad smoothed his balding head with his rough, working hands and circled his temples with his fingertips. "Yes, and it was a bad idea."

"Oh my god, how embarrassing, it's full of teenagers."

"Don't I know it, the last place we went, I had to pay a fiver to get in, and my shoes were sticking to the floor; they're ruined. You could have warned me Thursday was the new Friday."

"Oh, Dad."

"Sssh, my head's pounding, and my ears are still ringing."

"No gardening today then?" I asked, and he shook his head at me, screwing up his nose.

I watched him make his tea, leaving the teabag for way too long. Builders tea, that's how he liked it, me not so much. I was more of the teabag in, teabag out kind of person, with a bit of milk and no sugar.

"So, Dad…" I muttered, and he glanced back at me, furrowing his brows.

"What is it, Ashley?"

"Do you like Olly?"

I was up early, dressed, and ready to go out, considering I had a late prom night. Having slept soundly dreaming of, well, you can guess who, it only made me more eager to see him as soon as possible.

"Um, well, I can tell you do."

I smirked with a slight shrug, "Is that a yes?"

Dad leaned on the kitchen counter, facing me, holding his cloudy water. "I guess there are worse boys that could be dating my sixteen-year-old daughter."

"Worse?"

"Tattoos, drinking, drugs," he muttered.

I blushed a little. "Well, Olly isn't like that."

"That's what I worry about; he's *too* nice," Dad said.

"If he's not an addict, he will be into sex, and that's the last thing I want, a pregnant sixteen-year-old daughter."

Jeez, Dad's words horrified me; he had never spoken to me like that or about sex. I preferred it when we didn't talk as much; it was much less embarrassing.

"Oh my god, Dad, are you still drunk?" I laughed.

"What? I can see the glistening in your eye and that glow in your face," he paused. "You like him. That's all there is to it. Olly will be the boy who steals you for the summer and takes your innocence, just like I did with your mum."

I cringed. "Oh, dad, no, that won't happen, and anyway, when the time comes, I'm not stupid; I will be safe."

"Nooo, no ideas in my head, please. Just tell me you are watching a film or something, okay?" He downed the aspirin in two gulps before picking up his tea and heading back to the living room.

When he passed me, I looked up at him and said, "I love you, Dad."

"And you, Ashley."

The door went, and I was up out of my seat like a shot. I walked that fast on the laminate flooring; I nearly slipped over.

I had told Olly to walk in, but he was too polite.

My heart rate increased when my gaze met his, and my finger twirled my hair like a love-struck teenager going all gooey inside.

"Are you coming in?" I asked, and he stepped inside, removing his shoes before we headed upstairs.

"Uh-hum," Dad said, stopping us as we looked down at him and Mum standing in the living room doorway.

"Door open," they said in unison.

"Don't worry, Sir, we're just watching a film," Olly said. Dad's face dropped, and I couldn't help but burst into laughter. Mum and Olly, though, were utterly clueless on the matter.

*

The first few weeks of the summer had passed, and I had spent every waking moment with Olly. Either at my house or out venturing on his bike. He rides it and gives me a croggy. We'd been to town numerous times for lunch and wandered around the shops. We liked the small café upstairs in Waterstones, reading books we didn't buy. All our pocket money went on blockbuster films and twister ice lollies. We'd walked the parks, sunbathed in the fields, climbed the trees above the river, and managed to pry ourselves away from each other for football training on Wednesday nights. I'd had the most fantastic time with him, and I had lost count of how many make-out sessions we'd had. I couldn't keep my lips off him, yet the bedroom door rule still stood at my house, so we often went to his.

It was Friday night, and Mum and Dad were going out to the pub for a meal along with his parents. We had heard the never-ending, repeated warnings of "We're trusting you alone, no funny business." Each time was as humiliating as the first.

Being alone with Olly couldn't come quick enough. I could safely say I had found my confidence around him and was utterly smitten with the idea of experiencing something more than kissing. A warning didn't help the situation; it had become more of a rule I wanted to break.

*

"Nate and Zoe are watching a film downstairs," I told Olly as I entered my room, where he was lying on my bed, throwing the tennis ball up and down.

"Okay," he said hesitantly, giving me the idea that something was troubling him. So far, other than prom night, we'd had no issues, arguments, or worrying conversations.

"What's wrong?" I asked as I lay beside him, watching his hands open and close.

He stopped and gripped the ball, turning onto his side to face me. His gorgeous, tanned face was freckled more than before and shone under the light. He reached over, stroking where my stitches had now healed and curled a handful of hair around his finger. His body tensed up as he faltered. He took a deep breath and said, "I think I love you," which stole my voice. "I mean, I don't know what love feels like, but this feeling, this ache in my chest, I can't stop it. I can't get you out of my mind."

Olly was saying the three words I had wanted to say to him for weeks, and after what we had been through, what I had been through, he had no doubt been the only therapy I needed in my messed up life.

His words wrapped tightly around my heart, not causing pain, but instead, a silk bow hung gently around it. I felt serenity and pure bliss at that moment, a moment I had never expected myself to encounter.

"I feel the same way," I said in a near whisper, smiling as he stroked his hand down my cheek before touching my lip. "I don't want to be without you."

"You will never be without me, even if we are apart," Olly said as his deep eyes became glossy. "Cheesy, I know," he laughed, blushing as I agreed with a nod. "Just don't forget that, please, no matter what. You mean so much to me."

"Olly, you saved my life," I said. "Now kiss me."

I leaned into him, placing my lips on his, and as our kiss heated, I moved my hands under his top touching his bare skin. Excitement coursed through me as his kisses intensified and his grip on my body tightened. He was soft and warm, and my cheeks reddened as he allowed my touch to wander.

He opened my legs and placed himself between them, kissing me in a position he hadn't before; it was enthralling and sparked something deep inside me. Despite my hands trembling with nerves, I didn't want it to end.

When he leaned on me, his weight took the sensations in my body to another level. I could feel him, every inch of him, and only his clothes restricted us, which caused me to take a breath.

"Are you okay?" Olly asked, holding himself above me.

"I want to," I paused shyly, looking at him. "I want to experience new things with you."

"Me too," he said, nibbling his lip before getting up and shouting to Zoe and Nate, making sure they were okay. He shut the door as they responded before climbing back on the bed.

Olly was beside me and continued to trail his soft kisses along my neck and collarbone. I embraced how beautifully electric he made me feel as he tentatively unbuckled my denim shorts with his shaking hands. I was thankful his nerves showed, just like mine.

Lowering my shorts, we distracted our fumbling with kisses, entwining our tongues before he nuzzled into my neck. When his hand slid down the front of my panties, I gulped and bit the inside of my mouth, it tickled my bikini line, and my breathing instantly rose.

He lowered his hand, and I automatically took hold of his neck, pulling him closer to me. I kissed him passionately as the intense feeling of his touch made me feel sexy.

The rhythm of his zen-like breathing compelled my hands to roam to his football shorts. He pulled back a little hesitant, and I looked into his alluring eyes. He smiled and reassured me.

Beneath his layers, I felt him. My fingers softly trailed against his skin, touching him in ways I had never touched any boy. I treated him as fragile whilst spikes of sensations trembled the both of us.

His warm breath reached the most sensitive parts of my neck, the closeness of him being enough to drive the fear from my mind, and the idea of going all the way with him crossed it. "I want to have sex with you," I said as I became breathless, feeling a flutter within my stomach as he continued to touch me.

I realised we were not kissing anymore but instead studying each other. The silence between us was the longest time we had spent together without talking.

Olly moved on his back, allowing me to see him for the first time, and I didn't know what to think. I tried to keep my poise, licking my lips at how sensual I suddenly felt. I bit my lip as I watched his expression expose the pleasure he was experiencing as he became winded. His cheeks pinked as he rose to kiss me, removing his hand from my panties, and I pulled my shorts back up.

Raising his shorts a little, he puffed out his chest, stood up and headed to my bathroom, and I stayed on the bed with a Cheshire smile. I couldn't believe what was happening to me when just weeks ago, I thought I would never feel like this, in a bubble where I wanted to stay with the first boy I had ever loved.

I slowly trailed my fingers on my lips, down my neck and body, and rested them on my cartwheeling stomach. Every inch of me was electrified, and it felt incredible. I was confident in my skin for the first time, and I loved it. I didn't need to hide from Olly or myself anymore.

"That was nice," Olly said as he re-entered my room.

"It was," I grinned as he sat on the edge of the bed.

"What you said. I want to have sex with you too, if you are ready," Olly muttered, running his hand through his hair, looking nervous. "I just don't want you to regret it."

"I won't. I love you."

He took my hand, raised me to my feet and cuddled me tightly, "I have to go and put Nate in bed."

"I miss you already."

My emotions bounced from exhilaration, euphoria, anxiety, and despair rapidly and confusingly. They made me realise I had become the love-struck teenager my dad warned would happen. I had inevitably become a victim in my own romance story. And as I watched him walk down the driveway, I concluded that it would be painful even if fate brought us a happy ending.

From what I had learned in such a brief time, falling in love was unexpected and created the most undeniable ache for someone else. It was unquestionably, painful joy.

DISK TWO

1. Miss Independent – Kelly Clarkson
2. Seven Nation Army – The White Stripes
3. Good Charlotte – The Anthem
4. Heaven – DJ Sammy
5. Trouble – Pink
6. Buttons – The Pussycat Dolls
7. Sex on Fire – Kings of Leon
8. Vengaboys – We like to Party
9. Naked – Avril Lavigne
10. My Happy Ending – Avril Lavigne
11. Sk8er Boi – Avril Lavigne
12. Dilemma – Nelly ft Kelly Rowland
13. This Love – Maroon 5
14. Confessions – Usher
15. In The End – Linkin Park
16. Cry Me A River – Justin Timberlake
17. Unwritten – Natasha Bedingfield

JULY 2004

From...
To...

Name? Ashley Prince
Age? 16
Birthday? June 22nd
Hair colour? Brown with red highlights
Eye colour? Brown
Best friend? Alex, Sammy, Morgan, and Emily
Boyfriend? Olly
Crush? Olly
Celebrity crush? Only Olly
Favourite movie? Um, does Olly count?
Favourite subject? Olly
Favourite song? Wherever you will go – The Calling
Favourite artist or band? Avril Lavigne
Favourite animal? Dolphin
Favourite colour? Black
Favourite food? Cereal
Favourite tv show? Olly again
Favourite sport? Football
Favourite place? Anywhere with Olly
Tea or coffee? Tea
Bath or shower? Shower, it's quicker.
Hot or cold? Hot
Summer or winter? Summer
Birthday or Christmas? Christmas
Pets? None
Siblings? Sister
Tattoos? No
Ever smoked? No
Ever drank? Yes
Ever done drugs? No

Ever been in hospital? Yes
Ever broken a bone? No
First kiss? Olly
Had sex? Soon, I hope
Last thing you ate? Dinner
Last person you hugged? Olly
Last person you kissed? Olly
Last person you texted? Olly
Last person you called? Olly
Someone you miss? Olly
Something you love? Olly
Something you hate? Not being with Olly
Something you want? To be with Olly all the time
Biggest fear? Not being with Olly
Pet peeve? Being lied to
Where do you want to be right now? With Olly
What do you want to be when you're older? With Olly
Five facts about you?
1. I love Olly
2. I love Olly
3. I love Olly
4. I love Olly
5. I love Olly

Sent to: ...

CHAPTER NINETEEN

"My mum wants to know if you would like to spend the day with us tomorrow," Olly said through our kiss.

"Uh, huh," I muttered, raking my fingers through his hair. Our weekend plans were the last thing on my mind whilst he sat beneath me in nothing but a pair of football shorts with his tongue in my mouth.

"Ashley," he repeated, moving his luscious lips away from mine. I sighed, placed my hands on either side of him and looked into his distracted eyes.

"Do we have to talk about this now? Your parents will be back soon."

"Why can't we have a conversation?" He tapped my leg and moved me aside so he could sit up. His sudden distance worried me; usually, he was up for nothing more than a kiss and fumble when we were home alone.

"Okay, I'll spend tomorrow with your family; that's fine," I said. Although it wasn't, I only wanted to spend time with Olly. That was all I had wanted since I met him. And it wasn't only his family I wanted to blow off, but I had also turned down my family and the football girls over the past week to be with him.

I wanted new friends and had finally had some, but I was nothing more than a besotted teenager who wanted to spend every waking moment with her gorgeous boyfriend.

"Are you only saying that so we can carry on kissing?" he asked, running his fingers through my hair which fell around my face.

"Perhaps," I giggled, biting my lower lip. Olly smiled and kissed me on the cheek before climbing to his feet.

"I'll be back in a minute," he said before leaving the room.

In his bedroom, I sat and observed the sporty atmosphere around me. Inspirational quotes from Tiger woods and Rocky were on the walls, and trophies lined the shelves in height order. Eventually, I stood up and stroked my fingers across everything he owned, intrigued by the biographies of athletes stacked and the books about surfing.

The room's bright colours reflected his laid-back personality, whereas mine was dull. I turned on his CD player for a second to see what he was listening to, a R n B mix, which was far from what I enjoyed. Damn, did he think that my music was depressing like I just did?

These celebrities and icons inspired Olly, but I didn't believe anything they said. Did that make us too different? Are we opposites heading for the breakup I was expecting? Oh my god, where was he? I panicked. I needed his optimistic self back in my presence to stop my toxic thoughts from running astray.

His phone pinged on his desk distracted me, and my curiosity won me over. I took the Nokia in my hand and read a message from Lewis.

Why aren't you coming to the party tonight? Don't say it's because of Ashley. She is invited too.

What party? Why hadn't Olly told me about a party? I swallowed harshly.

"Ashley, what are you doing?" Olly said, making me jump.

"What party aren't you going to?"

"Why are you going through my phone?" he said curtly.

"Olly, what party? Are you embarrassed to be seen with me?" My heart pounded in my chest, anguished.

"Ashley, don't," he muttered, rolling his eyes.

I scowled, "So you *are* embarrassed to be seen with me?"

"No, I'm not." He edged towards me, taking his phone from my hand. "I just don't think a party is a good idea."

"A good idea for me," I huffed, staring into Olly's tormented eyes. He failed to find any other words to explain himself and sighed heavily. "You go to the party, Olly. I have suddenly decided I want to spend time with my mum, not you." I stormed past him, walked out of his bedroom and quickly down the stairs, slamming the front door behind me.

When the fresh air hit me, I had no desire to go home; instead, I jogged up the street, and my feet didn't stop. My steady pace took me around the housing estate and up to the field at the top of the steep hill, where I took a minute and sat down.

The feeling of the air in my lungs was calming, yet the fact Olly hadn't come after me, nor had he messaged, soon had tears rolling down my face. I cradled my knees tightly into my chest, looking at the large town in the distance.

I sat alone with my tormenting thoughts for as long as it took for the sun's warmth to leave my skin. The temperature had dropped a little, and as my phone battery had died, I guessed it was around six p.m. It was the worst day I'd had in a while, away from Olly for the first time. I felt insecure and questioned how or why I believed my opinions about myself had started to alter. My clothes hung loose on my body, having replaced food with the taste of Olly. And with the absence of high school and social pressure, my anxieties had reduced dramatically. So why did that message change everything so quickly?

Why didn't he mention the party?

I would have loved to go to a summer party and do something normal sixteen-year-olds do, and he knew that.

Standing up, I started to walk back down the hill, which, as I got halfway, seemed much bigger than it did when I was running up it. My legs ached, yet to avoid going past Olly's house, I walked the long way around, and for the first time, I didn't look up at his bedroom window as I entered the front door. I knew I was acting moody and childish, but he had upset me, and he was the one person I least expected to.

"Where have you been," Mum screeched at the top of her voice. Dad immediately stood from the sofa, both welcoming me with furious expressions.

"What?" I found myself saying, having not prepared myself for questioning.

"Olly came round almost four hours ago looking for you. It's nearly nine p.m., and you weren't where you said you were, and oh, I see you have your phone, so you have been ignoring us too," Mum shouted as she looked at my phone gripped in my hand.

"My phone died," I scorned. "And if Olly has been round, you know the story, so get off my back," I shouted before running to my bedroom.

"What the," I heard Dad say. Mum huffed.

I leaned against my bedroom door, inhaling and exhaling, gobsmacked at how I had spoken to my parents. I had never talked to them in such a manner. I wanted to apologise. Instead, I put my mp3 headphones in, distracting myself from the party. I could only assume Olly had gone without me.

Avril Lavigne's words got into my head, not sorrowfully, making me feel as worthless as they once did. Instead, they made me angry. I should be going to a party with Olly, why couldn't I? I *was* invited.

Pulling my headphones out, I sat at my desk and opened my drawer, taking out my makeup. I topped up my foundation, powdered my face and surrounded my eyes with my typical black mascara. Rather than black eyeliner, I bravely opted for a red eyeliner I bought the other day. My lips shone with gloss, and I had curled my thick bright coloured highlights, layering them on top of my straightened hair. I looked surprisingly good, but I was far from looking like Avril, who pulled it off better.

I took my phone from its charger and turned it on. No messages from Olly arrived, which hurt, but I was stubborn, still angry, and waiting for his apology.

I scrolled through my contacts and texted Lewis; he replied with an address, which I knew wasn't far away, even if I had to walk it alone in the dark.

Rummaging through my clothes, I had no idea what to put on. Should I wear jeans and a top, or should I dress up?

I had never been to a party, so I didn't know.

I looked around, and my posters told me to pick my low-cut black flares and a red vest, which I covered with a black mesh top. I heard recent words in my head, "You look rather emo, don't you?" I brushed the Lauren-shaped devil from my shoulder and held my head high.

I was comfortable wearing an outfit that suited me, and my reflection didn't disagree.

It was nearly ten-thirty, and neither of my parents had come up since I slammed my door on them. It was Saturday night, meaning they would have slumped on the sofa with a take-out, a film and too much alcohol, reassuring me they wouldn't hear me do my next reckless thing.

Leaving my bedroom light on, I walked to my window and looked at Olly's bedroom across the yard. It was dark, so he must have already gone to the party. Pulling myself up onto the windowsill, I pushed the window open as far as it would go. I turned around and lowered my legs outside, finding my footing on the trellis panels on the wall, praying it would hold my weight. Though I was that scared of falling, I quickly shut the window and moved so fast down it that my feet were safely on the floor before I knew it.

I exhaled rapidly as my adrenaline flowed through my body and tried to stop the shaking in my hands. I hung my hair on either side of my shoulders, looked back at my bedroom and then to Olly's and started to walk. I couldn't believe I had shouted at my parents and snuck out to a party all in one afternoon. What had gotten into me?

CHAPTER TWENTY

It was late, and the streets were empty. Scared of the dark, my mind ran awry, seeing imaginary, frightening things in the bushes beside me.

I walked fast, and the following eerie noises made me walk even faster, to the point my feet were burning.

My phone stayed silent, I had left the house ten minutes ago, and no one had noticed. Maybe I should go home? I shouldn't have snuck out; it was stupid, I thought.

Stopping, I hesitated and told myself to turn around and go back. But the smallest part of me kept me walking, wanting to experience a house party at its best; at the popular boy's house.

When I turned onto the street, and the laughter echoed, my stomach flipped. Looking up at the large house, I anxiously twiddled my hair, seeing how busy it was as silhouettes filled every window. I knew Lewis's family was well off, but I didn't expect his house to be so big.

I took a deep breath and apprehensively walked towards the front door, not bothering to knock, as people were everywhere. Entering the first-ever house party I'd attended, I hoped it would be as good as the films made out.

I didn't make it a few steps inside before seeing someone throwing up in a house plant, making me heave. I then realised I'd shown up so late that everyone would be drunk, and I was stone-cold sober.

Drinking hadn't even crossed my mind.

My chest suddenly tightened, and my vision blurred as the bottle of vodka I had last consumed flashed into my mind. I couldn't breathe, and I was panicking. Olly was right; a party was a bad idea.

"Ashley, is that you?" I heard over the god-awful rap music.

Calming myself, I turned around, "Hi, Lewis," I loudly said, swallowing hard.

"What are you doing here? I didn't think you wanted to come?"

Gesturing to my ears with a shrug, I shouted, "What? I can't hear you."

Lewis stepped closer to me, "I didn't think you wanted to come."

I looked at him and furrowed my brows, "Why wouldn't I want to come?"

"Olly said you didn't." Olly's lie aggravated me.

"I didn't know anything about the party until a few hours ago," I said. "Olly didn't tell me."

"Oh."

I shrugged my shoulders and looked around for Olly. Yet, all I saw was one massive, trashed house. People crowded the once cream leather sofas, drink spillages dripped, and crunched crisps trailed the carpet.

"Oi, dick head," Lewis shouted. "No smoking in the house. Get outside." He pointed as a cloud of smoke trailed behind a group of lads I didn't recognise, all dressed in black with tattoos and piercings.

I couldn't recall anyone like that at Bailey, and the more I looked around, the more I felt out of place.

Lewis tugged my arm and said, "If you're looking for Olly, he isn't here."

"What?" I shouted, but I couldn't hear him. The drunken rabble laughing and yelling over unbearably loud music was all that filled my ears. Glass suddenly smashed, a scream let out, and Lewis quickly disappeared.

"Lewis," I shouted though it was pointless.

I stood in the crowd. I didn't recognise anybody, not the group playing drinking games, the couples making out, and those dancing.

Where was Olly, and what was I to do now?

My hands trembled at my irresponsible decision, lost in a house with no familiar faces, wishing I hadn't turned rebel.

I pushed my way through the guys beside me; being much smaller than them, it was easy. I came out on the other side and attempted the stairs, which lines of people had comfortably taken as their seats.

It was ridiculous.

I took one step at a time, trying not to stand on anyone, holding onto their shoulders as I made my way through.

When I reached the top, I lost my breath, choking on, I don't know, it smelt like smoke and hairspray, and it was vile. But the idea of stepping back downstairs seemed tiresome, so I carried on, calling for Olly.

I stepped over the unconscious bodies on the stairs and tried not to stand in the puddles on the carpet.

"Hey," I tsked, looking at the crying girl who had just barged into me.

"Babe, it was a dare. Come back," I listened, stepping out of the way as her boyfriend chased behind her.

Holy crap, this was not how I imagined a party; maybe I had it all wrong.

"You! What are you doing up here? You should be downstairs," a tall guy shouted, pointing and walking toward me. I stopped and looked around, pointing at myself. "Yes, you. Come on. Before the coppers show up, and you get me in trouble. Fuck, did Lewis not tell you," he shouted, shaking his head at me.

What? What did I do? I thought, all sorts of confused.

The Boy Next Door

The boy took my wrist and yanked me through the crowds. My feet tumbled quickly, and I could barely keep up as he dragged me through the chaos, stepping in god knows what. I saw piles of liquor, alcopops, beer, and the scent of pizza cried my name as he hauled me through the kitchen. I was so hungry.

"Go," he shouted, and I looked at him, puzzled, shaking my head. He sighed and opened a door, showing me a staircase that told me to run home.

"I'm not going down into a basement with you, hell no."

"Go downstairs," he huffed, crossing his arms tightly. "Lewis," he shouted, and Lewis then appeared at the bottom of the steps.

"Ashley, come down." I reluctantly did as he said.

"Keep your friends down there, or they can leave," The boy shouted.

I looked at Lewis and back to the angry boy, "It's your brother's party?"

"Yeah. We have to stay down here. Just in case, you know," Lewis said, guiding me in. For the first time since arriving, I felt relief wash over me as I laid eyes on a small group of peers, though I still didn't recognise many.

"Here," Lewis offered, putting a blue WKD in my palm, cooling its sweaty state.

I rolled it between my palms, hesitantly looked at it and then took a sip. Its blue, mixed-fruit flavour went down like juice. It was delicious and instantly washed my fear of alcohol away.

As I observed my surroundings, it was a converted basement. It was quiet, much less hectic, and the music was more my style. A much more low-key affair was going on as pool cues had balls knocking, and a Tony Hawk video game was on the plasma TV.

"Are you going to sit down?" Lewis said, offering me a pizza box.

"No, thank you," I said, wishing the churning in my stomach would vanish to make me want to eat. Instead, I sipped my drink.

"Where is your boyfriend?" A girl then asked. I didn't recognise her, but she had a point, where was he?

"I don't know. I haven't seen him," I mumbled shyly to the blonde girl sitting on the sofa dressed in fishnet tights, boots, a short skirt and a no-fear t-shirt. With his sporty get-up and popularity, she didn't look the type Lewis would hang around with, but I liked her style and fingerless gloves. She had red-laced eyes like mine and a decorated nose which made me want to get mine pierced.

"He's not here. I told you earlier," Lewis said, scoffing his face with cheese pizza, washing it down with a beer in a few gulps.

"What do you mean?" I asked, cautiously sitting down on the sofa covered in coats, eyeing up the ice-filled tub full of bottles.

"Help yourself," he nodded. "Olly didn't want to come. I thought it was something to do with you, but clearly not."

Oh no, I thought. Why had I assumed Olly was coming? I was stupid, so, so stupid.

I opened another bottle of WKD, red this time, and put the opener back on the table. Its berry flavour was just as morish as the blue. "These are nice," I said, "But if Olly isn't here, I'm going to go."

I sipped the bottle quickly, placed it on the pile next to the others and went to stand up. "No, stay; it would be nice to get to know the prom queen," a deep voice said, appearing from behind me. He placed his hands on my shoulders and sank me back into the sofa.

I froze as his rude behaviour put me on edge, and as I looked at his hands to notice his black painted nails and sweatbands on his wrists, I knew I didn't know this person either.

Tentatively, I glanced up at him. He, too, was dressed like the girl in black, oversized clothes, dog tags hanging around his neck with piercings threading his bushy eyebrow and lip.

"Kyle, leave her," the girl snapped, and he released me.

Kyle moved around the sofa and sat on the table in front of me as his eyes tried to read me and my outfit choice. I seemed to fit in with them despite our apparent differences.

Picking up a bottle of brown liquor, I watched him line up four shot glasses and pour them slowly, looking back and forth at me with a mocking smirk as he placed the bottle down. He picked up a shot between his forefinger and thumb and shot it with ease.

"Your turn," he insisted, nodding my way, looking back at the girl whose eyes were on me. Her stare intimidated me as if to dare me to drink it. She could tell I didn't want to, and so could everybody else, which, stupidly, influenced me.

"Kyle, Ashley isn't into all this shit, go back over there," Lewis said, looking down at me warily.

I didn't think Lewis was into this either. He was always with the sports lads at school. And gazing around, none of them was there, nor were the popular girls: Lauren, Sophie, anyone I would have expected him to have invited. Who were these people? Were they from Bailey? I had never seen any of them. Maybe it wasn't only me who hid their true colours. Was this what Lewis was really like? After everything, I could suddenly see why the most popular boy in school was the most understanding and the least mocking.

I looked across at Lewis, noticed his ripped black jeans, plain black t-shirt and two silver rings lacing his fingers, and gave him a small smile.

"I beg to differ," Kyle grunted, taunting me.

"No, Lewis, it's fine," I said, picking up the shot glass.

"Ashley," Lewis paused. "Don't."

I looked back at Kyle, hesitant and took a deep breath, swallowing the brown liquid in one. Its smooth toasted oaky, caramel, vanilla flavour made me shiver and warmed my chest. Its heat swam over my body and into my blood, releasing me from my usual state of uptight and boring. "Wow," I coughed, smiling sarcastically at the girl and Kyle, whoever they were.

The girl sank in her seat, unimpressed and spun a wheel of a skateboard leaning beside her. I watched it roll until it stopped.

"Holy shit, you are that guy from Bailey who started on Olly and Lewis on the last day of school."

Kyle smirked, "And here I was, thinking I didn't make an impression."

I laughed sarcastically, "It wasn't a good one."

Kyle said nothing.

"What's Olly ever done to do? You don't even know him," I said, and his eyes intently bore down on me. His pupils dilated, and his smile was something villainous.

I found myself reaching for the bottle of Jack Daniels, and as I went to open the cap, Kyle reached out for it, placing his hand on top of mine. He pulled me closer and again said, "I beg to differ." I gulped, sweat dripped down my spine, and my entire body was on fire.

"Kyle," Lewis said. "Come on, not now."

I glanced at him and knitted my brows together, "What's not now?"

Kyle released my hand and shook his head, altering the cap sitting on it. "Nothing, Olly, isn't worth wasting any more of my time." He stood up, took a cigarette out of his pocket, and placed it between his fingers. "I'm going for a smoke."

I sat silent for a moment, not realising how tightly I was clinging to the bottle in my hand. "Lewis, what was that about."

"Nothing, just forget about it. Kyle likes to get under people's skin; he's tormenting you." I nodded in agreement and tried to clear my clenched throat. Opening the cap, I grabbed a shot glass but then put it down, swigging out of the bottle instead.

*

The music was blaring, Lewis was hollering my name, and everyone's laughs were deafening. And trying every flavour of WKD and drinking too many Jack Daniel shots to count was perhaps why.

My stomach was churning, empty yet full, though I couldn't stop. I couldn't pull myself away from the fun I was having, the dancing I was doing, and the singing I was attempting on the karaoke machine. This party wasn't what I half expected; it was probably more fun, which was odd being in a small crowd of strangers.

"Ashley," Lewis said, trying to tug me down from the table I was dancing on with Becca, the intimidating girl who eventually gave me her name.

"What?" I slurred.

"It's time for you to go," he said. "Olly will have my bollocks for this."

"Fuck Olly, he's a prick," Kyle said with a grunt.

I instantly stopped dancing and looked across at Kyle, scowling. He was sitting on the edge of the pool table with a bottle of vodka in his hand, looking irritated with how I hadn't noticed his return.

I clumsily climbed off the table and approached him, putting little distance between us as I placed myself between his legs, my nose nearly touching his. My confidence had reached new heights, as I wouldn't have dared do anything so upfront in other circumstances. But, at the same time, something about this boy did one over me.

"What the fuck is your problem?" I muttered.

His arms hung beside him, one tightly gripping his bottle as his eyes widened and burned into my blurry vision. If I weren't so drunk, I would have guessed they were some grey shade, dark and mysterious, yet glazed over with shock. As I investigated them, they sucked me in, as did his mesmerising scent. A hint of tar and hot pavement on a summer's day, interfering with zesty orange rind, sweetly delivering nostalgia and a touch of freshness.

I reclaimed the breath I unwillingly allowed him to take along with my balance. Stumbling back, I grabbed his black jean-covered thighs as he reached for me. He gripped my forearm, and I felt his body tense as I tightened my hand on his leg, regaining my footing. He groaned so quietly I could have misheard him. Kyle's handsome looks were more noticeable than earlier, with his messy brown hair and attractive face piercings. I suddenly forgot what I was saying.

He leaned into me, and I felt his breath on my neck, making me gasp, tremble, and weak at the knees. You name it, it happened. "Olly doesn't deserve you," he whispered.

My gaze locked with his, and curiosity ate at me. What did he mean? Did this skater boy even know Olly? I didn't even know who he was. How would Olly?

Everything around me started spinning, and my heart started to pound. I felt sweat pouring from my skin, and every sound around me dropped.

"Oh fuck," I heard as I bent down, puking on Kyle's stylish vans.

"Jesus, Ashley," Kyle said as I felt his hand on my back. And to my surprise, he didn't push me away, considering I'd ruined his expensive trainers, but instead performed slow circles, comforting me.

"How are we going to get her home?" I heard him mutter.

"No, I can't go home. I snuck out and can't get in," I slurred, standing back up and wiping my mouth. "Not unless I climb the walls like spiderman," I laughed. "God, my parents are going to kill me."

"You climbed out the window?"

"Yeah," I mumbled, with a wobble and a smile.

"There is more to you than I thought, Ashley Prince," he said, reaching out to me and moving my wet hair off my cheek. His touch had me retreating but also glued to the floor.

"How can you say that? You don't even know me."

"Ummm, let's see." He slid off the pool table and took a swig of vodka. "I know you go to Bailey and how you have been pushed around by your friends for your entire academic life. I know you have never had a boyfriend until now." His liquor-scented breath pinched my nose as he stood close to me, scolding me with his gaze as everyone else stopped to watch and listen. "I could continue if you'd like." I swallowed hard.

"Stop it, Kyle," Lewis said, stepping behind me.

Kyle looked at him, shaking his head with a tut, then moved his eyes back to me.

"And I know that because you don't even know who I am, and I've been at the same school as you since

I was five, and you are just like the other girls you pretend not to like. Just as bitchy, and as self-absorbed, who wouldn't have noticed guys like us unless we slapped you in the face," he snarled. His tone was harsh, and his gaze scolded me, as did his words. "Your scene in the park wasn't a cry for help. It was a cry for attention. It's just as well Olly is leaving," he finished, releasing my arm, where a mark now lay; I didn't even notice he was holding me so tight.

As a tear rolled down the curve of my pink cheek, I stepped away from him, looking at Lewis, Becca, and the faces I hadn't even spoken to and then back to Kyle. All of them said nothing.

I brushed my tears away and tucked my hair behind my ear, "What do you mean, leaving?"

"Ask him yourself," Kyla spat. "I told you, he's a prick and not as perfect as he makes out to be. And god, it felt good when I punched him the first time." He then picked up a pool ball and threw it across the room, letting out a frustrated growl before grabbing his skateboard and storming up the stairs.

"Kyle," Lewis shouted, going after him.

I was stunned. What the hell had just happened? Was everything Kyle said true? Was Olly leaving? Where was he going, and how did he know? Holy hell, it was all too much.

"Ashley, are you okay?" I heard Becca say as my vision altered all over again. I looked at her and reached my hand out, but she wasn't there. I stepped forwards, and the next minute I knew I was falling.

CHAPTER TWENTY-ONE

My eyes flickered, trying to open, but the light forced them shut. "Urgh," I said, covering my head with my hands, trying to rub away the ache. What did I do to deserve this headache? I thought. But then I suddenly remembered everything. From the minute I snuck out to the minute I saw stars, "Fuck," I shouted, instantly widening my eyes and sitting upright.

I brushed my hands through my dried-up, tangled hair and along my chest. I was still wearing the black mesh top I went out in and my flares. "Flowers, lilac flowers," I said, stroking the duvet covering me, "How did I get back here?"

Catching and releasing my lungs, I tried to figure out how I got home. I couldn't have possibly walked, and I wouldn't have called a taxi, would I? My mind was so foggy. The confusion arose warmth under my tingling skin, and my stomach turned a million miles per hour. All of a sudden, my cheeks flushed, and I heaved, "Urgh," I gagged.

Shoving the quilt back, I ran to my bathroom with my hand holding my mouth. I puked my guts up all over the toilet and in it. Its colourful design spreading over my floor wasn't looking as delicious as it tasted. Its grim taste burnt my insides more than when I was swallowing it.

"Oh god," I mumbled, cradling my aching head as I sat on my knees. My every nerve twinged like they were having their own party beneath my skin, except it hurt.

Every inch of my body hurt.

I took a deep breath and used the sink to guide me up; my muscles trembled, and nausea rose again, making my stomach tense, "Urgh." I spewed, crying as my sink got the artwork whilst my hands clung tightly to the rim.

Tears rolled down my cheeks, joining the sweat on my face. The aroma pulled my stomach, making every second of it worse, and vomit soaked my hair. I needed to clean up before Mum saw the rainbow-coloured massacre painting my bathroom. But seeing as I was home, I could assume she and Dad were fully aware of last night's antics. I was surprised they hadn't barged in the minute I made a noise.

Slowly standing upright, I gazed into the mirror; I looked like shit. I wiped my face and shook my head in dismay, holding my aching tummy before running the taps to rinse the sink. I used an entire toilet paper roll to wipe up as much as possible, flushing it all down.

Fumbling through the cabinet draws, I found a pack of face wipes and used them to clean the white ceramic, hoping it would smell a little nicer. It didn't. So I poured hand wash down the loo before flushing it.

Wiping the sweat from my forehead, I slowly stripped my clothes off, trying not to pain my tortured body. I didn't remember feeling this rough before; how was it so different? Why would anyone choose to drink if this was how it made them feel? Never again, I told myself.

Pulling open the shower door, I climbed in, preparing myself. I usually loved my power shower, but not then. It hit me full force, washing away every scent of alcopops, sick, pizza, and cigarette smoke.

I stood under the tepid water for as long as it numbed my body and appreciated the silence. Though the buzzing in my ears was another reminder of what was to come the minute I faced my parents. I tried to relax. I washed my hair and soaped my body gently, worried I'd be showering in vomit if I brushed too hard in its fragile state.

Climbing out, I took my nightgown from the back of the bathroom door, wrapped myself in it, and brushed my hair and teeth. I was soaked, but the idea of drying myself was too draining. Wiping the condensation from the mirror, I looked back at myself; I looked a little better, though my pale-coloured face told me I was in for a rough day. And when I opened the door back into my bedroom, seeing Mum and Dad sitting on my bed, it was about to get worse.

Here we go, I thought.

Their faces were sketched with blank expressions, not looking half as angry as I had anticipated, "I'm sorry," I tried through gritted teeth.

"What for Ashley?" Mum said in a disturbingly calm tone, tapping her foot with her arms crossed.

"Shouting at you, sneaking out and drinking."

"Right," she nodded, and Dad grunted and stood up, making me wince.

"How about going to a house surrounded by intoxicated hooligans and drinking way too much with no adult supervision," he snapped, looking down at me, worried, not angry. Genuinely worried, guilt-tripping me instantly.

"Dad, I'm sorry I am. I was upset."

"Upset!" he paused, "I was upset when I got a phone call from Oliver's parents in the early hours of the morning saying you had passed out at a party."

"Huh? What? Olly's?"

"And they weren't best pleased about being woken up either, and neither was Olly. You should be ashamed of yourself."

"I, er."

"Ashley," Mum said. Her deep brown eyes looked cautiously at me, and I watched them gloss over. "What you did last night was careless. From the second you left this house, you put yourself in danger. Anything could have happened to you, anything. Didn't you think?"

"No, I didn't." I put my hands in my pockets. "I'm sorry, I just wanted to be a normal sixteen-year-old and go to a party, and you never let me out."

"We know, and that's why, from now on, we may loosen the reins a little," Mum said, looking at me, then to Dad, who looked wry.

I let out a are you joking kind of laugh and said, "What's going on? Why aren't you screaming at me and grounding me?"

"Sit down, Ashley," Mum insisted, pulling the desk chair out, stopping the pacing I had unknowingly started to do. I looked at her curiously and sat, nervously scratching the nail polish from my nails. "We want you to be safe, and we want to know where you are, what you're doing and who you are with," she said. "Last night kind of put us in our place."

I listened with my eyes glued to them, dumbfounded, questioning who had cloned my overprotective parents and what they had done with them.

"When we were your age, we were doing things I don't even want to imagine you doing, alcohol, drugs, parties, sex." I cringed as revulsion cascaded over me at the thought of my parents having sex.

"I knew karma would come back and bite us in the ass," Dad added, shaking his head as he gazed around my room. "Can you not put ideas in her head."

"Let's face it; those ideas are already there," Mum said, looking to me, then to Dad and sighed. "Look at her. Sneaking out, hungover, and with a boyfriend."

"Olly," I blurted out. "I need to see him and apologise. We argued, and we haven't spoken since. I only went to that party, thinking that's where he would be. Oh, I'm so stupid; I bet he hates me." I started to cry and hung my head in my palms, and Mum moved closer.

"I wish he *was* there; then I could blame him for this," Dad muttered as he left the room.

Mum lifted my head and moved my hands aside, wiping my tears. "Ignore your dad; he's upset; he will come round."

I nodded with a sniffle, "Why aren't you angry with me?"

"Trust me, I am, but you need to learn from your mistakes, and I can see you have; I can smell it from here."

"Sorry," I sighed with a reluctant smile. "Can I go next door and apologise before you ground me indefinitely?"

"You're not grounded, and you can in a bit, you need paracetamols, food and fluids in you first," Mum said, rubbing my back.

"Thanks, Mum. I truly am sorry. I won't sneak out again."

"I know you won't." She smiled, running her fingers through my wet hair.

*

"I'm sorry," I blurted out as soon as the door opened.

"Morning, Ashley," Olly's dad said, and I recoiled. He must have had a right opinion of me after everything I had done in such a short time, and there was no doubt my mum and dad discussed it with him and Olly's mum every weekend.

"Oh, sorry, Sir, I was expecting Olly."

"Call me Calvin, not Sir," he insisted, and I agreed with a nod. "So, how are you feeling on this fine summer's day?"

Calvin was mocking me. Either because he was much less strict as a parent or lightening the tension written all over me. "Er, I'm okay," I muttered, looking at my feet and scraping my shoe against the floor. "I'm sorry about last night."

"No comment, Ashley; I was young once," he said, baffling me. I deserved to be punished for my reckless behaviour. Yet, my parents and even Olly's parents weren't telling me off, making me dread how Olly would handle it. He would be the most gruelling; someone had to be.

"Dad," Olly grunted, moving him aside.

"Bye, Ashley." Calvin smiled and walked away.

"Olly, I'm so sorry, so so so sorry." He looked at me and kept a straight face, it taunted me, but I deserved it. He grabbed his shoes, put them on, and shut the door, stepping beside me.

"Come on. Let's go for a walk," Olly muttered, ushering me down the driveway.

"Are you mad at me?"

"Mad? Of course I'm mad," his voice cracked. "You stormed out of my house, went missing for a few hours, and never contacted me. I then got a phone call and had to wake my parents up to wake up your parents to get you home."

Olly was pissed, and I had no idea how to get myself out of it; it was our first proper fight.

"I'm sorry, I don't know how many times you want me to say it, but I'll say it all day for the rest of the summer if I have to. The rest of my life even." I begged. "I'm stupid and stubborn. It just upset me you never told me about the party."

"And do you see why now?" he said sarcastically. "I knew it wouldn't be a party like you expected."

"I guess so. It wasn't even Lewis's party. It was his brother's. Who is super pleasant, by the way," I muttered, rolling my eyes. "Why didn't you go?"

Olly stopped walking, looked at me and puffed out his chest. "If you asked, I would have had the chance to tell you I'm not into drinking and parties instead of getting the wrong idea. You think I'm like Lewis, but I'm not. Just because I'm sporty, it doesn't mean I'm some party boy jock. I grew up on the coast with friends and had a childhood outside. I've worked my ass off to keep fit. That's who I am. That's all I am. I wasn't on the beach drinking as you imagine."

"I don't think that," I tried. Did I? Is that what he thinks I thought of him? Oh god, he did. Since day one, all I've gone on about is popularity and parties. I had never once asked him about his hobbies back home or his friends. He's right, I just assumed he had those experiences, and I was missing out on them. I was jealous, not only of my so-called friends but of Olly. I wanted anybody's life but my own.

"Sometimes, Ashley, I think you live far too much in your teenage films and magazines. It's not real life, and it's not good for you. Can we just forget about it?"

I nodded, not sure of what to say. Olly was right.

My perfect boyfriend had undoubtedly put me in place, and then it hit me. "Where are you going?" I blurted out, widening his gaze.

"Going? I'm not going anywhere?" he said, fiddling with his chord bracelets.

"A boy from last night told me you were leaving. What did he mean? Where are you going?"

My words altered his expression. His gaze dived deep into mine as if they were trying to relive my conversation with this so-called boy, saving him from asking questions. "And you believed him?" is all he said before stepping back, putting distance between us, and

I was suddenly the bad guy for questioning him. "A boy, who I wouldn't know, seeing as I have only lived here for five minutes."

Olly was more upset than ever, and I felt my heart crack. What was I doing? Why was I ruining the best thing that had ever happened to me over some stupid comment? Olly loved me, and I knew that. "You're right. I'm sorry, I don't know why I believed him. I don't know him," I said, closing the space between us.

I cupped his face and leaned in, kissing his unbearably tempting lips, and he kissed me back. "Can you forgive me?" I asked, and he smiled, kissing me again.

After twenty-four hours without him, I was back where I belonged.

*

"I can't believe you snuck out and went to a party," Alex laughed, "Was it good?"

Was it good? How would I know if it was? I had never been to a party to compare it with. I had fun, but it was far from what I expected. There were no spin-the-bottle games, truth or dare, and if rude boys and intimidating girls were fun, then maybe? But was the hangover and argument with Olly worth it? No, I guess not.

"Erm, it was okay, mediocre at best, but I had to spend all day yesterday grovelling to Olly and my parents," I shrugged as I flicked through the clothes rail.

"Oh, a bust then?"

"Pretty much," I nodded. "You wouldn't believe how my mum and dad have been; they haven't even grounded me. They said, and I quote, they would loosen the reins a little."

"What, really?"

"Yeah, they said they would rather know where I am than me sneaking out."

"That's crazy; what's gotten into them? Even my parents would have locked me in my room, and they don't sound as bad as yours," Alex laughed, and so did I.

"I keep asking myself the same thing, but I might as well go with it rather than question it. They could change their minds," I shrugged. "Do you think these suit me?" I asked, picking up purple cord flares, then held up a T-shirt with a tie attached to its hanger, "Or this?"

"Erm, I like them both," she agreed. "I think you should get these; they're pretty and would suit you." I took the black lace gloves and ran my fingers down the floral pattern.

"Umm, they are beautiful," I said, putting my fingers into the gap and my thumb in the thumb hole. I instantly liked how my hands fit perfectly into them. They ran down my forearms and covered up my knuckles. I looked in the mirror, and with black nail varnish, they would look great.

"You're kinda into the skater look, aren't you?" Alex asked, fingering the small badges on the accessory section.

Looking around, I had unconsciously wandered into the clothes section where no fear and quicksilver labels hung, and no bright colours existed. And with black tights and dark t-shirts filling my shopping basket, she had caught me out.

I did like that Becca girl's outfit, and there was no competition for preference over Lauren and her fashion sense. I didn't need to read magazines to blend in with that crowd. It came naturally. It was me.

Even with the likes of Kyle, who was downright the most intimidating person I had ever met, I would pick his company over anyone at Bailey. Somehow he knew me, even when I didn't know him. The more I questioned how the more he intruded into my mind. His hands on my shoulders sent shivers down my spine more than I would have liked. His mysterious grey stare pulled at my stomach, and his breath on my face rose warmth in places only Olly should. Yet, with never seeing him again and his imprint of harsh words in my mind, I could only hope I had stained his expensive vans.

"Ashley?" Alex said, nudging me.

"Huh, yes, yes I am," I grinned. "I know it isn't what everyone likes, which means I won't fit in with the majority, but I'm okay with that. Being true to myself has made me the happiest I've been in a long time."

"I like it," Alex smiled.

"You do?"

"Nothing new to me, there are loads of kids like that at Oakley, and they're no different."

"Huh," I muttered, furrowing my brow. "I wish Bailey were like that; it's so stereotypical. If you don't fit, you don't belong."

"Don't go back then," she said, and I wished I didn't have to.

"Transfer," we simultaneously shouted, jumping up and down, nearly losing half our baskets.

"Oh my god, why didn't I think about that before," I squealed.

"It's such a good idea. Move to Oakley for A levels, screw Bailey." Alex laughed.

"There is one problem," I mumbled, fiddling with my hair. "Olly, I can't leave Olly."

Alex tutted and shook her head, "Surely, he would understand."

"Yeah, he would, but I know I'll lose him if I leave. I can't imagine being apart from him."

"Erm Ashley, he's your neighbour," she smiled as we walked to the tills and stood in line. "Nothing would change."

And I guess she was right, Olly would understand, and he would still be right next door. He knew how Bailey made me feel. Just thinking about going back made me anxious. A clean slate and new friends would be a fantastic way to finish my school life before university. But seeing as Olly was my only set plan for my future, I quickly brushed the idea aside.

"Is there anywhere else you need to go?" Alex asked, hovering in the doorway as I sorted my bags.

"Erm, I don't think so. I told Olly I would be back at his for five."

"I'm surprised he let you out to see me," she joked, shoving her shoulder against mine. "Sammy thought he had kidnapped you."

"Ohh, Olly's not like that. If anything, I'm the one who hasn't wanted to leave him. But I think I've been getting on his nerves a bit lately. He wants to talk more, whereas I want to kiss him all the time."

"I've seen him. I understand," Alex snorted. "So, I guess that means you don't want to come to my sleepover at the weekend?"

"What?" I beamed. "No, I'll be there."

"Good, I can't wait." Alex hugged me and twiddled with my hair before letting go and said, "Think about Oakley; I think you'd be much happier, and I'll see you on Friday."

I nodded and said, "I will," and waved, walking in the opposite direction towards home.

I thought nothing more of Oakley. Olly wouldn't be there, so there was no point in getting hung up on the notion, even if it was a great idea that could change my school life forever.

CHAPTER TWENTY-TWO

"Olly, we're going now," Marie shouted up the stairs.

His gloriously tasting lips pulled from mine, moving me aside as he got up. I sighed and followed, standing at the top of the stairs as he hovered halfway, sitting on the step.

"You two, behave," Calvin said, looking at Olly and me.

"Ashley, home by nine with Zoe, please."

"I know, Mum," I muttered, drumming my fingers on the stair rail.

"No later," she pointed. "And in the living room with them, no funny business."

"Liz," Dad butted in, tugging Mum towards the door.

"Sorry, I just worry," I heard her say.

"Right. See you later," Marie said with a small smile. She looked warier than usual as she glanced back at me before shutting the front door.

"Have a good night." I waved.

Laying on Olly's bed, I listened to his voice echoing downstairs, talking to Nate. When he reappeared, shutting the door behind him, he puffed out his chest, leaning against it. "Do you think our parents are mind readers?" I said, and he smiled, walking towards me.

"Are you sure you're ready?" he asked, and I nodded shyly.

I was ready. Ready to give Olly all of me. I would give him the world if I could. At least, I thought I was. How was I supposed to know?

I knew that whatever I felt for Olly stole my heart whenever I was with him. Even when he was with me,

I missed him. When Olly was close to me, he wasn't close enough. His kisses weren't intense enough, and his hands didn't hold me for long enough.

I simply couldn't get enough.

I don't know what to call it. Love, lust, maybe even a little obsession. Either way, he made me feel not quite right. It was what I wanted; I wanted to experience the closeness, the magical first time with no one other than him. I was ready.

I took a deep breath as he looked down at me and tried to hide the trembling in my hands. The butterflies in my stomach were fluttering rapidly, and I felt sick.

"Are you okay?" he asked, laying back beside me, stroking my cheek.

Silence had suddenly bound me, and I worried I might throw up if I opened my mouth, so I tentatively nodded with an "Uh-huh," biting my bottom lip.

He dived his gaze into mine and wrapped it tightly around my soul, banishing the fear in my mind, and when he leaned in, our kiss was electric. His lips were gentle on mine, tingling every nerve, beautifully waking them.

Slowly moving his hand to the small of my back, his probing tongue deliciously entwined with mine, and his fresh vanilla scent filled all my senses. Olly had me lost in a moment where nothing else existed. He was gentle and perfect, making my dreams come true.

The beating of his heart thumped under my palms as I ran them under his football shirt, pulling at him eagerly. I was in control and powerful, but I also felt a rush of helplessness.

I slid my hands up his neck, toying with his hair as I breathed wildly, experiencing the warmth he kindled all over my body. As I stopped and took a breath, he smiled and kissed me softly, then intensely, making me dizzy as I clung to him. I gave him access to my neck, and as his tender lips sent tremors through my body, I was swimming in giddiness. My shaking hands drifted down the perfect crease in his spine and grasped the bottom of his shirt. I faltered, then pulled it up, guiding it over his head, and the sight of his body provoked sensations on an entirely new level. I was drenched in euphoria.

Olly moved back, leading me from the bed, and we were standing opposite each other, as nervous as each other. His fingers threaded my hair and brushed down my cheek, moving to my top. He gently removed it above my head, and my long locks brushed against my skin like feathers, shivering me. I watched him with glee. His breathing was deep, and I sensed his anticipation as I inhaled his scent.

Undoing the button on my shorts, I let them fall, stepping out as trepidation tingled my toes. Moving back to his bed, I got under his covers, and he turned the light off. He was now a kept secret as his shyness took over.

Olly climbed under the quilt after me and ran his hand up my thigh, raising goose pimples, quickly soaring my excitement. His lips fell on my shoulder, startling me. I instinctively grabbed him, taking my hand on his back as he moved between my legs, and I felt his arousal against my stomach. Before now, it had been foreplay, and I was happy wandering. Now I needed him.

His kiss grew deeper and deeper the more his hands caressed my body. As they lowered, he picked up the lining of my panties and fumbled with them, removing them hesitantly. In the serenity of his room, I heard nothing. It was the quietest I had ever heard it, and when he opened his drawer and the sound of a wrapper disturbed it, fear hooked my stomach.

I caught my breath, and a million questions went through my head. My heart hammered ten times faster in my chest. Exceptionally nervous, aroused, and confused.

His warm breath hovered over my skin as his presence moved back above me, not daring to move. My hands cupped his face, and I kissed him, pulling him down, and he relaxed a little. "Are you ready?" he whispered, and I swallowed hard, saying yes.

My heart exploded as he slowly became a part of me, taking me beyond places I had ever been. Olly tenderly touched my body with patience, and his worry showed, and it cast a spell over me. It was surreal, warm and the opposite of what I expected and imagined in its entirety. I thought I felt alive, but I hadn't experienced true happiness until then; it felt like it couldn't get any fuller.

I couldn't stop looking at him, and the glistening in his eyes looked like a little milky way spinning slowly. I had never felt this way before and couldn't imagine feeling any different. Olly completed me, bewitched me, and had shooting stars surging through me and trembling my body. Pure bliss ached in my chest, and from that moment when all I could feel was him, I was the closest to heaven I'd ever be. I wanted him to hold onto me and never let me go. Nothing in me was mine anymore. It was his.

I failed to part from Olly for the rest of the night. We cuddled as his heart's steady pace soothed me, relaxing me from the realisation that I had lost my innocence and become a woman. If anything, I had become the new me, as suddenly I felt like someone new. I had been reborn and was no longer the loser nobody noticed, and I loved this Ashley, every inch of her.

I couldn't stop thinking about what had just happened, and my body was still to stop tingling as my heart shined brightly about the entire thing. There was a party under my skin, and I hoped it would never end.

We didn't talk about it. Nothing needed to be said.

The night was like a dream.

Magical.

Out of this world.

Indescribable.

My heart was bursting at the seams, and I feared it wouldn't be able to contain anything more. It was ready to explode at any minute. That's how Olly made me feel, and I couldn't imagine feeling like that for anyone else.

When I reached my driveway with Zoe clinging to my hand, I looked up at his bedroom to find him watching me and beamed as he blew me a kiss.

*

"Ashley, are you happy?" Zoe asked as I tucked her into her covers. I stopped and sat down on the edge of the bed.

"What do you mean?"

"I hear Mum and Dad sometimes saying you're not happy. That your heart is broken," she said, shrugging her shoulders.

I smiled and stroked her hair, "I am happy, Zoe."

"Are you only happy when you're with Olly?"

I blushed, and my heart glowed as I nodded and wrapped my hair around my finger, "I am mainly happy when I am with him, but that's a grown-up thing."

"I'm happy and not a grown-up," she muttered inquisitively.

"You have lots to be happy about, that's why. Now go to sleep," I said, hushing her as I stood up and walked towards the door.

"Ashley," Zoe called again. I sighed and looked back. "You have lots to be happy about, too; I love you."

"I love you too, squidge." I smiled and gripped the door handle tighter as my emotions got the better of me. They sure had taken a battering in the past twenty-four hours.

I shut her bedroom door a tad and went into my bedroom across the hall. As I turned on the light and looked at it, wondering what to do, it stripped me from my contentment. What was meant to be my safe haven was a disguise for who I truly was. The flowery bed covers weren't me, nor were the lilac curtains. The glitter and outfits hanging beside my new ones I would never wear again and the pile of magazines sent me down a path I wished never to return. Gone were the days of pretending. I would no longer wear a cover-up. Olly loved me for who I was, so I should love myself too.

I texted Alex and arranged for her to come shopping with me. If I had to, I'd spend my allowance to escape the shadow I had lived behind. If I had learnt anything, I was ready to embrace being me. I wanted to change, and it was finally my time; nothing could stop me now.

Nothing.

*

My mind was running on overdrive as I tossed and turned, so instead, I stood at my window looking out into the sheet of blackness, watching the stars light the sky.

Wearing the tiara Olly had given me, I listened to the songs we danced to and put my new lace gloves on.

I tried to think of a style between who I had been pretending to be and the girl I felt myself becoming. Fearing if I completely let go of who I had been, who I was when I met Olly, I may risk losing him along with myself. But then again, he never said he loved me based on my choice of handbags and gladrags.

CHAPTER TWENTY-THREE

I miss u 2. XXX, I read, brushing my thumb over the screen as my smile sketched wider over my face.

"Ashley," I heard, bringing me from my thoughts.

"Huh. Sorry," I said, looking back at Alex.

"Have you got everything you wanted?" she asked, looking at my full basket and hers. They were piled with posters, pillows, quilt covers, and accessories.

"Yeah, I think so." I altered the basket handles, stopping them from pinching my skin. "Maybe we should mention Woolworths needs trolleys."

"Yeah, that would have made this easier," she laughed, heading to the tills.

"What's the plan for tonight?" I asked, piling my items into the carrier bags.

"Ooh. You are going to love this," Alex squeaked. "So, last-minute change. Mum and Dad are having a BBQ with loads of their friends," she paused. My expression altered, imagining the kind of party my parents would throw, shoving me in my bedroom out of the way. "No, it's not as it sounds. My parents throw the best parties. They open the pool and hot tub, and Harley brings her friends and slips me drinks."

My eyebrows raised, and my smile returned, "Harley?"

"She's my older sister. She's back for the weekend."

"Oh, okay. So she's older, older?"

"She's twenty. She goes to NYC."

"Wow, that's far."

"Yeah, she went as far away as she could. She's pretty cool, and I think you'll like her," Alex said. "Actually, I *know* you will like her."

"Come on, let's go back to mine. Sammy, Morgan, and Emily are coming round, and we need to pitch some tents up in the garden."

"Tents?"

She nodded, picked up one of my bags, and tugged me along as I dawdled on my phone, reading my text message.

I'm going 2 Lewis's. Enjoy ur sleepover. I love u, xxx.

My heart sank a little, quickly taking me back to Lewis's hidden identity. Though, seeing as Olly made it clear that partying was not his scene, I knew I had nothing to worry about.

I love u. C u tomoz xxx

"I don't have a swimming costume?" I muttered, putting my phone in my trouser pocket.

Alex laughed. "You don't need one; I have loads or wear your clothes."

I loved how free-spirited Alex was. She was nothing like anyone else I knew. She went with the flow and was insultingly honest, which was her best quality. Being around her eased me. She didn't question anything I bought, not the black pillows, red and black chequered bed covers, Avril, Good Charlotte and Pink posters. Nor did she comment on how I dressed, talked, or felt. She was my best friend, and I was glad to have her. And since she mentioned it, I hoped she wouldn't follow in her sister's footsteps and leave for a distant university too.

*

"This one attaches to that one," Morgan shouted over the pile of twisted fabrics and poles.

"Oh my god, we have been doing this for hours," I huffed, dropping my poles and stretching my back.

"It says fifteen minutes on the bag," Morgan laughed.

Alex glanced at Morgan, Emily, and then me. She dropped everything and burst into laughter, stepping out of the mess in the middle of us, "Dad," she shouted. "Can you come here, please?"

I took a breather and checked my phone; Olly hadn't texted me back. I didn't want to bother him or seem needy, but something made me want to check in. I knew I shouldn't; he was entitled to time without me. I told myself to stop worrying, shut my phone off and put it in my bag.

"What's the matter, girls?" Alex's dad, Phil, asked, walking into his enormous immaculate garden. "Christ, you still haven't done it?" He wiped his brow. "Go inside. Your sister has just arrived. I'll sort this."

"Thanks, Daddy," Alex said, with a beaming smile, kissing him on the cheek and handing him the instructions, which he tossed aside.

We went inside, following the giggling coming from the kitchen. And when we got there, Alex's mum, Maxine, Max for short, was smothering a slim woman, ecstatic, bouncing her up and down.

"Mum, that's enough," the woman chuckled.

"I've missed you so much," Max said, wiping a small tear from her cheek.

As I watched on, enjoying the family reunion, I noticed the woman's leather jacket with studs up the sleeve. It complimented her short, cord black skirt, fishnet tights and bulky black boots.

It wasn't until they let go of each other that I saw the blue streaks in her brown crimped hair, styled in a high, crimped quiff, falling long down her back. Her hoop earrings were large, and her nose stud was red. Bulky headphones hung around her neck.

She looked amazing.

"Welcome home, Harley," Alex muttered, hugging her. "Did you bring me anything?"

"Is that all you care about? It's not that we haven't seen each other in months." She rolled her eyes as Alex tutted. "Fine, I did; all the American sweets you like are upstairs."

"Oh yes! Thanks, you're the best."

"Don't I know it, you spoilt brat," Harley Joked.

Alex let go and looked at me, "Harl, this is Ashley, my next bestie. She is kinda into the fashion you are. I bet she would love some advice."

"Hi. Hi," I choked, nervously tucking my hair behind my ear.

"I like your outfit," she said. I looked down at my baggy cargo pants and red vest. It was basic and nothing to like, but I smiled anyway.

"I have loads of stuff upstairs. You're welcome to look through it," Harley said. "I was going to chuck it but take first dibs, seeing as Alex doesn't want it."

"What? Really?" I beamed.

"Of course. Come up. I have the perfect outfit that would suit you for the party."

I smiled and swallowed, eager to go upstairs and see her wardrobe, in awe of her charisma and style.

"I told you that you would like her, didn't I," Alex muttered with a nudge and smirk. I agreed, unable to take my gaze from her sister, wishing I had such an iconic role model. I now knew why Alex wasn't bothered about my style.

"Come on," Harley said, peering around the kitchen. She sneakily took a pack of WKD from the stash on the table without her mum seeing it and winked at me, nodding upstairs.

*

"Do you like it?" Harley asked as I gazed in the mirror.

"Oh my god, I love it," I said, looking at myself in black ankle-length capri pants and a white vest top covered by a waist jacket. The thick strapped pointed heels wrapped around my bare ankles, and the entire outfit made me look slimmer.

"Eek," I gushed. "I wish I knew how to dress like this all the time. How did you get so good at it?"

Alex and the others were sitting on her bed, piling all the clothes which were going home with me. All of it; I loved every unique, quirky item.

Harley stood behind me, gulped down her WKD and fiddled with my hair. "I have always liked the grunge, skater style, but it helps that I study fashion."

"Really?" I said more enthusiastically than expected.

"Yeah," she paused. "Why did you say it like that?"

"Erm, I didn't mean to," I stuttered. "It's just."

"Assumed someone dressed like me, with piercings and tattoos, can't have a career in fashion?" She sighed.

"No," I said, suddenly panicking I had insulted her. "But I get judged just for wearing black and fishnets. How do you not let it bother you?"

Harley passed me another bottle of WKD. I took it, enjoying the berry flavour sliding down my throat, surprised my vomit-painted bathroom hadn't put me off.

Never again, what a joke; this was how people drank regardless of the hangover. It was fun, and I was young, enjoying my life, not wasting time worrying about the aftermath.

"I ignore them and don't give a fuck." She laughed, and I giggled, wishing she could lend me some of her personality.

"So, what do you think about a piercing?" Harley muttered.

"What?" I said.

"What?" Alex repeated.

"What? I think a nose piercing would suit you." Harley shrugged. "Can I do it?"

"Erm, I don't think my mum would allow that," I cautiously replied.

"Your mum isn't here."

"Harley, stop it," Alex muttered.

"Stop what? She knows she wants to." I pondered the idea; I had wanted it done since seeing Becca's. I never expected to be given the opportunity.

"It doesn't hurt for long," she insisted. "I did Alex's."

I glanced over at Alex and the others who had fallen mute and raised my brow.

"Urgh, she did it last year. I don't wear it," Alex mumbled, and Morgan looked closely at her, observing her tiny hole.

"Oh yeah, I see it."

"Put it in and let us see," Emily insisted, but Alex shook her head.

"Okay," I blurted out. "Do it."

"Really?" Harley asked.

Alex disagreed and said, "You'll get in trouble, but whatever."

I nodded, bit my lower lip, and drained my bottle dry, suddenly full of nerves.

"Great. I'll go and get a needle and some hot water."

"Ashley, what are you doing?" Morgan whispered as I sat beside her, tentatively waiting.

"What? I wanted to get one anyway. This saves me having to ask my mum." I said. "She can't say anything if I already have it done."

"She is going to kill you," Alex tried. "And what about Olly?"

"What about him?"

"Will he like it?" Emily asked.

"I don't know. It's only a stud."

Alex rose from the bed. "Fine, if you're sure it is what you want, you will need something stronger than WKD to numb the pain." She opened Harley's desk drawer and pulled out a bottle of Gold schlager, handing me the bottle as I watched the visible flakes of gold float within the clear liquid.

"Does it hurt that much?"

"Nah, not really; your eyes might water, that's all."

"Right, are we ready?" Harley squeaked, rubbing her hands excitedly, re-entering her room. "You!" she then scorned Alex, wide-eyed. "It's you who has been drinking my alcohol."

Alex pursed her lips and wrinkled her nose, "Nooooo," she said half-heartedly, laughing. "But Ashley needs more than WKD if you're piercing her nose."

Harley looked at me and relaxed her shoulders. "Yeah, I guess you're right." And Alex grinned, pretending to wipe her brow, mouthing phew behind Harley's back as she took the bottle from my hand.

She took six shot glasses off a shelf and lined them all up. I watched her pour the liquid into the shots perfectly and patiently waited.

"Take one," she insisted, looking at me, Alex, Morgan, Sammy, and Emily.

They all took theirs, giddy and eager. I looked at Harley, then at them, apprehensive.

"Come on, Ashley, it's nothing you've not done before," Alex mumbled.

I exhaled profoundly and took the small glass between my fingers.

"It's going to be a great night," Harley cooed. "Cheers." We clinked our glasses and shot back the cinnamon flavour.

"Jeez," I said, laughing as my cheeks warmed and my body lightened.

CHAPTER TWENTY-FOUR

"Girls, are you coming to play truth or dare?" Harley asked, squatting down as we sat on the poolside, paddling our feet.

I looked at her, then at Alex and around the bustling garden. "How can we play truth or dare? There are only six of us."

Harley grinned, "My friends are here now. They're upstairs."

"No, not a chance," Alex muttered.

"Come on, Ally, don't be a spoilsport," she pouted, ruffling Alex's hair.

She sighed. "Harley. You know I don't enjoy it. I'm boring and never do any dares."

"Okay then, how about seven minutes in heaven?"

I glanced at Harley, inquisitively chewing the inside of my mouth, "What is seven minutes in heaven?"

"Are you joking?" Harley gasped, looking at me gone out, and my lack of knowledge embarrassed me.

"You basically get locked in a cupboard with someone in the dark and have seven minutes to kiss or whatever," Emily explained.

"Ashley has a boyfriend. She won't want to play," Alex added.

"Ooh, well, what happens in the cupboard stays in the cupboard." Harley winked.

"Harley, we're staying here."

"Suit yourselves. We have a stash of alcohol, though. But, stay with the old people if you prefer," Harley mocked. "Good luck getting a drink off, Mum and Dad." She stood up, wobbled a little and stumbled off. I watched her talk to everyone around as she passed through confidently. I wanted to be like her, and I wanted to follow.

Part of me wanted to experience the games I had never heard of; it was what I had wanted to do for so long, but Alex was right; I had a boyfriend. What were the chances of having a boyfriend and the opportunity to party and play simultaneously?

I certainly never saw it coming.

"Alex, let's go and play," I found myself saying.

"What? Why? They are lame games."

I looked at her and the others, who seemed as bored as me. Our alcohol disappeared the minute we left Harley's room. My nose was also throbbing, and I needed something to numb the pain.

The minute that needle jabbed through my nose tissue, my eyes watered. It was quick and painful, like a sharp pinch, and until the effects of a few shots of Gold schlager wore off, it was smooth sailing. Now the dull ache pained my face.

"I have never played any of them *lame* games," I admitted, and they all looked sorry for me. It made me feel pathetic.

"Never?" Sammy asked. "Never ever?"

I shook my head and looked at my feet, watching the water surround them and then fall as I lifted them in and out.

How could I feel embarrassed about not playing silly games when I have had sex and have a boyfriend? Why did I care? I shouldn't have wanted to kiss someone else. I didn't want to. But I also couldn't explain why I was so eager to get up and experience it to say I had and not be the only one in school who hadn't.

"Fine, come on," Alex muttered with a roll of her eyes, rising to her feet. "But I promise you; these games *are* lame. None of Harley's friends will want to kiss us; we are too young."

"Yes," I shrieked excitedly, standing up, picking up my heels, and following her inside along with the others.

"Didn't take long to change your mind," Harley smirked as we walked into her bedroom.

Every inch of the large room was full of faces. All spread out amongst the floor, chairs and king-size bed.

My chest tightened, observing the tattooed guy spinning an empty bottle, pointing and laughing. Some stylish girls on the bed glared at us, and I swear I heard one tsk.

"Alex, are you sure you and your friends are up for this?" Harley said.

"It's nothing I haven't done before," Alex mumbled. Her words surprised me. Was there more to Alex than I knew? How many parties had she been to with older teenagers?

"You have done this before?" I asked, tugging her arm. "I thought you had never kissed anyone until prom?"

"I've played once or twice, but I never kissed anybody," she said like it was no big deal. It had me wondering, what had she done?

"Are you sure you don't want to go back downstairs?" Emily whispered to Sammy and me. They both looked as nervous as I felt.

"I thought you had played before?" I asked, catching the eye of a guy staring at me sitting at Harley's desk, flicking through a magazine. He licked his lips and smiled seductively, and I was suddenly out of my comfort zone.

"I never said I had played. I just knew what it was," Sammy muttered apprehensively.

"Can we go?" Emily retreated, rocking back and forth on her heels, wringing her wrists.

"Right. Sit down in a circle." Harley insisted. "Come on, Ashley, Emily, Morgan, Sammy, sit next to Alex."

I looked at Morgan and took a deep breath, catching the cigarette smoke surrounding us. It was not regular smoke, making me cough and my eyes water.

"Erm, we're going to go back downstairs," I mumbled, looking down at Alex, who had already joined the circle. She glanced at me, embarrassed by us backing out after talking her into it. It made my stomach ache and my palms clammy.

"No, you're not. Come on, sit down." Harley prompted us to the floor.

There was nothing I could do without looking idiotic, so I mouthed, "I'm sorry," and took Sammy's hand, sitting beside Alex. Morgan and Emily sat down too.

"What are you doing? You wanted to play?" Alex whispered.

"Yeah, my bad," I said, leaning my elbows on my trembling knees.

"Here," Harley offered, handing us all shot glasses and a bottle of peach schnapps.

"Don't be so scared," the guy from the desk spoke up, now sitting opposite me. Shit. My body sank lower, and my cheeks burned.

"Give me that," I said, taking the bottle from Alex. I poured a shot and, without hesitation, drank it. I gasped, poured another one and drank that, letting out a slight cough as my chest burned

"Come on, girls, we're at a party." I smiled. "Let's relax."

"Now that's more like it," Harley grinned. "I like her." She laughed, reaching her arm over Alex and giving me a playful push.

I took Alex, Morgan, Emily, and Sammy's shot glasses, poured a drink, and passed them back. I then sorted myself another one. I smiled, slightly apprehensive about what was coming and swallowed it.

"Let's play," I said, nibbling my bottom lip as it tingled.

Harley took the empty bottle from one of the boys and placed it on the floor.

"I thought we were playing seven minutes in heaven?" Alex asked.

"We are, this to spice it up a bit," she said, looking at everyone, taking the lead. "So, the rules are, if the bottle lands on you, you go in the cupboard, we spin again, and that person joins. For everyone else, you have to take a shot. Understand?"

"So the person who goes in first doesn't know who joins until they come out?" Alex asked.

"You got it," she winked, and Alex puffed out her chest, flaring her nostrils. My stomach knotted tighter.

I had a million questions but stayed silent, not wanting to look like the inexperienced teenager I was in front of all these twenty-year-olds. Who were, quite frankly, already intimidating.

Watching Harley spin the bottle, we waited. It turned rapidly and started to slow.

Every inch of me trembled as all I could think about was Olly. What was he doing? Would he kiss someone else? Oh my god, what was I doing?

"Holy crap," Morgan reacted. I looked at her, and her cheeks were flushing red. I then glanced down at the bottle, and it was pointing her way. Oh shit, that was close, I thought.

"Eeeek," Harley said, rubbing her hands together. "Morgan, in the cupboard, go."

"Oh, erm," Morgan tried, but Harley pointed, giving her no option. She got up slowly and made her way, and it was nerve-wrenching to watch as she looked anxious as hell.

"Has Morgan ever kissed anyone before?" I asked Alex.

"Nope, never," she said, shrugging her shoulders. "Neither has Emily."

"Oh god, why didn't you say something?" I mumbled, twiddling with my hair. "They are going to hate me."

"No, they will thank you later. It's not every day you can say your first kiss was with a twenty-year-old," she laughed.

"You're right. Well, at least I hope you are."

"Oooh, Jake. You're up," one of the girls said.

A blond-haired boy stood up. Tattoos covered his forearms and neck, and he had a pierced lip. Black vans matched his baggy black jeans and an oversized t-shirt.

"Be gentle," Harley insisted, smirking.

"Right," his deep voice said, winking at her. He opened the cupboard and joined Morgan.

"Shot, shot, shot!" The boys bellowed.

I looked around, and they were all pouring their drinks. Alex handed me one, and I drank it. I was buzzing. My body was tingling all over, and the pain in my nose was long gone.

"Seven minutes is a long time," I said, giggling.

"You can do plenty in seven minutes," the guy opposite me said. "Trust me."

"Ewww," I mumbled to Alex, who spat out her drink as she couldn't contain her amusement.

"Times up, times up," Everyone bellowed as the timer rang.

Relief cascaded over me when Morgan left the cupboard with Jake, and more so that a huge smile was on her face.

She sat back down and took a shot.

"So?" Emily pried.

"It was good," she sighed, almost melting to the floor.

"Good?" Sammy asked.

"Yeah," she said, swooning. I laughed, as did she, lost for words.

*

"How have you gotten away with not going in the cupboard yet?" Emily said.

"I have no idea," I slurred, laughing, toying with the empty schnapps bottle in my hand.

I had escaped the cupboard for over an hour. Emily and Sammy had been three times, Alex twice, and Morgan four times.

"Shall we go in the pool after the next round?" Harley said. "I have some more friends joining in a minute."

"Oh, thank god," I muttered.

"Does playing count if you haven't actually participated?" I asked Alex.

"Oh, don't make me laugh. I'm dying for a wee."

"I wasn't joking." I laughed. I was a little disappointed I never got seven minutes in heaven, though at least I had no guilt running through me when it came to Olly.

"About bloody time," then took my attention. I looked at the circle, which was all staring at me. Most were drunk and resorted to snogging, in or out of the cupboard.

I caught the gaze of the boy who had been giving me the creepy eye since walking into the room, and he bowed his head down. My eyes followed where I found the bottle pointing right at me.

My heart instantly climbed into my clenched throat, and my hands rolled into tight balls. I let go of the breath my fear had taken hold of and looked at Alex, mortified.

"Go. Go, Ashley. Then we can go downstairs," Alex prompted, pushing me from my sitting position.

Oh my god, I didn't want to; I panicked.

I wished I could say so, but I couldn't. No one had the entire time, and I would not be the first and only one. So I found my feet, leaning on Alex for support, wobbling as I struggled to balance. All eyes were on me. I'd fallen into a nightmare; I knew I had.

I tried to avoid looking around and prayed to god the guy licking his lips at me didn't follow—anyone but him.

Opening the door, I stepped into the dark, holding onto the door frame as I closed it behind me. I peered around, but it was pitch black. I couldn't see a thing and could only feel the clothes hanging behind me as I leaned on them, trying not to pass out or puke.

My ears picked up as it suddenly sounded loud on the other side of the door, tempting me to open it.

I moved from my position and went for the door handle, but it opened. I quickly closed my eyes and turned around, allowing them in.

Anxiously, I bit my lip, not knowing whether to say something or not. How was it fair that I didn't know who it was, but they did?

When they touched my shoulder, I flinched and froze simultaneously. Their hand was warm, gentle, yet firm. I pivoted my feet and faced the mystery in front of me, which smelt deliciously fruity. What was that?

Orange or peach? I had shot so many peach schnapps that it was likely me; it was all I could taste.

I listened to his breathing for a second, which was therapeutic and slow, whereas mine was erratic; I was breathing way too hard.

My body was statue-like, and I had already wasted two minutes thinking about kissing him. And just as I went to move, I was startled when something touched my face. It was his hand stroking my cheek. Considering it was a game, his touch felt more than it should have, igniting butterflies in my stomach.

He pulled me closer to him, and I did as I should. I leaned in but bashed my teeth against his. Pulling back, I tried not to laugh but, at the same time, wanted to cry with humiliation. Damn it. I heard him sigh, and I wanted to say sorry, but my voice had vanished.

I then felt his hand touch mine. His touch slid up my forearms and shoulders, standing the hairs all over my body, dripping sweat down my spine. His fingers moved to my chin, cupping my jaw, rubbing what I thought was his thumb across my bottom lip, and I stopped myself from licking it. Even though it was dark, he knew my exact shape and where he was going with his hands. And when his lips softly touched mine, I melted to the floor.

The kiss tasted as good as it felt. I enjoyed it, forgetting everything: Olly, my friends, and the alcohol flowing through me. I banished my subconscious and didn't allow her to intrude for five minutes. I stepped entirely into this guy's aura.

Setting my hands free, I moved my hands to him. He was taller than me, and I had to tiptoe a little. I slid my fingers along his broad shoulders. I wrapped my hands around the back of his neck, gasping as his kiss became more intense the minute I held onto him, entwining my tongue with his.

My fingers moved to his hair; it was long, and I didn't know what colour it was, but I was yanking at it as if I owned him. My focus fell on him and the way his lips were devouring mine. He wasn't kissing me like Olly. He was kissing me hungrily and experienced, like the twenty-year-old he was.

His hand moved down my body, and I didn't stop him. I didn't know if it was my drunken state or him, but his delicate touch made me feel sensual and confident. Sexier than I ever had before, like a harlot trying to break free.

His hand gripped my thigh, pulling it to his waist, and he guided me to the back of the cupboard, pinning me against the wall. I didn't falter. I didn't want to move; I was having too much fun. I pulled his hair harder, and he sexily groaned in my ear. Without knowing this body, I knew this boy leaning against me was sexy and undoubtedly a bad boy. At least he was kissing me as one would expect.

"Holy fuck," he sighed as I felt his arousal against me. It sent shivers down my spine and into my every nerve—I was weak at the knees, clinging onto him desperately, feeling powerless.

"Times up, times up!" I heard, and he let go. That guy was right, you can do a lot in seven minutes, and that was only five.

My cheeks burned as my breathing slowed, aware I'd know who took me to heaven and back in a second.

Light entered the cupboard as he pushed the door open, and I exited, readjusting my eyes to the light.

Everyone stared at me, then at him. My gaze moved from the now crowded room, where even people my age sat, and I looked at him. My stomach flipped, and my skin set on fire. I caught my breath and let it go, screaming at myself as my subconscious returned.

"Kyle!"

CHAPTER TWENTY-FIVE

"Ashley," Kyle paused. "I didn't...."
"Did you know that was me?" I cut him off, crossing my arms over my body.

I was horrified, shocked, confused, and downright angry that I was swooning over this mean-ass skater boy. Only Olly should have made me feel those emotions, but Kyle went and did it anyway. What's worse, I let him. He affected me exactly as he did before. I lost control of myself, all sense of reason, and so effortlessly.

I felt so guilty.
Olly was going to hate me.
I hated myself.

"No, I didn't," he snapped, hanging his thumbs in his shorts pockets. "Don't make a big deal out of it, even if I know you enjoyed it." He smirked, taking his lip piercing between his teeth, which thinking about it, I hadn't noticed was there, or did I?

"I did not," I spat, gritting my teeth and rolling my eyes away from him.

Harley pushed through the crowd, looking back and forth at the two of us as Alex and the others joined. "Ash, how do you know Kyle?" she said curiously, and I said nothing, looking to the floor.

"She doesn't like being called Ash," Kyle butted in, his words regaining my attention as I suddenly fell back into his grey stare. I observed him in more detail and noticed a small faint scar on his cheek and near his eye, taking me to his brow piercing, then to his lip bar, captivated by his glossy lips.

I swallowed hard when I managed to pull myself away from his glorious face, five-foot-nine stature, and charismatic style. He was too striking for my liking, and I hated that he captivated me without trying.

"How..." I stuttered. "How did you know that?" He said nothing, shrugged his broad shoulders and looked back to Harley.

"We met at a party. And no, Ashley *doesn't* know me," Kyle snarled. "And Harley babysits my little sister before you ask or get the wrong idea," he snapped before barging past and out of the room.

"Bloody hell, what's his problem?" I asked.

"Not a clue," Harley said. "He's always been like that, but more so lately."

"Kyle's a jerk," Alex added. "Come on, let's go get in the pool."

"Pool party," Harley shouted above the crowd, and we all left the room.

"Ashley, how *do* you know Kyle?" Alex asked as we walked into the kitchen. The atmosphere was bustling, filled with well-dressed men and women, laughing and dancing all over the place.

I peered outside the double patio doors, and it was dark; fairy lights and solar lamps were everywhere, lighting the garden. It was beautiful and relaxing, not blaring and out of control like Lewis's house party.

Stepping onto the patio, I watched Harley's friends jump in the giant lit-up pool, fully clothed, well, most of them anyway.

"Ashley?" Alex repeated.

"Huh, sorry. I met Kyle at that party the other night. He was a jerk there, too," I said, scanning the crowd, unconsciously finding myself looking for him.

"Does he go to Bailey? He's not at Oakley. Does he know Olly?" Morgan asked.

"That's what's confusing. Kyle does go to Bailey, but I never noticed him until the last day. I swear I would have, look at him. He's...."

"Scary," Sammy butted in.

"Stunning," I said.

"Ashley," Alex nudged me, "How can you say that when you have Olly? Olly is stunning, not Kyle. Urgh."

"What? It's only an observation," I muttered, twirling my hair around my finger.

"Plus the seven minutes in heaven with him," Emily joked.

"That too, oh crap. What am I going to tell Olly?"

"Nothing, you're going to tell him nothing. It was only a game; it didn't mean anything. And with a guy like Kyle, I doubt you will be the only girl he kisses tonight," Alex said.

I don't know why, but her words hurt a little. I didn't know Kyle, so why did I care who he kissed? I had a boyfriend. A perfect, gorgeous, sweet boyfriend. So why was I standing there wondering where Kyle had gone? What had he got over me? All I had seen was a bad-tempered, bad-boy attitude, yet instead of scaring me off, it was pulling me in more by the second.

"What do you mean, a guy like Kyle? Do you know him well?" I asked, narrowing my brows.

"No, I don't, and I don't plan to," she said defensively. "Harley tells me he's always got different girls around when she babysits, and he talks to his parents badly. Anyway, come on, let's get in the pool."

"I don't think I want to. I've had too much to drink," I said, backing off. The idea of stripping off in front of all these people was enough to change my mind.

"Don't be a spoilsport, Ashley," she muttered as she took off her denim shorts and jumped into the water, wearing only her top and undies. Morgan, Sammy, and Emily giggled, looked at me and shrugged their shoulders, jumping in after her, mixing in with the crowd.

I shook my head in refusal and stepped back as they splashed me, tumbling into something behind me.

"Ashley," I heard. It wasn't something; it was someone.

"Kyle," I choked as I turned and looked up at him. His gaze melted me to the spot, and his stern expression had me warily biting my lip.

"Being boring?" he asked as he fiddled with the sweatband clinging to his wrist.

"No," I retorted. "I just don't want to go in. I don't want to get my piercing wet or infected, and I don't need to explain myself to you."

"I never asked you to," Kyle said, stepping nearer to me and making me move back a little.

He raised his hand towards me and closed in on me, and for a moment, it seemed like he was going to kiss me. I stepped back again, but his ever-moving stride met mine, rubbing his thumb near my nose and along my cheek, "It suits you. I like it," he said. "Harley will have a lot to answer for. You know, my mum was fuming when she did my piercings."

"I'm not worried," I lied.

"Yes, you are," he muttered in his deep voice.

"Don't tell me what I am and am not. You don't know me."

"That could change if you wanted it to," he smirked, and I moved back again, but I went too far. My feet reached the edge of the pool, and I was suddenly falling in.

"Ashley," I heard, feeling his grip on my arm as my palm reached for any part of him. Though it was too late, my grip grabbed his shirt, and I pulled him straight in with me.

I hit the water, and it was warmer than I initiated, going straight under, as did Kyle. It was deep, and I panicked, forgetting I knew how to swim. I tried to see, but it burnt my eyes, and it was damn near impossible.

But then I felt a hand on my back, pulling me up, but not to the surface, closer to him instead. I saw the silhouette of Kyle in front of me, and I was still holding my breath, but he then stole it, planting a kiss on my trembling, cold lips for no one else to see. The intensity hit me hard in the chest, and my hands gripped him for dear life. His breath filled my lungs, and I wanted to stay submerged even though I was kicking my legs hard to get to the surface.

He let go of me and pulled me up with him, and the minute I reached the air, I gasped, wiping my hair back from my face. I glared at him, he stared at me, and we said nothing for what felt like an exceptionally long minute.

"Thanks for that," I said, splashing him.

"I'm a good kisser, I know," he toyed.

I rolled my eyes, "I meant pushing me in."

"You're welcome," Kyle said, making me smile and almost giggle. "It was as good for me as it was for you," he teased, splashing me back. And despite being in the wrong place with the wrong guy, I wished we were back under the water, not being watched by everyone.

"Ashley," I then heard from the side, where I spotted Alex, dripping wet, looking right at me with a perplexed expression on her face.

I glanced at Kyle and said nothing more as he stared at me, then at her, and his usual serious face returned. I swam to the side and pulled myself up, squeezing the water from my clothes.

"What are you doing with Kyle?" she asked as the others also burned me with curiosity.

"I fell in the pool, he tried to grab me, but I pulled him in." In my defence, that was the story, almost.

"It looked like more than that. You have a boyfriend, remember."

"Back off, Alex, it's true. It was an accident, not that it should matter; it's not like they are married or anything," Kyle cut in, stripping his shirt off in front of us. His muscular body and toned six-pack were not helpful as my knees weakened and my heart clenched.

"Kyle, Ashley has better sense than to ruin what she has with Olly with some bad-mouthed skater boy like you," she scorned.

"Bite me," he retorted, and before I knew it, Kyle stormed past me, baring his tattooed back as I watched him disappear.

CHAPTER TWENTY-SIX

"Alex." I huffed. "You didn't need to be like that. Kyle wasn't doing anything wrong; you got the wrong impression."

"I was just looking out for you. Trust me. Kyle is bad news," she said, looking at Emily, Morgan and Sammy, "Isn't he girls?"

Emily glanced at me, Morgan looked to the floor, and Sammy did nothing but nod.

"Only from what I've heard Harley say," Emily spoke up. "But I don't know him to judge."

"Thank you, Emily," I said, shivering as my clothes tightly tied to my body shape.

"I'm sorry, Ashley, I think he's a bad influence," Alex continued. It was tense between us, the entire atmosphere was thick, and I hated it. Everyone around us was partying like we weren't there, whereas I suddenly felt sober and wanted to go home.

I crossed my arms tightly over my body. "Do you know him enough to say that?"

I didn't know him either, and I didn't understand why I was so defensive when what they were saying seemed so accurate.

Kyle was mean and intimidating with his rebellious ways, but there was something more to him. It wasn't only about his good looks, his fantastic kissing skills, or the way he smelt of tar and hot pavement on a summer's day with zesty orange. My gut was telling me there was more to him than he made out, and for some stupid reason, he had me hooked.

"I guess not," Alex muttered, shuffling her feet as she looked at them.

"Guys, what's going on here? It looks so tense; what's happened?" Harley cut in, rowdy, grabbing

Emily and dancing as she sipped her drink. It made me laugh and relax.

I looked at Alex and stroked her arm, "I'm sorry, let's not argue," I said.

"No, let's not. It was horrible, never again." Alex smiled.

"Never. Especially over some boy." I hugged her. "I'm freezing. Can we go and change?"

"Erm, no, we're going back in. We're going to play some games now Mum and Dad's lot has moved inside. They have the karaoke on, and I would rather not listen to that," Harley slurred, giggling. "Come on. You guys need drinks. You're bumming me out."

"Your sister is a nutter," I laughed as we followed her into the kitchen, and she was right; all I could hear was screeching from the living room. No one could get as high as Frankie Valli, not even with a tonne of alcohol in their system, but they sure were trying hard.

"Right, jello shots for each of you," she said, handing us all one.

"Finally." I licked my lips, took a red one and shot it back; it slipped straight down and soothed me instantly. "You got another one?" I asked, and Harley raised her eyebrow at me, as did Alex.

"What?" I shrugged. "This is a party, isn't it?"

They giggled, and Harley pointed to the fridge. I went over and opened it, and the entire contents were alcohol and trays of jello shots.

"Jeez," I said, taking six more and handing them out.

"I told you my parents know how to throw a party," Alex replied, shooting her shot.

"Right, let's go, chicken fight it is. Who's first?" Harley shouted, pushing us all outside.

"Chicken fight?"

"Oh god, Ashley, don't tell me you don't know what that is either?" And my silence answered her question.

"Right, that's it, Ashley, you're up first. Jackson, get over here; you're taking Ashley; who's going against her?"

"I will," Sammy stepped up.

"What? Against me? What's going on?" I asked. Then, before I could refuse, Harley pushed me towards the shallower part of the pool, where one of her friends stood near the edge, waiting, shirtless, with his back to me. I looked back to Harley, apprehensive.

"Relax, Ashley. Sit on his shoulders; you'll be fine, Jackson is strong, and you're tiny."

"Tiny, I'm not tiny." I tried, but she was having none of it.

"Come on, girl, come here," the long blond-haired boy said, tugging me by my leg.

I looked at Sammy; she was already climbing on another big guy, so I did as they said and thought to hell with it. The next minute, I was resting my entire body weight on his shoulders, with his arms tightly holding me.

"Now what?" I shouted, laughing, trying to hold onto him for balance, but there was only his head. I didn't want to fall, but I also didn't want to drown him with my weight which I was paranoid I was squashing him with.

"Grab Sammy's hands for a second," Harley shouted, and the two guys drew closer.

"Right on my count, you must try and force each other off whilst the guys keep you up. The winner stays on, understood?"

"Wow, this will not end well," I snorted, and Sammy giggled so hard she nearly fell in.

"I hope you are strong, Ashley; I'm a sore loser," Jackson warned, gripping my thighs tighter. "Are you ready?"

"Right, three, two, one, go," Harley yelled, and my grip on Sammy's hand tightened. I used all my force to move her to the left, then the right, whilst balancing simultaneously.

"Ashley, Ashley, Ashley," I heard, and those also chanting Sammy.

My face ached from smiling so much; it was the most fun I'd had in a long time. I never thought I would be sitting on some huge twenty-year-old lad's shoulders wrestling my friend into a pool, and I didn't care if I won or lost.

"Yeah," Jackson cheered, letting go of me for a split second as Sammy splashed into the water. I nearly went in with her but grabbed tightly onto him as I hailed, trusting him to hold my legs as I fist-bumped the air.

I beat Alex.

I beat Morgan and Emily.

I even beat Harley and that lad who gave me the eye during seven minutes in heaven. I had to try a little more as he twisted my hands in all different rotations. Still, no one budged me with Jackson as my 'vehicle' and his unquestionable strength and grip.

"Let me have a turn," a deep voice came from the crowd.

"Kyle," Harley said. "I thought you had left."

"No, I'm here, have been the entire time," he slurred. "I want a go."

She went over, looked closely into his eyes and shook her head, muttering something under her breath.

"No, it's a bad idea," Harley said, but he had already taken his shoes and top off and climbed on Ben, who he ordered with a point of his finger.

My throat dried, and I forced my eyes not to look any lower than his perfectly shaped shoulders. Not at his chiselled chest or his cute, swirled belly button surrounded by dainty brown hairs trailing down under his black knee-length shorts. Nor did I question how he came about the massive gash in his left knee and right shin.

"Take my hands, Ashley," he ordered, and his masculine voice brought me back to reality.

"Ashley, you can beat him," Harley bellowed, nudging Alex as they sensed what I believed to be my first true competitor.

"How are you with losing Ashley?" Kyle teased. "I'm the reigning champion, you know."

"I don't know; I haven't lost yet, so we shall see how *you* are with losing," I smirked, leaning towards him, entwining my fingers with his.

His large grip covered my knuckles, and his ring dug in a little, but his touch was enough to send a bubbling mess right through me.

Kyle looked into my brown stare with his enchanting grey gaze, sending me crazy. I couldn't help but feel I was looking at him like he was me; I was obsessed.

"Go," I heard, nearly missing Harley's voice as Kyle moved first.

My squeeze tightened on his hands, and my legs tensed around Jackson, using my entire body and core to stay up. I knew all I would get was grief if I lost to Kyle, which would undoubtedly come from him.

"Kyle always wins at this game," Jackson muttered, making me try harder. I moved his hand forwards, backwards and all over; our match seemed to last forever.

My grip became looser, my palms became clammy, and my wrists were tired. I pushed my arms with all the strength I had to give, and it hurt my shoulders slightly, and as I felt Kyle beating me, my legs loosened a little.

"No, Ashley," Jackson shouted. "You have got this." He crossed his arms over my legs, gripped my calves with his large palms, and I was secure; there was no way I would fall now. But there was no way I would beat him on pure strength.

I gazed at Kyle, lost my grin, and he narrowed his eyebrows. "What?" he asked.

"It's just," I mumbled.

"What? What's wrong?" he said, sounding eerily concerned, relaxing his grip a tad.

I tensed my hands, used my back, shoulders, and legs strength, and forcefully pushed him sideways. As I knocked his balance, I shoved him some more and watched him splash into the water.

"Yes," I roared, and the audience went wild, the music blared louder, and everyone jumped in the pool. Jackson tapped my legs with his palms and squeezed them a little as he gestured his hands to me. I took them and moved my legs behind his shoulders, sliding down his back into the water. High-fiving him, "What a team," he cheered.

"Ashley," I heard and turned around, looking at a dripping-wet Kyle brushing his hair back with a somewhat amused smile. "Well done." He offered me his hand. "I don't lose well, but you gave it your best, even if you cheated."

"Cheated? No, I never." I shook his hand.

"If you hadn't distracted me, I would have beat you."

"I don't know what you are talking about." I cleared my throat. "Perhaps you shouldn't care so much, and then I wouldn't have distracted you."

"Oh, but I do care."

"What?" I said, darting my eyes as his hand moved towards my face. I shifted my head back a little, but my body resisted. He picked up my hair stuck to my cheek and tucked it behind my ear. His touch had fear hooking my stomach and pulling towards my chest. My heart was beating rapidly, and I nearly choked on it as it made its way into my mouth.

"I may not act like it, and you can say I don't know you, but I do care. I care more than you will ever know." Kyle's words were soft, genuine, and confusing. He then turned and climbed out of the pool.

My eyes didn't leave him, and my words had done a runner. I took note of the several tattoos inked into his skin, mainly skateboard-related, and a bull that intrigued me.

What did he mean when he said he cared?

CHAPTER TWENTY-SEVEN

"I can't believe you lost," Alex mocked, snickering as she looked at Kyle, who was strangely quiet. "So much for the king of chicken fight."

He shrugged his shoulders, wrapped his hand around the bottle in his hand tightly, sank lower in the camping chair and lifted his eyes to me. "I let her win," he mumbled. "It's the least a gentleman can do."

"You a gentleman?" Alex howled. "That's rich."

"Think what you like, Alex," he huffed, moving closer to the bonfire.

After a long time in the water, my bones were frozen to the core, and my nose pounded. If Mum weren't going to kill me for piercing it, she was sure as hell going to for getting it infected. Harley had given me some antiseptic, and Alex insisted chilling by a bonfire would help ease the pain. I was the first to jump at the chance to roast marshmallows, providing that no singing was required. And when Kyle came over and sat with us, I was slightly surprised. And, despite his presence, I sat, slumped in the chair, warm, at ease, and dry.

"Ashley, we're going in the tent. Are you coming?" Emily said as they stood, yawning. I looked up at her and nodded.

"I'll nip to the bathroom, then be there," I said as I rose to my feet.

I glanced at Kyle, sitting alone, and part of me wanted to stay, though I knew I shouldn't, perhaps more so for my own sake than for Olly's.

His head was leaning comfortably against the neck of the chair, and his eyes were closed. I was unsure if he was asleep, so I said nothing.

Quietly walking past him, he exhaled profoundly, "I'm sorry about what I said at Lewis's," he mumbled. His eyes were still shut, and his hands were tucked under his armpits as they firmly crossed his body, "I was out of order and didn't mean it."

I swallowed hard, replaying the abuse he gave me and inhaled as my chest tightened, "It's okay; forget about it."

Kyle fluttered his long, dark eyelashes open and glared up at me. His misty, alluring stare swallowed me whole, taking any following words. He relaxed his arms and reached for my hand, fiddling with my fingers as I lost all sense of reason, "No, I can't; you didn't deserve it."

His clutch grew tighter, and he tugged me closer, nodding his head to the chair beside him. I looked to the tent across the garden, then at him, and the mystery in front of me won.

I sat down, unsure, and for a moment, nothing but silence surrounded us.

"Why did you do it?" he gently asked, and I knew what he was referring to without saying the words.

I hadn't spoken to anyone, not Mum, Dad, Olly, or the GP, about it. But then again, no one had point-blank asked me the question like Kyle did. I didn't know him; he was a stranger to me, and considering the constant warnings, I felt like I could talk to him about anything. It came easily; he seemed somewhat familiar and unnervingly trusting.

I crossed my fingers over one another, twiddling with them and looked away. "I don't know," I quietly said. "I thought it would take away my problems. I hated school. I hated being invisible, laughed at, and different. I got to the point where I was fed up with not being good enough and thought, seeing as no one would notice, I wouldn't be missed." My emotions choked me; the backs of my eyes were pinched by forming tears, and I was trying my hardest not to look at Kyle, who I sensed was burning me with his gaze. My throat bobbed as I gripped the chair tightly, scratching my nails along the fabric.

"Is that really what you believe?" he said softly, moving his chair closer to mine before grabbing my hand.

My eyes lifted to his, and how he looked at me was like nothing I had seen before, a rarity. His gaze was almost delicate, gentle, and safe, and so was his slight smile, which creased his cheek. It enhanced a scar embedded in it, and I wanted to know how he got it; I wanted to know how he got all of them. He was covered in secrecy and an untold story.

Kyle pulled the metal in his lip between his teeth and held it there momentarily as I watched his chest puff out hard. "You couldn't be more wrong if it is," he muttered, squeezing my hand. "A lot of people would miss you. You have been hanging around with all the wrong people all this time, that's all. The likes of them, the popular girls, may look incredible and well-liked, but to girls like you, or boys like me, they are toxic and undermining. You don't need them in your life."

"Lauren has been my only friend for my entire life. Without her, I wouldn't even be on the map."

He tsked, "And look where that got you. Stop kidding yourself and be who you really are. Forget about Lauren, Sophie, and the rest of them. Be the Ashley I have seen today, the fun, confident, pretty Ashley who won't take shit from no one." Kyle blushed, jaw clenching and chest puffing.

I tried to hide my smile; I had just made Kyle blush, a badass skater who makes his own rules and has zero respect for anyone, and no one here to witness such an achievement.

"Did you call me pretty?" I muttered, and he let go of my hand, looking down at his feet.

"Do you want to end up in the pool again?" he smirked, and I grinned. "You know, I'm not as bad as everyone makes out."

"Right, like I believe you." He took a sip from the bottle and offered it to me, but I declined, so he put it down.

"You don't know me to say that. No one does." Kyle's altered tone caught me off guard, making me look him up and down past the charisma he carried, and I attempted to dive into his soul. Beyond the danger, the fearless attitude and the rebellious streak, I questioned if this Kyle, the one who was holding my hand, was the honest Kyle no one knew. Was he a genuinely nice guy, charming inside and Dorian Gray on the outside?

"Let me then," I warily said, and the garden lights suddenly turned off, leaving only the spotlights in the pool, which barely lit the garden. I looked around and could hardly see anything, and when my eyes returned to Kyle, he was gone.

"Kyle," I whispered loudly, suddenly frightened. I then heard him breathe and saw him on the poolside, taking his vans off. His pencil dive made no sound, barely rippling the water.

"Kyle," I said again, rising from my camping chair and peering in. I couldn't see him; it was so quiet I couldn't shout.

"Kyle," I grunted, pacing up and down the edge. "It's not funny, and I'm not coming in after you."

No response came.

I stood shivering and unexpectedly worrying.

"Kyle."

"Ashley," he said, making me jump as he then placed his hands on my shoulders.

I went to turn, but he didn't let me. His wet hands slowly moved down my arms, soaking my skin and making me tremble. His touch took my waist as he wrapped his arms around me tightly. Protectively. I breathed in, unsure if it was to conceal my body or because he'd stolen my breath.

"Relax," he whispered, and I did nothing but obey, having lost all control and power of my mind, body, and soul.

I leaned my head back against his chest, listening to the steady beat of his heart, which quickened the minute I let my guard down. We stood in silence for as long as it took for me to forget about everything and focus on nothing but the oxygen filling and escaping his lungs.

"Get in the water," he said, and again, I was in no place to deny him. The way he talked to me was compelling, hypnotising in such a way it seemed he knew what he was doing and knew whatever the outcome, I trusted him.

I found my bearings and turned as he let me go, not taking my eyes from him as I stepped back and lowered myself into the pool. He climbed in after me, and as I leaned against the edge, instantly shaking, he moved in front of me. He placed his arms on either side of my body, locking me in. I was trapped in no place to move; even if I could, I knew I wouldn't.

"What do you want to know?" Kyle asked, his warm breath reaching down my neck, standing every hair as he leaned closer.

I gasped, pulling my lip between my teeth and ignoring the sensations running through my entire body, right down to my every nerve, "Anything."

"That's not specific enough," he said, and as I failed to respond, it appeared he'd lost interest, which scared the hell out of me.

I grabbed him, taking my hand to his waist as he moved away and muttered, "How do you have tattoos when you're only sixteen?"

Kyle looked back at me, "I have my ways of persuading people to do what I ask," he smirked. "Why? Do you want one?"

I laughed a little, "God no, my parents would kill me. I'm yet to face the wrath I will get for getting my nose pierced first, let alone if I got a tattoo."

"Chicken."

"But seriously, how?"

He looked into my eyes, "With parental consent, some places let you at sixteen."

"I didn't know that," I muttered. "What does the bull mean?"

As he bowed his head and flicked the water, I realised my grip was still tightly on his waist, gripping his shirt as my fingers turned to prunes. I let go, nervously threaded my hair, and my teeth chattered.

"It's your turn to tell me something."

Pulling my lip between my teeth, I toyed with the water, trying to think of something.

"Something real," he insisted, and his eyes had me swimming in them, diving as far as they would allow. I suddenly wasn't scared anymore. Scared of whether I was skinny, good enough, and well-liked. The only thing I worried about was him disappearing and not being with me in a raw moment like this again.

It was then that I realised something had changed the day I first saw him across the school grounds. Kyle had gained every ounce of my attention, and I didn't care about anything or anyone else. It made me a traitor. It made me something I never thought I would be. But it was like he knew me, really knew me, when he didn't know me at all.

"I want to know everything about you, past that scary bad boy persona you try to portray."

Kyle straightened his posture, knitting his brows together, "So, you don't find me scary?" he asked.

I shook my head with a small smile, "Do you hate that? Is that why you are so mean to me and unwilling to tell me the truth for one split second."

His thumb reached my quivering lips, holding them still, and I swam in his stare as I fell into it, "If only you had noticed me before Olly showed up," he muttered. "Then I would have all the time in the world to tell you what you want to know, all my secrets and show you who I really am, but seeing as I don't, I'm not going to."

"What? Why are you like that?" I asked. "Why are you nice one minute, then ruining it the next with some snide, uncalled-for comment?"

"It's the easiest way," he muttered, stepping away, ripping my heart from my chest as he took his touch with him.

"The easiest way to what?" I asked, moving towards him. "You do know everything you say makes no sense to me."

He scowled, an expression I had seen before, and I knew it was time to back off, but I couldn't. He was hiding so much, and I wanted to know what it was. I thought I saw an opening, but then he mentioned Olly, and it reminded me I shouldn't have even been there. I shouldn't have been with him. I shouldn't have been thinking what I was or feeling what I had been.

One more word would take my curiosity too far, and I was in trouble if I took one more step. Kyle had made one thing clear. He was particularly good at persuading people to get what he wanted. And with the glistening in his dark, mysterious eyes and his irritated expression, me begging for answers was what he wanted. Even an unpopular, kept-in-the-dark girl like me could figure that out.

"The easiest way to what?" I repeated as he said nothing.

He stared down at me, squinted his eyes and clenched his jaw. His hands moved swiftly beneath the water and grabbed my forearms tightly; it hurt, and as he lifted me a little, it frightened me more than I would admit.

"Kyle," I gulped as I tried to deny the thrill rising in my body as his hands roughly held me.

"To stop people getting too close to me because when they do, when everything seems perfect, everything changes," he growled and let me go, pushing me back a tad. "If I gave you a chance, it wouldn't be any different. I already know how this is going to end."

"How, what is going to end?" I asked, unable to stop with my million questions.

"Ashley, stop it. Why are you still here? I saw the fear in your eyes just then. You should be backing off like everyone else," he snapped, then climbed out of the pool.

I exhaled, watching his mesmerising body exit the water, fascinated by how it washed over his muscles and dripped down the perfect crease of his spine. I owned the moment with my stare as if it was the last time I would.

"You already said I'm different to everyone else, you know it, and so do I, and believe me when I say it, you don't scare me, so get used to it."

I stayed, frozen to the spot, looking at the silhouette I could barely see and rang the water from my hair. Kyle left without saying a word, bursting the exhilarating bubble he effortlessly built every time I saw him.

*

I returned to the tent, soaked again and late, dreading explaining myself to the others for my disappearance. It wouldn't take a genius to work out where and who I was with, seeing as they left me with him in the first place.

I tried to think of a logical explanation, but nothing came to mind, and why should it? I should feel guilty. I deserved to. I was letting Kyle, a rude, disrespectful, angry boy I barely knew, get in my head. And no matter how much I hated his bad attitude, I liked it when he lost his skater-boy personality and was honest and pure. Something about him had hit me like an Ollie gone wrong on the sidewalk, hard, fast, and painful. It was wrong, lousy timing, and ruthless, but it felt right. Terrifyingly right.

Creeping up to the tent, attempting not to trip over the cords, it was dark and still, and when I entered, everyone was asleep. "Damn it," I muttered. I missed the end of the night and hoped it didn't last too long.

I clambered over the sleeping bags, sprawled out girls, and found my bed. Standing up, I tried to take my clothes off, but as they clung to my body with no space, it was tough to balance after drinking too much. I wobbled all over the place, stripping down to my undies; they weren't that wet, well, they were, but I'd been cold for that long; I'd already risked my health.

I fumbled in my bag and found my phone, turning its pathetic torch on, noticing many messages and missed calls.

Olly
Olly
Olly
Olly
Olly
Olly

My stomach flipped, and my heart sank into the acid forming in its pit as I suddenly felt nauseous.

I ditched the idea of finding clothes and got into my sleeping bag before reading them all. What further could a night in the bare minimum clothes do? Anything Olly had to say was more important.

R u having a gd time?
U nva told me u knew Kyle.
Ashley, txt me bk!
Dn't listen 2 anything he says.
Ashley!
I'm sorry

"What the hell?" I gulped, trying to relieve the dryness in my throat as I started to panic. Something was wrong. What had happened? Was Olly okay? And Kyle? What? What? Just what?

CHAPTER TWENTY-EIGHT

"Alex," I whispered, but she didn't budge. "Alex," I tried again, poking her.

She moved a little and murmured, "Ashley, what's the matter?"

I handed her my phone and said, "I don't know, look at this."

Alex flicked on her torch, sat up and wiped her eyes before taking my phone. She mouthed the words as she read them and looked at me, confused, dizzy, and half asleep.

"Huh?"

"I know, right? Something is up?" I asked, hoping it was me being paranoid.

"I don't know. What's Olly got to be sorry for?" Alex said, pulling her long blonde hair over one shoulder and twirling it. "I can't believe I'm saying this, but what has he got against Kyle? Does Olly even know him?"

"That's what worries me. I don't know, but something must have happened between them."

I took my phone back, rereading the messages.

R u having a gd time?
U nva told me u knew Kyle.
Ashley, txt me bk!
Dn't listen 2 anything he says.
Ashley!
I'm sorry

What could Kyle possibly say to me that had Olly so worked up? I had never witnessed him so fretful, and it put me on edge. There was no way I was going to be able to sleep now.

"Have you texted him back?" Alex said, lying back in her sleeping bag, and I considered doing the same.

I shook off my arms, tried to relax my shoulders, took a deep breath and laid down, resting my head on my palm on my pillow, with my other holding my phone as I stared at the screen.

"I don't know what to say. Should I?" I whispered as one of the girls turned over, muttering something in her sleep.

"You said he was at a party; maybe he is drunk?"

"No," I hesitantly replied, shaking my head. "No, Olly said he doesn't drink or do parties. He said he was going to Lewis's house. I don't think it was a party." I then panicked, rubbed my hands over my face and cringed. "Oh god, it was a party? Wasn't it?"

"Ashley, stop worrying. I'm sure it's a misunderstanding; get some sleep," she said, closing her eyes.

I moved onto my back, put my phone beside me and pulled my sleeping bag up as far as it went. "Okay, okay, forget about it. Go to sleep, Ashley, go to sleep," I said to myself, closing my eyes tightly, and before I knew it, the taunting thoughts in my mind went blank.

*

"Rise and shine," A deep voice echoed through the tent's thin walls, waking me with a startle.

"Urgh," I grunted, folding my pillow over my head as it pounded. "Who the hell is that?"

"A fucking moran, that's who," Alex mumbled, throwing her pillow to the zipper as it opened. "Get lost, Kyle."

Kyle opened the zip, poked his head in, and woke the others with his rustling and joyful morning mood. "Now, now, Alexandra, it's too early to start name-calling."

I sat up, wiping the sleep from my eyes and stretched out my aching muscles.

"Wow, Ashley, look at the tits on you," he smirked. What the, I thought, then looked down. My eyes widened, and I pulled up my sleeping bag, covering my body. Shit. I had forgotten I went to bed in only my bra and pants.

"Kyle," Emily shouted, looking at me, then at him, then back to me, raising one eyebrow as the others stared. "Ashley, where are your clothes?"

"Oh, erm, I couldn't find them in the dark, so I slept like this," I said, blushing as Kyle kept his eyes peeled on me.

"Why didn't you sleep in your clothes like the rest of us?" Morgan queried, lowering her sleeping bag and showing me her top from the party. Oh god, how am I going to get out of this one?

I glanced at Alex, Morgan, and, regrettably, Kyle, whose smile had altered.

"She fell in the pool," he spoke up, taking their attention.

"You fell in the pool again? How?" Alex asked.

"On the way to the tent, I tripped on a chair and went straight in because, well yeah, I'm a clutz," I explained, unsure why I was lying.

"Is that how you hurt your arms too?" Sammy asked, leaning over and glimpsing at my forearms where a red mark lay on my skin.

With no explanation without adding Kyle to the story, I was short for words and looked suspiciously guilty of hiding something. It was too early for such an interrogation, and my spinning head didn't agree.

Neither did my stomach as my nerves took a hammering; I hadn't been awake fifteen minutes, and I already had to defend him. And with the way he left things, I shouldn't have been so kind to do.

"That was me," Kyle butted in, still looking like a hovering head. A gorgeous one at that.

"What. You hurt Ashley?" Alex scowled through gritted teeth launching towards him, although her sleeping bag restricted her.

"No, Alex. It wasn't like that," he snapped, looking at me.

I watched him observe my arm, then the other, both of which were marked a little. When he grabbed me, it hurt like a Chinese burn, but I didn't expect there to be evidence of it.

"When she fell, I grabbed her arms, but she went in anyway. But thanks for the accusation, Alex. I appreciate it," Kyle sarcastic retorted.

"Argh, I hate that my sister likes you," Alex growled. "What did you want anyway? Why are you even here? Do you have a reason to have woken us up so early?"

Kyle licked his lips and laughed, "Nah, I was bored," He sneered, stood up, and disappeared from the tent.

"Prick," Alex muttered.

"I heard that."

Preparing myself for the grilling I was about to get, I avoided looking at Alex. She may hate Kyle, but I was yet to feel so strongly about him, even if I denied feeling anything for him at all. I didn't want to keep things from her, I never wanted to be that person, but with her doubts about Kyle, it was the only way for me to stay on mutual grounds.

I sighed, laid back and threaded my fingers through my knotted hair. My gaze fell to my arms, and my lungs tightly squeezed as I recalled the moment in my mind. I had never been spoken to in the way Kyle had. It was scary, frightening, and abusive. Yet, simultaneously, how he lifted and scolded me with his fierce eyes was provoking, exciting and dangerous. He ordered me, read me effortlessly and drained the very soul from my body the minute I saw him. I couldn't reject it any longer; even if I wanted to, something about him had me addicted. I craved to run from my life to live a more adventurous, thrilling one like his.

I hated to admit it, but I forgot about everything when I was around him. I forgot about Olly, and I needed to confess my sins. But I needed to know what he seemed to have to tell me first.

*

"Has he texted you since?" Sammy asked as she scrolled through my messages at the kitchen table.

I shook my head, chewing a mouthful of toast and swallowing it with a sip of tea. "I haven't texted him back."

"If you don't want to ask him, there is always someone else you can ask," Emily pointed out, brushing her thick brown hair. I looked into her pretty freckled face and knew she was right. Seeing as he had no respect for me, asking him wouldn't ruin any sort of friendship we had.

"Where is he?" I asked, brushing the crumbs from my face.

"Are you sure you want to go there?" Morgan added as I drummed my fingers on the table.

"What other option do I have?"

"Mum, have you seen Kyle about?" Alex asked her as she unloaded the dishwasher. She tried not to make a noise, kneading her temples between each item.

"No need to shout, sweetheart. My head is rather delicate this morning," she responded.

Alex looked at us and rolled her eyes, and I tried not to laugh. "Good night then?" she asked.

"Yes, great. Did you enjoy yourselves, girls? I'm sorry we weren't around much. Harley tends to host whilst we socialise in the sitting room. I'm afraid I drank way too much wine to recall the evening. I hope you didn't do anything stupid. Your parents won't let you round again if I have some explaining to do."

"Our parents are used to it, Mrs Young," Morgan giggled. "But I won't elaborate on your party antics, especially the singing."

"Oh god, you didn't hear us?" she groaned, sipping some water with paracetamol.

"Hear you? The entire street heard you," Alex snorted, making us all burst into merriment.

"What's so funny?" Harley asked, strolling into the kitchen, also looking worse for wear. I got off lucky; I didn't feel half as bad as expected. Nothing a cup of tea and food managed to fix, but I had consumed just as much chlorine as alcohol.

"Oh, nothing," Alex finished. "Have you seen Kyle?"

"Oh, erm, yeah," she faltered. "He's in my bedroom."

Alex stood up from her chair, and my posture straightened as jealousy suddenly flew through me, and I hated that it did.

"Upstairs? Why is Kyle upstairs? Oh my god, you're sleeping with him!" Alex spat.

"Oh Alex, don't be like that, and no. No, I'm not; he's way too young for me," Harley snarled, slamming her glass down. "You seriously have that boy all wrong, and *me* for that matter."

"You, maybe, but him, no f in way," Alex said, rolling her eyes at me. "Come on, let's go and ask him."

Rising from my chair, I gestured to the others to do the same but then started to think it was a bad idea. Questioning Kyle would be embarrassing. Asking Olly would be the better, less aggressive option.

"Ask him what?" Harley wondered, piling her bowl with crunchy nut cornflakes.

Alex looked back to her sister and scowled, "It's nothing to do with you."

Harley tutted, "Well, just so you know, he isn't in the best mood. You may want to save it for another day if it is going to piss him off."

"We'll take our chances," Alex huffed, dragging me out of the kitchen as the others warily followed.

"Alex, are you sure about this?" I muttered, having seen Kyle angry twice as much as I had planned in one evening; I'd had my quota.

"Kyle," she shouted up the stairs, and no voice returned. "Kyle."

Pushing open Harley's bedroom door, the whiff of liquor, smoke, perfume, and sick caught my nose; I heaved, holding my mouth.

"What do you lot want," Kyle muttered, turning his head in our direction as he lay front down on the bed. His eyes were red, bloodshot and puffy, and he didn't look half as well put together as he did at first light.

"Jeez, look at the state of you. It's a bit early to be stoned, isn't it?" Alex jibed, and I recoiled. I loved how Alex was upfront, but sometimes I wished she would have assessed the situation before opening her mouth.

He sat up straight up, the vein in his clenched jaw jumped out, and his nose flared, "Give it a rest, Alex. You have no idea what you're talking about," he scorned. "Back the fuck off with your opinions." He rose, pushed past us all and went down the stairs.

Alex looked at me, shrugging her shoulders, "What the hell was that about?"

I bit the inside of my mouth and twiddled with my hair, "I think Kyle has been crying."

"I thought that too," Morgan added, and Emily nodded in agreement.

Alex disagreed, "Kyle isn't like that. He hasn't got an emotional bone in his rock-hard body."

My foot tapped on the ground, and I turned to the door. "Where are you going?" Alex asked.

I turned and puffed out my chest, "I'm sorry, I know you don't like him, but I need to know if he's okay."

"What? No, you don't."

"Yes, Alex, I do."

I strolled down the stairs and through the house, observing every empty chair before entering the garden.

"What have you said to her?" I overheard. "I told you to be her friend, and that's it," A voice muffled through gritted teeth; it sounded familiar.

"Don't flatter yourself." I listened as I stood still, unsure if I planned to continue. "I don't waste my time talking about the likes of you." The response spat, and that voice I knew, the hostility I heard a few minutes ago. It was the voice I was looking for.

I hesitated, scared to walk around the corner.

"I never wanted to be part of this, and I can't believe I let you drag me into it. You should have told Ashley the first day you met her."

The mention of my name pulled my interest. My bare feet continued to pad across the grass, and cigarette smoke overwhelmed my nostrils. "Olly," I gasped. "Kyle," I huffed. "What is going on? Tell me what?"

My eyes darted back and forth between them. Kyle swallowed hard, throwing his half-smoked cigarette on the floor, and Olly rubbed the nape of his neck, unable to look me in the face.

"Olly?" I muttered, furrowing my brow. "What are you doing here?"

"Tell her, now is a better time than any," Kyle snapped as Olly stood mute, turning his cap round and then back again.

"Ashley," Olly paused, gesturing towards me. "I need to tell you something I should have mentioned a long time ago, but with everything you have been through and how much I love you, I didn't know how to say it."

"Love her," Kyle snickered. "You don't love her."

"Like you care about her, Lewis told me how you spoke to her. I should have never considered you could ever be nice," Olly growled.

"Don't push me, Olly; you know how it will end," Kyle muttered, clenching his fists and stepping towards him.

Fear hit me. I didn't want them to fight. I was clueless and in the unknown, and as I stepped forward, placing myself between them, stuck defending them both as my back was to Olly, and my hand pushed on Kyle's puffed-out chest.

"Kyle, I don't know what's going on, but back off." His heartbeat was rapid beneath my shaking hand, and his stare burned me, melting me to the ground.

Kyle's hand moved to my arms, covering the proof of his temper, gripping them firmly. I heard Olly sigh, and his hand pulled my shoulder, driving me back. Kyle's grip didn't falter, only the disgust in his eyes as he scolded Olly with displeasure. He leaned toward me, and my stomach flipped. The scent of hot tar and orange pinged my nose as he closed in on me, and my cheeks flushed. I tried to hide every effect he had on me in front of Olly, although I knew it was a losing battle.

"Olly is leaving. He's going to break your heart," he whispered, and I said nothing as I raised my hands to his and gripped them tightly, and he let go.

Turning to Olly, I noticed the grief in his glossy brown stare, "Is it true? Are you leaving?" I asked.

Olly stepped closer, leaning his forehead on mine, threading his fingers through my hair, and cupping the back of my head. "I wanted to tell you."

My head tilted, resting on his forearm. "Tell me then." I waited.

"I'm going to college, not sixth form. My parents moved here because it's closer, but I'm only here for the summer."

I stepped back, pushing him away from me as he ripped my heart from my aching chest. I looked at Kyle, slumped in a chair, watching as if this was a comedy show. The pleasure in his expression angered me.

"You knew, and you didn't tell me?" I snapped, pointing towards them both. "I asked you, and I asked you."

"Ashley, what's going on?" Alex said as she and the girls appeared in my eye line.

"You have lied to me all this time. Acted as if you cared about me. Like you loved me. When you were leaving anyway. How could you not tell me you were never here for the long run and let me fall for everything you said like some fool," I yelled, shaking my hands wildly.

"Ash."

"No, Olly. This must be a joke; it's a joke, right?" I laughed in disbelief. "I gave myself to you. I know you. There is no evil bone in your body to make you do something like this."

"Oh god, you didn't," Kyle cringed, flaring his nostrils. "That was a big mistake. But hats off to you, Oliver."

My body tightened, my emotions were intense, I was confused, so puzzled, and I couldn't breathe. I couldn't feel my body, not the ache in my chest or the anger bubbling through me.

"Ashley, are you okay? You need to calm down," Kyle said as he stood up, reaching out to me.

I retreated, pushing him hard in his chest and his eyes filled with sorrow. "You! I barely know you. How on earth do you know all this before I do," I quizzed, trying to compose myself, breathing slowly.

"He's my cousin," they said simultaneously, both with regret and loathing.

"Cousin?" I retorted. "So you're in on this too? Trying to woo me with your ridiculous charisma, so I would forget about him, is that it?"

"Of course that's what I have been doing," Kyle shouted, shocking me. My eyes widened, and my senses began to return. It all became more apparent as I figured it out. I knew there had to be a fucked-up reason why Kyle tried to gain my attention, and I couldn't believe I had fallen for it. I was angry. Angry with myself. Infuriated. I had never felt my blood boil so hot beneath my skin. I wanted to shout at them both, but more so myself.

"I can't believe this; you have made out you were better than him all this time. Well, this tells me you are exactly the same."

Kyle grabbed the camping chair beside him and launched it across the garden, morphing back into the foul-mooded, dangerous bad boy I kept meeting.

"No, I'm nothing like him," he growled. "I know you say you don't know me, but you do, and I know you. I've known you since we were little. I've seen you cry and crumble at school. I've watched you hate yourself and fall for those stupid popular girl's lifestyles and the boys, and then he showed up, and I knew he would have the same effect."

Kyle moved towards Olly, and Olly moved back a little, holding his arms firmly in front of himself. "Yes, I've been trying to get your attention, but only because."

"Kyle, don't," Olly cut in, glaring at me, tugging on the nape of his neck.

"Because your perfect boyfriend asked me too," Kyle finished. He watched a tear roll down the curve in my pinked cheek and barged past Olly, forcefully knocking his shoulder as he stormed off.

"Ashley," Olly tried.

I looked at him and said, "I trusted you." I cried and left the garden.

I was no longer angry or heartbroken. I wasn't sad, and I wasn't surprised either.

I didn't know what I was.

CHAPTER TWENTY-NINE

"Olly has called around again; he's upset," Mum said. "Do you want to tell me what happened?"

I turned on my bed to face her, hugging my pillow tightly as a tear slid over my nose. My words choked my throat, "Upset? He has no reason to be upset. He is a liar, and I never want to see him again."

"Now, Ashley, that's a bit extreme. Whatever it is, I'm sure you can work it out."

"No, there is no point," I mumbled, squeezing harder as my stomach panged.

I hadn't eaten since breakfast and barely ate at the party; marshmallows and jello shots weren't exactly substantial, and it was way past lunchtime. I had left Alex's house in a hurry and said nothing to Mum on the way home. Olly went, Kyle disappeared, and the girls had no idea what to say.

I didn't want to see or talk to either of them, and I wished I could get both of them out of my head.

"You should talk to him," Mum continued, shuffling everything into a neater pile on my desk.

"No, I shouldn't."

"Olly won't be around for long, and I doubt you will want to say goodbye on these terms."

I sat up, narrowed my eyes and held the black cased pillow on my lap, "What?"

Mum straightened her posture and placed my Avril CD on the top of the pile. She swallowed hard and blinked rapidly.

"Holy shit, you knew, didn't you?" I stood, throwing my pillow aside. "Why didn't you tell me?"

"Now, Ashley, let me explain."

"No, there is nothing to explain. You knew all along, and you let me fall for him knowing he was fucking leaving."

"Watch your language, young lady," Mum threatened, pointing her finger at me. "I was only protecting you."

"Protecting me from what, heartbreak? You didn't do a very good job," I shouted. "No wonder you have been so forgiving lately. I knew something wasn't right. You knew this was coming. You knew Olly would break my heart, and guess what, you have to."

"Ashley, calm down."

"Get out. Get out of my room," I shrieked, stamping my foot and thumping the air beside me.

Mum didn't move; I'd shaken her to the core. Usually, I would have felt guilty for such an episode, but I didn't in the slightest. I'd had my limits pushed, and something was different. Like a switch had clicked, and I didn't care anymore. If no one cared about me and could lie so easily, even if it was to protect me or not, I no longer had time for them. I just never expected to be adding Mum to the list.

"Ashley, we need to talk about this. You acting like this isn't like you."

I flared my nostrils and ground my back teeth. "If you won't get out, then I will." I grabbed my phone and stormed out past her.

"Ashley," she yelled, but the front door slamming masked it.

I didn't look back or glance at Olly's house. I speedily walked down the street with no destination in mind. Anywhere else but there.

*

Walking around blockbuster, I'd exhausted every shelf. It was empty for a Sunday; the town was usually heaving all weekend.

I trailed my finger along the boxes, Get Over It, Save the last dance, Mean Girls, and A Cinderella story, all of which I had watched.

"There isn't a lot out, is there?" a girl's voice said, and I turned towards her.

"Mila," I smiled, hugging her.

"Hey stranger, how are you? Where have you been? I've texted you over the summer, but you never replied."

I wished I didn't have to lie about ignoring her messages; I'd not been too busy to see her; I'd chosen to spend my time tonging Olly instead, which now, I wished I hadn't got too caught up in.

"Sorry I never texted you back; I've let the summer get away with me."

Mila passed me a DVD case, "I understand. I wouldn't want to leave my boyfriend either if he looked like Olly," she laughed. "Have you seen this one?"

I glanced at the DVD case in my hand, Bend it Like Beckham, and it took me right back to Olly, quenching my stomach. "No, and I would rather not," I tutted, putting it back on the shelf.

"Are you okay?"

I pulled my hair over my shoulder, playing with a chunky highlight and looked away, "I don't want to talk about it."

"Okay, then don't. Let's get a drink and sit at the park if you're not doing anything. Might make you feel better?"

I beamed. "Yeah, okay, cool."

We left blockbuster and headed a few shops down to Woolworths. I bought a Dr Pepper and pick-a-mix. We then went to the nearest park just outside the high street. It was empty, sunny with a breeze, and the silence was bliss.

We lay in the long grass beside the swings and discussed our summers. Mila told me where her new denim jacket was from, and she asked about my new clothes and Alex's party.

After all this time, I didn't know why I was worried about everyone's opinions. Alex and the girls, Harley, Mila, and even Olly and Kyle, had accepted me for who I was. I had hidden behind a shadow for no reason to please a few popular girls. And if they didn't like me for who I was, screw them; the days of trying to be somebody else were long gone. No popularity or social status was worth being as miserable as I were. For once in my life, my friends or appearance weren't the problem; it was boys.

Handsome, sporty, tattooed, lying boys.

Infatuated with one and deeply intrigued by the other was one thing. But from the same family, sharing the same blood was another.

Cousins, I couldn't believe it!

The sun on my skin eased me so much that my eyes drifted. A late, eventful night was not my usual weekend antics and too much to hack for the regular early bird like me.

A sound pricked my ears, and I jolted with a start, flicking my eyes towards the roadside.

"What is it?" Mila muttered, sitting up.

I listened to the wheels turning and the bearings rattling; it was therapeutic but also had my tiny hairs standing. My gaze moved to his baggy clothes and tanned, toned arms, then to his face hidden under his cap. Headphones in, headbanging in a world of his own. Precisely who I didn't want to see. Kyle.

He pushed his foot off the ground, gaining speed and leaned his body forward, perfectly balanced. He dodged pedestrians, using the path as his playground, ignoring the disgust on their faces. He sneered back at the tuts he gained with his zerofucks-given attitude and carried on.

The force on his next glide was more powerful; he moved faster, standing straight as he approached a bench. The next minute he was bending, defying gravity as he jumped in the air with the board firmly hooked to his feet as he ground along a bench. The loud bang rang in my ears as he landed. He skidded to a halt, and my heart throbbed at the slight raise of his head.

I watched intently, unable to move my gaze as he placed his feet in a more specific position on the board. He bent his legs and then pushed the back of the board down with his foot before jumping in the air using his front foot first. His front foot caressed the board, and his knees raised to his chest, levelling it before landing. For a moment, he had me captivated. I didn't think about what he and Olly had done to me. I didn't see him as the rebel who destroyed public property like every other bitter person.

He was glorious, talented, and committed.

"Wow," I let out.

"Kyle is a great skater, probably the best around here. The Ollie is hard, but he does it effortlessly," Mila said, and I glanced at her.

"Do you know him?"

She shook her head, "Yeah. No. Well, I know *of* him. I live next to the skate park; he's always there, many of them are. I could sit there all day and watch them; I bet he's going there now."

"He's dedicated, I give you that," I paused. "If only he were more compassionate about everything else."

"Too right, he's a brute, but his devotion to that board is, I dunno."

"Enchanting," I cut in, and she agreed.

"Do you fancy going to the skateboard park? I like watching the rollerbladers too." Mila stood, brushed the grass from her denim skirt and straightened out her pigtails.

I fiddled with my fingers and sighed. "I don't think that's the best idea. I should go home. I ran out on my mum after an argument; I have…" I peered at my phone and read the notifications. "A lot of missed calls and texts from her, my dad and Olly."

My eyes rolled back towards the path, and the way Kyle was no longer there, marking it with his incredible ability, made me nauseous. I wanted to follow him and see more, yet I knew I shouldn't. I should be talking to Olly, making everything okay; that's what I wanted, even if I was angry at him.

"Come on, text your mum back and tell her you're with me."

I looked up at her, nodded and stood up. She linked her arm through mine and grinned, "You can tell me what happened on the way and how you know Kyle."

*

Sweat dripped down my back as we approached the large, dark blue gates at the top of the steep hill, past the school, on the town's highest point. You could see acres of land, housing estates and the high beam of the church. Seeing it reminded me of how big the town was. Despite constantly feeling small, there was more to it than I realised. Its natural beauty made it look like a middle-class fairy tale.

I didn't appreciate it enough.

I had lived there all my life and had never set foot in the skateboard park.

Crossing the gate was as if I had stepped out of bounds. The territory was not for me, and the hordes of crowds on wheels were proof of that. Music blared through several boom boxes, and a mixture of painful groans and excited cheers caught my ears.

Mila grabbed my hand and took me towards the large concrete bowl benches.

"This is crazy; it's so busy," I said as I sat beside her.

"I know, it's always like this. It's like a community of all ages, children, youths and adults. You see over there," she pointed, and I followed her fingers. "That's where the pros are; notice the sunken floor, quarter pipe, grind rails and two tall, gloomy black slopes facing each other. That's bank to bank. It's dangerous but thrilling to watch."

"Check you with all your skating lingo," I laughed.

Mila grinned, "I've picked it up by watching, that's all."

"It's weird. I often see skateboarders and how they glide around town but forget about the danger and the tricks."

"I know, it's very underrated. You forget the talent with the reputation of being rebels and vandals they gain."

"What's that bit over there?" I pointed.

"That's more for the newbies, can't you tell? They're all dressed similarly, with their loose fitted jeans, brand new boards and sparkling white vans."

"Ouch," I cringed, watching a boy fall off his board trying to jump over the iron rails. He stood, rubbed the blood pouring from his arm and laughed, trotting back off to claim his wheels.

I smiled, almost glowing at the contentment around me. The atmosphere was calming and happy. Like caged animals, this place stood behind tall gates and kept the nuisance from the streets, yet it was the opposite. These skaters were persistent and brave, taking the leap of faith and living in a place full of dreams. They were safe and secure. I was inspired by how they practised, as if it were all that mattered. As if there would be no tomorrow.

They never gave up on their skateboards, and they trusted them.

"Come on," A guy shouted to the crowd of lads on BMXs beside us.

"What's going on?" Another called, taking his feet to his pedals before riding down the bowl towards the crowd forming.

"It's Kyle. He's on the halfpipe."

Kyle. I began to sweat, rubbing my palms on my knees.

"Come on, let's go watch," Mila pulled at me. "I told you he would be here. I bet he's been warming up all day."

"Huh? Warming up?"

"Jeez, don't you know anything? Do you not follow Tony Hawk?" I shook my head. "This park is like a playground. The skaters warm up here, all day long, then hit the streets; that's where they perform properly."

"And you know this by watching them?" I walked with her squeezing through the crowd, finding a spot with a perfect view down the halfpipe.

"I live right there," Mila said, pointing to the house on the corner with front-row seats to the park. "I can't miss much."

I gazed across to the top of the halfpipe, where Kyle stood. He looked enticing in his skater oversize shorts and quicksilver t-shirt. His vans weren't as white as everyone else's, used, worn, loved, and the billabong cap he wore sat backwards, framing his handsome face and dark eyes.

He couldn't see me, and I was glad he didn't know I was there. There was no way he would. The skate park was not my scene. I didn't fit in; it was the last place he would find me. Kyle and I had nothing in common, and I knew I was better off sticking to the swings and ignoring the gravity pulling me towards him. It was safer for me to bury those unwanted feelings and back away, but five minutes more wouldn't hurt.

My eyes stayed on him as he stood on the edge, preparing himself for a drop I wouldn't dare try. He picked up the dog tags around his neck and placed them between his teeth. As his front foot pushed down, and he dropped, gaining speed, riding up the opposite pipe, my lungs tightened, and I wanted to look away, but I couldn't. He went back and forth, faster and higher. My heart filled my mouth as he spun in the air, taking the skateboard from one foot to the other. He was happy, flawless, and perfect, whereas I was uncomfortable and unable to cheer like the others.

Fear coursed through my body. My anxiety made my heart race, my legs tingle, and my gaze wouldn't move. The idea of Kyle falling was threatening and nauseating. It was hypnotising and safe on the floor; now, it was scary. I was unsure if it was the skateboarding or the emotions rising whilst watching my boyfriend's cousin, which was all the more terrifying.

"Kyle, Kyle, Kyle," the crowd chanted.

His sweat-covered skin glistened in the sun as he flipped, performing one-handed handstands and spins, keeping everyone hooked. He was in deep concentration as if it was just him, the halfpipe and his white graffitied board.

I wanted to be him, focused, ambitious, and living in a wonderland.

The board slowed, the crowd quietened, and the tick-tack, tick-tack, tick-tack of his skateboard trucks hitting the floor spread through the park. His vans pressed tightly against the board, gliding up the half-pipe one last time before he pushed his front foot down on the edge, coming to a halt. He stepped off and turned to his crowd. He smiled, not the tiny sarcastic smile I had seen, but a beaming wide, glossy-eyed smile.

It was magnificent, and the applauding of everyone told me he was a god to them, an icon. I didn't look at him and see a defiant punk. Instead, I knew he would go far, and nothing would stop him, not if he had anything to say about it.

CHAPTER THIRTY

My phone buzzed in my back pocket, dragging me back to the reality of my problems which I had ignored all day.

Leaning over to Mila, chatting to some tall, older, tattooed guy, I warily smiled at him and then at her and said, "I need to head off. I need to talk to Olly; I'll see you soon."

"Don't be a stranger; you know where I am," she said, waving me off with a nod.

I scanned the crowd, enjoying the black, white, and red patchwork of people that made it feel like a safe place. I knew no one and was illiterate about skating and what came with it, yet it felt like a haven. I could see why Kyle went there; it was a place full of hope and no judgment, making it more difficult to leave as I stepped back into the street.

I strolled down the hill, eyes fixated on the scenery in the distance, releasing the air from my lungs as I took a deep breath. A smile sketched my face, feeling free and invigorated, but I didn't know why; the minute I got home, I would return to hating life again.

Mum would ground me forever after my outburst, and now I had Olly to deal with. What was I supposed to say to him? I didn't have a clue. He was leaving me, and he had been all along. His secrets made me angry, downright furious, yet I missed him already. I loved him and hated him at the same time.

And what about Kyle? I had ignored Olly all day and instead spent the afternoon watching him. He deserved no friendship from me, yet I had butterflies swirling in my stomach the minute I set eyes on him.

Like two best friends, they had lied to me and treated me like some child who couldn't hack the truth, which evidently, I couldn't. But what bothered me most was why they hated each other. What was all that about? What had happened between them, and why did Olly get him involved?

Boys were so complicated, unlike girls and the more involved I got with one, the more I started to question why I ever wanted a boyfriend in the first place.

"Ashley," I heard panting over my shoulder.

I turned and stumbled, tripping on an out-of-place slab in the pavement. My hand reached out, grabbing onto his forearm, securing my balance as he gripped me. I blushed, and he grinned, mocking me with his shimmering grey stare.

"Do I always have this effect on you, or are you really the clutz you seem to be?"

I let go of him, brushed my hair from my face and tucked it behind my ears. "Don't flatter yourself, Kyle," I said. "I tripped. I still would have if you weren't here."

"So, you're a clutz. That's all you needed to say."

"Why are you such a dick?" I paused. "You could have asked if I was okay instead of insulting me."

Kyle took his cap off, ran his fingers through his messy brown hair and looked away as he balanced on his board, slowly moving beside me. If I didn't know better, I'd put him on the spot, and he didn't like it.

"I can't help it. It's who I am," Kyle muttered, stepping to the ground, claiming his board as he tightly clutched it in his hand.

"Well, perhaps if you treated people as delicately as you do that board," I gestured towards his wheels and watched his grip tighten. "Then perhaps people would think there is more to you than just talent."

"Ahh, so you think I'm talented," He sneered, glancing at me. "Did you enjoy what you saw?"

I looked to the floor and pulled my bottom lip between my teeth. "I did. What you do is terrifying and reckless, but I guess you're quite good at it."

"Quite good? Everyone would disagree with that statement."

"Fine, it was incredible. Is that what you wanted to hear?" I said, and he smiled.

"I knew it."

"Knew what?"

"I saw the look in your eyes and the fear; you were in awe, mesmerised, but also scared."

"I wasn't scared for you; why would I be?" I faltered; he had caught me red-handed. "Hang on, you saw me?"

"Of course I saw you. Who wouldn't."

I looked at him and stopped walking, crossing my arms across my body. "What is that supposed to mean?"

Kyle stepped forward, closing in on me. I stepped back, and the rough bricks of the wall behind me grazed my skin. I gasped and gulped simultaneously.

He placed his free hand on the bricks beside my head as I watched his chest tuck in and puff out. He glanced to the right, left, and back to me, "Stop assuming I'm insulting you all the time. I'm not," his hoarse voice muttered, and he stepped nearer.

His breath was warm on my skin, and his aroma sent me into a tizzy. My body trembled as I denied my knees from buckling beneath me, "You are beautiful. That's why I notice you, and that's all there is to it."

I chewed the inner of my mouth, staring at the scars on his cheek, fighting the urge to stroke the small white lines. I looked away and muttered, "You are more of a liar than I thought."

Kyle moved his hand and retreated, narrowing his eyes. He looked slightly hurt, "Think what you like,

Ashley Prince. I never wanted to lie to you; that was your boyfriend's doing. If anything, I was protecting you. Blame him, not me. I only did what I had to because he practically begged me."

I wanted to say something, words, to argue, ask questions, anything would have done, but words failed me.

Protect me? If Kyle was protecting me, he had a funny way of showing it. He was nothing but mean, insulting and aggressive, and his temper was disturbing.

Olly was soft, gentle and kind. From the minute we met, he treated me like a princess and saw me for who I was. He loved me and made my heart dance, and I knew everything would be okay when I was with him. But that was before. Now I questioned who he was and what his plan was all along.

Olly was supposed to be the one protecting me. But instead, he was looking out for himself and somehow dragging Kyle down with him. And despite Kyle's brute attitude, he *was* the innocent one. If anything, I needed to protect myself from him, maybe them both.

Kyle sighed at my silence as I did nothing but stare at him. I could sense he wanted to argue, but it only built the unspoken, growing tension between us. It added fuel to the fire burning within me, but as long as Olly was around and I saw sense, I needed to dig deep down and find every reason to stay away from him and put out the flames. But then again, was that Olly's plan all along? I don't know, the situation was too unclear, and I needed answers from no one other than Olly. He would tell me the truth.

I shook aside the notion and swallowed hard.

"What is it, Ashley?" Kyle muttered as he put his skateboard down beneath his foot. "Tell me, what's bothering you?"

I moved away from the wall and started walking, "Nothing, I'm going home."

He slowly skated beside me and said, "Let me walk you."

I let out a small laugh and furrowed my brows, "No, that is something Olly should be doing, not you. Besides, I don't want you to."

Kyle was near sulking, "Suit yourself," he said. "I'm sorry I never told you about Olly. Whether you believe me or not, I mean it." And before I could reply, he stopped his board, turned on it and went in the other direction. I didn't look back at him. I hoped he didn't look back at me.

*

I knocked twice, hesitated, and then knocked again. My foot scraped the floor as I waited, picking at my fingernails before hooking my thumbs in my flared jeans pockets.

The door opened, and the look Olly gave crushed every part of me. His eyes were red, and he was undeniably upset. "I'm sorry," he mumbled, gently taking hold of my arms and stepping out. "I'm so so sorry; this wasn't supposed to happen. I never meant to hurt you."

He cupped my face as I stood still, seeing his lip quiver and his eyes tighten, "I never expected to fall for you, I would have stopped it if I could, but my feelings for you took me by surprise. Please believe me when I say I love you. I want to change my plans and go to sixth form with you, but I can't, not unless I give up on my future. I wish I had the guts to tell you from the beginning; I really do. I'm sorry. Please forgive me."

I gulped, raising my hands to his forearms. His big brown doe stare locked onto mine, and I fell into it, banishing the anger I wanted to feel. I was naïve, but I could tell he never intended to hurt or desert me by how he looked so regretfully at me. I believed him, and when I was with him, I had no chance of hating him; it wasn't in me; he effortlessly and foolishly made me weak.

Thinking about the time we had spent together, he had managed to make every minute beautiful. He was the only one I could imagine doing such a thing. I knew all I could do was cherish the time we had left.

I moved towards him and cuddled him tight, and he wrapped his arms around me, playing with my hair as it fell long down my back. The scent of suncream pinched my nose, reminding me of the sea and sand, imagining him on the waves. Free and untroubled.

I was going to miss how he made me feel so secure, and I didn't want to imagine my life without him. I was lost, not knowing what path he was on; I just knew that I didn't want it to be different from mine.

CHAPTER THIRTY-ONE

"So, it's a sports college?" I asked, reading the college prospectus in my hand, leaning on Olly's chest as we lay on his bed.

"Yeah, a sports academy."

"So what will you be studying, football?" I questioned.

"I'll do BTEC sports-related qualifications, then possibly a higher national diploma. I will study for fourteen hours each week and train with elite and ex-professional football coaches for fifteen hours. There are weekly matches in a competitive league."

"Wow, that's good."

"Yeah, it is. It's what I want to do; if I'm lucky, I might get a scholarship or something. My dad reckons this route is more suitable and that A-levels would be a waste of time."

I turned my head and glanced at him, feeling my throat clench, "It's exciting. I'll miss you, though."

"I'll miss you too," he replied, toying with my hair.

"I wish I knew what I was doing with my life like you do. Two more years of school is my worst nightmare."

His hand stroked my forehead and then kneaded my temples, "At least you have transferred now; no more, Bailey."

I nodded and turned on my front, slightly digging my chin into his chest. "You're right. It will be better with Alex and the other girls. But English, Business and Media Studies, that's crap compared to what you're doing."

"It's not. You could do loads with that," Olly tried. "Why didn't you pick P.E like you did for GCSE?"

I shrugged my shoulders. "I don't know. Mum swayed me with her opinions, she never did A-Levels, but it made sense to do qualifications I'll use. What would I use P.E for? I only took it in GCSE for exercise. Before that, I was always forging notes and skipping it." Sitting up, I placed the booklet down, crossed my legs and faced him. "Can we talk about you and Kyle?" I needed answers and closure before he left.

Olly straightened his posture and took his cap off, "I'd rather not," he said, rolling his eyes. He caught my body stiffening, watched me frown, and exhaled. "Fine, what do you want to know?"

I thought about everything I wanted to know, from their hostility to their secrets, "Why do you hate each other?" I asked first.

"Because he's obnoxious and full of himself, haven't you noticed?" He put it bluntly.

"I think there is more to it; I can tell."

"Sometimes, I wish you weren't so observant."

I smiled, cleared my throat and twisted my earrings, waiting.

"We used to be close. We spent every school holiday together, and we were inseparable. Every half term and summer, his family would stay with us, he made friends with mine, and we both learnt to surf."

I rested an elbow on my knee and leaned my chin on my palm, "So, what happened?"

"I don't know. Something happened between my auntie and Mum, and they stopped coming down. Kyle changed overnight. He stopped talking to me, switched his surfboard for a skateboard and the only time he was in the water was when he came to compete against me. His sports clothes became black ones, and his tattoos and piercings appeared. He became aggressive, started smoking and drinking, and didn't care anymore. His family and mine only started talking again last year. Kyle and I will never be the same."

"Didn't you ask what happened?"

Olly stood from the bed and sat on his desk chair, swivelling it to face me, "I wanted to. I tried to ask my mum, but she brushed it off every time. I asked Kyle once, but he got angry and defensive and started fights with me for no reason." He sighed.

"If you hate each other so much, how did the secret between you come about?" I said curiously, and Olly strained a little.

"I said I was sorry about that."

"I know. But you never told me."

He picked up the photo frame casing our prom photo and slid his finger up and down the glass. "Before we moved here, my dad got our families together to sort out our differences and make peace. Kyle was, as he always is, untrusting and rude. He told me to stay away from him at Bailey, so I did," he paused. "Until I met you."

I looked at my hands and stroked my clammy palms up and down my trouser leg.

"Ashley, I don't regret meeting you, so don't think it for a second," he muttered, sounding threatened by my thoughts.

I shook my head. "I never thought that. But I feel like an inconvenience. I made things hard for you."

Olly moved off his chair and towards me. He bent down and rested on his knees as I looked into his glossy chocolate eyes. His shimmering red lips took between his teeth, and he expanded his chest, "You are not and never will be an inconvenience to me. I know we're only sixteen, perhaps young and foolish, but I know how I feel; this is real. I love you, and I would never change meeting you."

"So why bring Kyle into it?" my voice quivered, denying the tears pinching the back of my eyes.

"I got scared. I didn't want to hurt you after what you have been through this summer. I thought telling Kyle, asking him to make friends with you, may have had an effect, that may be, in a way, it would be easier if you had someone else to hang out with when I left." He rubbed the back of his neck, squeezed it slightly, and then put his cap back on backwards. "I didn't think he would be mean. I'm sorry; I should have thought better. Kyle is a prick, and I'm glad you don't have to see him again."

"Yeah, me too," I warily agreed, thinking about the idea of never seeing him again. Was that what I wanted? Yes, it was. It was for mine and Olly's sake.

"Is there anything else?" Olly asked, stroking my knees, and I shook my head.

He raised towards me, planting his lips hard onto mine. He tasted glorious, and I couldn't believe I thought Kyle kissed me better. It was only a kiss, and I wished I could tell Olly about it, but I couldn't, not after he'd opened up like that. He was right; I didn't have to see Kyle again, so I needed to stop thinking about him, even if he may have had more effect on me than Olly had planned. I'm sure many girls have experienced the same with a boy like Kyle, regretting it too.

Olly kissed me again, placing himself between my legs and pushing me back on the bed. My hands moved up his body. He took his cap from his head and put it on mine. I grinned, biting my bottom lip and then his. He pecked my neck, nibbled my ear lobe, and I took his shirt off. He took me as I was, and I took him as he was, more naked and emotionally vulnerable than ever before.

CHAPTER THIRTY-TWO

I smoothed out my dress, looking at my reflection. A dress. I couldn't believe I was wearing a dress. Besides my prom dress, I had worn nothing other than capri pants, baggy shorts, vest tops, and flares all summer. I'd entirely ditched any feminine style.

Lauren and Sophie wouldn't know what hit them if they saw my dark wardrobe. They would be beside themselves.

Running my hands through my long, curled hair, I picked out the chunky highlights and laid them on top. Adjusting my diamanté choker wrapped around my neck, I gulped, setting my bottom lip between my teeth as I grinned. I looked pretty. My mirror and I were finally friends.

It liked me.

I liked myself.

My strapless dress hugged my chest and gave me a waistline. The top half was black and laced with a corset style running down the front. The bottom was black and white striped and flared out. It matched my new platform boots, adding to my never-ending collection.

Switching off my Avril CD on the way to my bedroom window, I glanced into Olly's garden. His parents were throwing him a leaving party, music was blaring, and people were beginning to crowd. With his college allowing residential pupils, he would only be back on weekends; he promised he would be.

We had a few more weeks until summer ended, and I planned to spend every minute with Olly. He had other plans and was leaving early for a summer football camp he had signed up for. We only had two days left together. And instead of spending every minute alone with him, I had to endure a party surrounded by people I had never met.

"Ashley, come on," Zoe squealed, barging into my room before coming to a stop, "Wow, you look pretty."

I turned towards her, and my cheeks pinked a little, "Thanks, squidge. So do you."

Zoe wore her first pair of small chunky heeled sandals and a flowery dark blue summer dress; it highlighted her red hair, which I curled earlier. She looked older, more mature. I couldn't believe she was nearly ten.

"Come here," I said, opening my desk drawer, where I had shoved every glittery hair accessory I owned and was yet to get rid of. I pointed and said, "Pick a colour." Zoe beamed, eagerly grabbing the drawer and tipping it out on the bed.

Rummaging through the pile, she went for the big pink glittery butterfly clip she had always had her eye on. She clenched her jaw, waiting for me to say no like I usually would.

"You can have them," I said, picking them up and placing them into a pink playboy makeup bag.

"Really?" she squeaked, and I nodded.

"Here," I insisted, taking the clip into my hand. I stroked the wings and watched them bounce, reminiscing the time I bought it with Lauren, a time that didn't feel real anymore. I placed it into her hair, "It suits you better."

"Thank you, Ashley," Zoe said, squeezing me tightly, and I hugged her back.

"Come on, let's go. Mum and Dad are waiting."

"Gosh, where did my sweet sixteen-year-old go?" Dad said as we walked down the stairs hand in hand, "And look at you, princess."

"Thanks, Daddy," Zoe said before dancing around the hallway.

"Dad," I blushed. "Are you sure it's not too much?"

"No, sweetheart, you look beautiful," Mum added, squeezing my hand as I reached her, giving her a tentative smile.

We had barely spoken since finding out about Olly, and her keeping secrets from me and apologising made it no better. She had lied to me, knowing it would hurt me. Sure it seemed the kindest way to keep me from heartbreak, and I probably would have done the same, but if I had known the truth from the beginning, perhaps I wouldn't have let myself get so close to Olly. My heart wouldn't be facing heartbreak that way. Instead, it was twice over, once by Olly and then mum. I trusted her. I trusted them both.

It was easier to forgive Olly when he stood before me, grovelling and compelling me with his handsome face and charming ways. But mum had to work a little harder. Since knowing how she was in the wrong, she had let me do whatever I wanted and go wherever I wanted with no argument. That advantage I would hold onto for a little longer.

"Finally, where have you been?" I heard Olly say as Mum, Dad, Zoe and I walked through the door in a huddle.

"Olly, you should see Ashley," Zoe squealed, pulling on his arm as I entered behind her.

Olly looked at her, then spotted me, and his jaw dropped. I smiled, looking at my feet and pulling on the hem of my dress. He walked straight up to me, took his arms around my waist and kissed my cheek, whispering in my ear, "You look gorgeous."

"Thank you," I said, linking my fingers around the back of his neck, toying with his hair.

"Come on, love birds, outside," Calvin said, and I pouted, wishing no one else was there. I didn't like sharing Olly with anybody.

Interlacing my fingers with his, I followed his lead and made my way through the unfamiliar faces. "You have a big family," I muttered as my grip tightened, smiling at the men and women enjoying cans of beer and glasses of Pimms.

"A lot of aunties, uncles and cousins. My five aunties have eighteen children between them. You see." Olly pointed to the bouncy castle full of children.

"Zoe fits right in, obviously," I smirked, rolling my eyes, and he laughed.

"Mum, Ashley is here. Can she have a drink?" Olly said as we approached the refreshments. The BBQ smoke made me cough slightly, and my eyes watered as I wafted it away.

"Why, Ashley, don't you look lovely," she said, kissing my cheek. Olly will miss you; you shouldn't make it so hard for him by looking like that." My cheeks burned, and a metallic taste reached my tastebuds as I chewed the inside of my mouth too hard, not knowing what to say.

"Jeez, Mum, thanks for that. You are so embarrassing," Olly muttered, straightening the collar on his Lacoste polo before putting his hands in his beige shorts pockets.

"It's fine, Olly. Don't worry, Marie," I laughed.

"Mum... drink, please," Olly repeated.

"What would you like, Ashley?" she asked. I eyed up the Pimms jug and stroked my finger along the rim of one of the glasses beside it. I had never tried it before. The fruit swimming in it made it look delicious and tempting. I shouldn't, but I wanted to.

"I'm sure your mum won't mind, would she?" Marie added. She could have tried and stopped me, but she wouldn't have gotten very far.

"No, she wouldn't," I agreed, and she poured me a glass.

"Ashley," Olly warily muttered.

"It's fine, don't worry about it." I raised the glass straight to my lips and took a sip, holding it in my mouth for a moment, then let it slide down my throat. It was fruity yet mildly spiced and tasted like a hybrid of iced tea, apple juice and something else.

"What do you think?" Marie asked.

"It's nice. It's more bitter than I imagined," I said, taking another large gulp. "Thank you."

*

We sat on the bench the furthest away from the adults all afternoon. The sun was low, hot and blinding. "Are my shoulders red?" I asked Olly, sitting opposite me with his legs wrapping mine under the table. He leaned over, brushing his soft fingers along my collarbone and shoulder.

"Yeah, a little. Do you want to sit in the shade or go inside?"

My eyes moved to his gloriously dark stare, and I gave a flirty smile, "Inside and upstairs."

"Okay, you go in. I'll clear the table and say my goodbyes. I won't be long."

Clinging to the bench, I took my legs over the seat, wobbling and slightly dizzy. My one glass of Pimms had turned into four or five, which seemed to happen too easily and regularly lately.

Gaining my balance in my high boots, I took a deep breath and hurriedly passed Mum and Dad, nearly falling into a bush on the way. "Oi, watch where you're going," I heard as I stumbled into someone in the doorway, knocking their drink all over me.

"Arrr, that's cold," I gasped, wiping the liquid from my chest with my palm. "I'm sorry," I muttered, looking for the nearest cloth on the kitchen unit.

"Here," they said, handing me a kitchen towel roll.

"Thanks." I dabbed myself, then looked up. My lungs squeezed extra tight, and my knees buckled. Not only did they go weak and shaky, but they also had me stumbling right over.

"Are you okay?" he said, quickly grabbing my waist and wrist, stopping me from hitting the floor.

I placed my feet firmly back down, not letting go of him until I knew I was safe from falling.

Exhaling profoundly, I gripped his forearms so tight that I could feel his skin beneath my black-painted nails, "Since when did you care, Kyle," I said curtly.

He rolled his eyes and sneered, pulling me closer to him, and all I could think was pull me closer. "Since you told me to ask if you were okay," he whispered.

"Wow, you must be drunk or stoned; whatever it is, you're completely out of your right mind," I gulped, and he stayed silent.

I moved back, letting go of him, but his hands remained where they were. I observed his tight grip on my arm and then gazed into his mysterious stare. "The last thing I want is for you to be nice to me. What are you even doing here? I thought you hated Olly?"

"Why's that?" Kyle asked, pulling his lip piercing between his teeth. I tried to step back and lose his grip, but he didn't budge. "Scared of me replacing your boyfriend?" he smirked, intimidating me with his grey glare and large pupils.

"That will never happen," I scorned, "Now, let go of me."

I pushed my free hand against his chest, and he tensed, using his strength to hold himself firmly to the floor. I looked away, sighing, glad no one else was in the kitchen, but at the same time wishing someone would rescue me. "Kyle, let go of me. I don't like it," I begged, taking my hand to his arm and pulling it from me. He was solid and intense, like a lion, and I was like a tiny kitten trying to break free from his clutches.

"Don't lie to yourself," he teased, and I burned him with my scowl, pushing him off as hard as I could.

I didn't think I was lying; I told myself I wasn't. But the truth was, I was frightened of being seen with Kyle by Olly. I was afraid of finding out if the way Kyle made me feel was too obvious to hide. That's why I was panicking. I hated that Kyle was the reason I suddenly couldn't breathe.

Something smashed, and I hit my back on the kitchen unit as someone pushed me aside. "Holy shit," I gasped, watching Olly tackling Kyle to the ground.

"Get off me," Kyle growled, forcefully pushing Olly from him, pulling on his clothes, "You'll only lose."

"Olly, Kyle, stop it," I yelled, not knowing what to do or who to shout at. I was horrified, clinging to the kitchen unit for dear life.

Olly looked at me, then back to Kyle, "Give it your best shot," he mocked. "It's the least you deserve."

Kyle sneered, climbed to his feet, brushed the creases from his top, and picked up his cap. He moved towards me, and I flinched a little as he put it on my head and winked. My stomach flipped, and my hands were shaking uncontrollably.

"Winner takes all?" Kyle said to Olly. Considering I didn't play many games, it was a phrase I understood.

"Ashley isn't a prize," Olly bit back, pushing Kyle into the kitchen cupboards.

"Is that right? You were trying to palm her off on me the other week. What difference does it make?"

Olly said nothing. He closed into Kyle and punched him. I winced, and tears swelled in my eyes. I wanted to shout for help, but I'd lost my voice. I'd lost control of my entire body.

"I'm not going to let you win anymore. I did nothing to you for you to be such a prick," Olly yelled, punching him, throwing them one after another as Kyle stood there unprotected, letting him.

Olly looked scarily possessed, and as Kyle's face started to bleed, I feared for him for a moment.

"No, you didn't," Kyle grunted, grabbing Olly by his arms and shoving him back as they moved around the kitchen. Kyle attacked him, punching left and right like Olly was nothing but a punching bag.

My fear switched sides.

He grabbed Olly by the collar, forcefully took him from his feet and onto his back, and winded him. Kyle took Olly's shirt into his fist and pulled him up, scolding him with his fierce glare, "Your whore of a mother did."

He punched Olly, thudded his back against the floor, and then let go. Kyle wiped the blood from his mouth and stood above Olly, looking down at him as he caught his breath.

I cried.

I was helpless.

I physically couldn't move.

"What the hell is going on here," Calvin shouted, storming through the kitchen door, helping Olly to his feet, and glaring at Kyle. "I have had enough of this behaviour towards my son. What did he ever do to you."

Kyle swallowed hard, tightened his fists and remained alone whilst I moved towards Olly.

"Oliver, baby, what happened?" Marie shrieked, sobbing as she walked in, seeing Olly bleeding with a split lip and his top covered in blood.

"She did it," Kyle spat.

"Did what?" Olly's dad said, and Marie suddenly looked worried. Kyle's stare moved to her, and my gaze followed.

"She ruined everything."

"Kyle," Marie faltered. "This is not the time or the place, don't," she warned, stepping towards her battered nephew and reaching out.

"Don't you touch me," he shouted, backing off. "My dad may like it, but I don't want you near me."

"What?" Calvin grudgingly said.

"Yeah, you heard me," Kyle scorned. "I walked in on your wife fucking my dad years ago."

Holy hell. I had fallen into one of the soap dramas my mum watched, and I had no way out of it unless I was to be killed off or kidnapped. A scene had broken out in the kitchen, and I was in front row seats. I was stunned, unsure of what to do or who to talk to.

Hatred surrounded Kyle as they scrutinised him like a burning witch in Salem, yet he was innocent *again*.

I knew I should stay beside Olly, but part of me was pulling towards the boy who needed some kind of protection. No wonder he turned out the way he had. No wonder he didn't trust anybody.

"Watch your mouth," Marie stepped in, slapping him around the face, embedding her prints into his bleeding cheek. Kyle took it and just stood there.

"Is it true?" Olly asked stern. He let go of my hand, which I hadn't noticed he was holding and moved in between Kyle and his mum. His breathing was erratic, and the colour had drained from his face, "Is it true?"

"Olly," she muttered. Looking up at her son, who stood tall above her, then at her husband, who shook his head with disgust.

Did he know? It didn't seem like it, even if he stood remarkably calm, mute and shaking.

"Kyle, there you are," his dad said, entering. I gulped, knowing things were about to get worse. I needed to leave, but I couldn't feel my feet. "Someone told me you were smoking around the front. We have spoken about this."

"You rat bastard!" Calvin yelled, running towards him, thudding him against the kitchen door.

He hit Kyle's dad with a blow, who tried to defend himself as he threw punch after punch. His fists quickly swelled and were covered in blood, most likely cracking with each hit. Anger surged through him, and he wouldn't stop. The adrenaline in him wouldn't let him.

I was frightened. All I could hear was screaming, shouting and crying, and I couldn't work out which one I was doing.

People had begun to leave, dragging their curious small children out of the front door. And I could see the horror on Nate and Zoe's faces as my dad ushered them back outside, calling my name, telling me to follow.

"Stop," Marie begged, and Calvin paused, looking at the beaten man within his grasp. He took a deep breath before launching one last hard punch. He walked out of the kitchen, slammed the front door behind him, and Marie followed.

It fell silent. The commotion had stopped, and my ears were ringing a little. I was piecing together what had happened, working hard as if it didn't make sense, but it did; Kyle hated Olly because of what he knew. A secret he had kept this entire time. The aggression, the substance abuse, the rebelling, I understand it all. He was a volcano, having sat waiting to erupt, and I witnessed the final blow.

I felt sorry for him.

I loosened my grip and moved away from the unit, looking at Kyle and Olly, who were side by side, hostile, cut and bruised.

"Are you okay?" I asked, although I was unsure as to who I was asking.

Kyle glanced at me, then back at his dad, who had blood pouring from his face. My mum was helping him as he looked close to blacking out. Kyle picked up a vodka bottle, sat on the table and opened it.

He took a large sip, exhaled the warmth rising in his chest, and muttered, "You always wanted me to be like you, Dad. Well, I kissed my cousin's girlfriend, and look where it got me. You were right; I'm nothing but a violent cheating prick like you."

My eyes tightened, and the sigh I heard from Olly was deafening, as was the door slamming behind Kyle. My clammy palms clenched, and my mind ran a million miles per second.

"Ashley, you didn't?" Mum said.

"Ashley?" Olly mumbled as a tear rolled down his cheek.

"Olly..." I paused.

CHAPTER THIRTY-THREE

"Olly," I yelled as he stormed upstairs. I followed as fast as my boots would take me, screeching his name through my cries. With a thud, his bedroom door slammed in my face.

"Please, Olly, it's not how it sounds. Please let me explain." I slammed my hand on the door, trying the handle, but it didn't move.

"There is nothing to explain. You kissed another boy. You kissed my fucking cousin," he shouted back.

"It's not like that. It was a game at Alex's house. I didn't know it was him, and I didn't know he was your cousin." I wiped the tears falling from my cheek. "Please let me in."

The handle loosened, and the door slowly opened. Olly's lip was swelling, cut and blue, and his knuckles looked painful. I wanted to care for him, aid him, but I'd hurt him even more; I knew I had. If I'd learnt anything, heartache is more painful than anything physical, and I couldn't just fix it with a plaster either.

He looked at me with sorrowful eyes, burning me inquisitively, "Was that the only kiss?"

I panicked, swallowing to ease my dry throat. My hands ran through my hair, and tears soaked my face. I could taste them. Something was wrong with my tongue; my words were missing. I stuttered and stumbled with nothing to say as Olly didn't need an answer; he already knew it.

"You've changed. I don't know who you are anymore," Olly muttered.

"No, I haven't," I sobbed. "I love you. I'm still the same Ashley you met; if anything, I'm a better person, and you did that. I'm the Ashley you love."

"I want to believe you, but I don't." Olly puffed out his chest, sucking it back in as he choked on his words. "I knew love hurt, but you've ripped my heart out. I can't do this. Not after everything I have just heard."

I reached out to him, but he stepped back. My lip quivered, and my head shook, forcing my words out as my emotions bound me, "What are you saying?"

Olly put his hand in his pocket and pulled out a cord bracelet. "I planned to give this to you tomorrow before I left as a promise we would never part, but now, you can have it as a memento."

I cried, "No, Olly."

I ugly cried.

He took my hand and opened my palm, placing the red and black bracelet into it. I didn't look at it; I squeezed it tightly, "I have too much to figure out, and I don't want to think about you being here with Kyle," Olly said.

"I'm not going to be here with Kyle. It's you I want. I need you, Olly. Please, you can't leave me now. I won't let you."

"If you truly love me, you will because this is what I want."

"Don't say that. I know that's not true," I wept. "What about everything we have been through?"

"Ashley, none of that matters. There is nothing you can do or say to change the truth."

"I love you," I begged, "That's the truth."

I was out of breath and words. I didn't want to give in, but I could feel it in my gut, Olly was inches away, yet he was disappearing, closing the door on me.

"I love you, Ashley, but I think I know where your heart lies."

I broke down and fell to my knees. I tried to figure out what to say, how to fix and undo what I had done, and how to banish my unwanted feelings for Kyle.

I hated him.

I wished I had never met him.

I loved Olly, and he was the one who had my heart.

"Promise me something, Ashley," Olly then mumbled.

I raised my head to him as he crouched down to me. He kissed my forehead, and I knew it was goodbye. It was just like the movies, heart-breaking and sudden. "Promise me you won't do anything stupid."

Olly stood back up, and the following cries streaming down my face weren't because I was sad and heartbroken; they were from anger and devastation. Olly's last thoughts were not how he loved me but how I was still that girl he needed to protect. That sad, lonely girl from the park. And boy, he was wrong, and his words made it so. If I could put up with his secrets and Kyle, I knew I could prove I was stronger than he thought.

I stood up, straightened out my dress, smoothed my hair and said, "I promise." He shut the door on me, saying nothing more.

The white paintwork stared me in the face. My insides screamed, cried and abused me as I clung to the doorframe until I regained control.

I turned and leaned against the door, sensing he was doing the same on the other side. I'd broken his heart, and he had mine, shattered into a million fragments, and each piece missed him already.

I was guilty of kissing Kyle, but Olly was far from innocent. From the beginning, he had lied. He was leaving, yet let me fall for him anyway. I'd given myself to him in every way I could.

He had changed my life as well as saved it.

Yet still, Kyle wouldn't have come into my life without Olly, and it was his fault for me feeling so confused. Things wouldn't have been so complicated without him and his stupid plan.

Instead of talking, he shut me out and banished me from his life, and all so quickly, so easily. I told myself that when the tears weren't so raw, and the pain wasn't so intense, the only way through the heartbreak was by holding onto the frustration I had surging me at that moment. I would prove him wrong and not be the sad little girl he thought I was, that everyone thought I was. Not anymore.

I would prove him wrong and stay away from Kyle.

Wiping my eyes, I slowly walked down the stairs. I hesitated as I walked to the front door, observing everything around me, the memories, the smell, the layout, and the photos. I preserved them in my mind for safekeeping, doubting I'd be coming back in. "Bye, Olly," I whispered and shut the door behind me.

Every step away I took was painful. I couldn't breathe, and I could barely see. The further I went, the more my heart bled, pounding hard in my chest. I couldn't feel Olly with me anymore, and I had lost all sense of purpose.

There were only tears.

CHAPTER THIRTY-FOUR

Olly was gone. I watched him drive past, and he didn't look up at my window. I needed him to look me in the eye and give me hope, but it didn't come. He hated me, and I had to live with that. The only problem was I didn't know how to.

I hadn't stepped foot out of my bedroom for the past week. My conversations with Mum, Dad and Zoe had been minimal, and my stomach was rumbling hard, but even the plates of food on my desk seemed too good for me.

The first boy I had ever loved had a broken heart because of me. I didn't deserve anything but to feel the same.

I kept thinking of ways I could have changed the end of our story, the conversations we should have had, and the confessions he deserved once I met Kyle.

How could I have been so stupid to risk the one good thing in my life?

The day I saw him standing on my driveway, my world stopped. The first kiss he planted on my cheek made everything seem possible, and for a while, I conquered everything. I faced my fears and my enemies whilst learning to love myself. I saw what was important beyond popularity and being skinny. None of that mattered anymore, and with Olly by my side, all I wanted was to be ordinary. I wasn't invisible to him. He saw right through me when I was hiding from everyone else, and once I let my guard down, I wasn't afraid anymore. I had never felt the way I did around Olly. He was a stranger who stole my heart, the prince who rescued me.

I was going to miss how he sent sparks of static dancing over my skin every time he touched me. Our time together was magical and enchanting. I could only explain the shivers of pure ecstasy we experienced as nothing comparable in this world.

What I read in all those stories was true. True love was the most beautiful thing you could experience, even if it slapped you in the face. But watching it crumble and feeling your heart crack was the hardest, most painful thing I'd ever endure. Olly and I were over, but I didn't see it as the end. Time and distance were not on our side, but anything could happen in two years; look what happened in a few months.

The for-sale sign outside his house and his dad moving out may have been the end for his parents, but what I had with Olly was different. I knew it was. I'd see him again. He'd be different, and so would I. I couldn't say how I'd feel when I did, be it tomorrow, next week, next month or years to come. Either way, different days were ahead of us. Time is what we need. Time is what *I* needed to figure life out.

*

"Ashley," Mum gently said with a knock at my door.

I let the tennis ball fall back into my hand and sat up. "What is it?" I said, and she walked in.

"I, Ashley," she stuttered, and it clenched my chest. Why had things got so difficult between us? There was a wall, a big eight-foot brick wall I wanted to bash down standing in the way. If only I had the strength.

"I'm sorry," she muttered as her lip quivered. "I'm so sorry about everything. I shouldn't have kept Olly's secret from you, I was wrong, and I know it now. You are in here like this because of me."

I bowed my head, gripping the ball tightly, "No, I'm not; this isn't all your fault. I did most of it. I'm sure if

I knew, I still would have fallen for Olly anyway. I'm young and naïve, remember." I cried.

Jeez, I was so fed up with crying. My eyes were burning, swollen and puffy, and pouring like taps the instant I allowed myself to talk or feel anything. I was not strong; I was grieving and had more to come before I felt more optimistic.

Mum sat beside me and grabbed my hand, "You're not. You are your mother's daughter, unconditionally loving and passionate. You see the world as a fairy tale, as you have always done, just like Zoe does. When I was a teenager, I also fell in love, and look where he is now, outside in the garden." She smiled. "It doesn't make you naïve. You have a lot to learn; unfortunately, heartbreak is one of the most agonising things to go through."

"How would you know?" I said, brushing my tears with the back of my hand.

"Trust me, even before your dad, I had my heart broken. I also dressed a little like you too."

"No, you didn't," I snorted.

"Oh, I did. Your grandma hit the roof the day I went home with a piercing and an older boyfriend."

"I don't believe you."

"I wish she were here to tell you, but it's true. We are more alike than you think. The mum you hate, who I am now, is who I became once I learnt all the lessons and became a parent. I'm sorry I'm not the type of mum you want, but I'm still learning, failing, and trying." She brushed her hand down my hair and began to sob.

"You're not failing," I stuttered, pulling her tightly into my arms. "I haven't been the easiest, but I'm learning too. I need to find out who I am and what I'm supposed to be doing. It's hard trying to be perfect."

"You're not perfect, Ashley; no one is. There is no such thing; the sooner you believe that, the better. You'll get there. I promise."

"Mum..." Zoe said, walking into my room. She looked at Mum and me and backed out.

"Come here, squidge," I said, reaching my arm out.

Zoe ran over, climbing between Mum and me, cuddling us both, "I'm going to miss Nate too," she said in her squeaky voice.

"Oh honey, I know," Mum said.

"I'll never have a boyfriend again."

"Oh god, not you as well," I cried and giggled simultaneously.

"What, he's a boy and my friend," she said, and I looked into her innocent, shimmering eyes.

"That's the best way."

TWO WEEKS LATER

"Good luck, sweetheart; I hope you have the best first day," Mum said, handing me my bag as I climbed out of the car.

I put it on the seat, brushed down my flared black jeans, adjusted my thick chunky belt and straightened my red vest top at the waist.

"Are you sure I look okay?" I asked, bending down to her, and she nodded with a smile.

"Oh, that reminds me, I got you something." She leaned back and took something from her jean pocket. "This was mine. I want you to have it, seeing as it's a fashion trend now."

I took a red sweatband from her, and my eyes glossed over, "For real?"

"It will match your outfit."

I bit my bottom lip, climbed back in, and hugged her, "Thanks, Mum. I love it."

"You're welcome," she said, running her hand down my newly chunky, highlighted straightened hair, more reds and dark blues this time. "Right, now go, don't be late."

I grabbed my bag, waved, and fiddled with the sweatband. Adjusting the cord bracelet Olly gave me, I held the letters A and O in my hand, which hung on small tan cubes. I took a deep breath and blinked, keeping my eyes closed for a second before placing the sweatband on top of it.

Shaking myself off, I looked at the vast school building, listened to the bell and walked up the steps.

Here goes the last, first day of school.

I walked down the corridors, and panic suddenly hit me. Pretty girls were strutting down the hall, clinging to each other, with short skirts, heels and flawless make-up-filled faces. Sporty boy's wolf whistles followed behind, making them gush.

Catching my breath, I stepped back, trying to escape, bumping into someone behind me.

"Gosh, I'm sorry," I said, picking up some books.

"It's fine," a girl said, adjusting her glasses and curly hair.

She took the books from me and clung them tightly to her chest. She wore pink knee-high socks and a skirt and cardigan, an outfit I would have tried back in the days with Lauren. She made it look good. My smile grew, then altered as I saw her glance at the girls nearing us.

I wish I were invisible. I wish I were invisible. Please don't say anything to me. Please, please. I thought. Oh god, where was Olly when I needed him?

"Nice socks, Ams," the middle girl said with a smile, blowing a bubble with her gum. Her eyes rolled to me, and her strut slowed. I looked to the right, left, and then my feet. She looked me up and down, and I gulped, gripping my bag strap harder and harder and then she stopped; all three of them stopped.

"Hi, you're new. I'm Nikki," she said. "You're pretty, and I like your outfit." I was mute for far too long.

"Erm, thanks," I muttered, looking at her, noting her long shiny blonde hair, flawless makeup and piercing blue eyes. She lifted my wrist, looked at my sweatband and nodded, "I like this. Rebecca will copy this, won't she, girls," Nikki laughed, looking to the others, then let go. I put my hand into my jean pocket and tentatively grinned. Who is Rebecca, and what is happening?

"What's your name?" Another girl asked.

"Oh, erm, Ashley."

"Have a good first day, Ashley. If you need anything or get lost, just ask," Nikki said, and they turned and continued on their way.

"Oh my god," I muttered under my breath.

"Are you okay? You look like you saw a ghost," the girl standing beside me warily said.

I closed my mouth and licked my dry lips. "Yeah, I think I am," I said. "I'm not used to girls like that being nice to me."

"You're from Bailey, aren't you?"

"How do you know?"

"So was I," she said, shrugging her shoulders. "Come on. I'll show you to the reception. You'll need your timetable."

I smiled, and my feet slowly moved, "I'm Ashley, not Ash."

"Amelie, but everyone calls me Ams."

*

I had survived the first half of the day without complaint, with more hellos and waves than I ever received at Bailey in one morning. And with my first two hours of media studies done and a new friend, I was less sceptical about how the next two years would go. I had English in the afternoon, which I had with Alex. I hadn't seen her yet as she'd been off at lunch arranging some football stuff, which I didn't feel like joining at the moment. I needed to find my bearings first.

I entered the dining hall, and there were tables full of teenagers. It was mayhem. In typical circumstances, I was prey walking into the claws of predators, but Oakley was not like Bailey, where the sports lads were on one side, the popular on the other, with the geeks in the middle. There was a small order, but everyone was talking to everyone. It was like the school was breaking the expectations of high school and college clicks. I wasn't sure what to make of it but went with the flow anyway, unsure if it was because it was the first day.

With Alex, Morgan and everyone all together elsewhere and not seeing Amelie, I didn't know where to go, so I stood in line to buy a sandwich and a bottle of water. I thanked the lunch lady and took my change, turning to the room I used to hate stepping into, where all my worst high school memories happened.

Taking a deep breath, I went to the empty table near the door and sat down. Placing my headphones in, I put my music up loud and listened to Pink whilst skimming through my notes from Media studies.

I was in a world of my own, ignorant of anyone and anything around me, exactly how I liked it.

Something pulled at my headphones a few songs in, taking my attention. A tray dropped down, and a casted hand caught my stare. I bit my bottom lip as I watched him put one of my headphones in his ear. He nodded and raised his pierced eyebrows with approval.

With a roll of my eyes and clenching in my stomach, I cautiously said, "Kyle, what are you doing here?" I wasn't even shocked.

"Nice to see you too," he said with a mouthful of food. Kyle smiled, nodding his head to my music and drumming his fingers on the table. His glorious grey stare swallowed me whole, and I sank into oblivion, not knowing where I was going or where I'd end up. I had so many questions.

"Seriously, why are you here?"

Kyle took a sip of my drink and then leaned back, adjusting his skateboard on his lap and spinning the wheels. "Come on, did you think Olly would let you go to a new school without protection? Give the guy some credit. We may hate each other, but there are some things we have in common."

"You're lying. Olly hates me," I said. If what Kyle was saying was true, it was odd but sweet that Olly was protecting me from afar, keeping me safe. But since when did the prince of the story send his princess into the arms of another charming? Especially when he loathed the idea. And which one was the prince, and who was the villain?

"Believe what you like," he shrugged. "It's not like you would care if I'm here of my own accord, is it? We both know I don't have a nice bone in my body, so let's say it was part of Olly's plan, for argument's sake."

Moving my tongue around my mouth, I hesitated, unsure which scenario to believe or which one was more likely. Either way, he was messing with me, and I wasn't going to give him the satisfaction of letting him know I needed to know the answer. I tilted my head, fiddled with my water bottle label, and said, "Your politeness isn't what you share in common, so what is it?"

Kyle leaned forward, looked around and then back at me, "We're both very protective and committed to getting what we want," he paused. He stroked his fingers over my sweatband and whispered, "I'm just a little harder to break and seeing as he's out of the picture, I will do whatever it takes to win this little game he got me playing."

"Good luck with that," I sneered. "There is one problem, though." I rose from my seat, took my headphone out of Kyle's ear and looked down at him as he pulled his lip piercing between his teeth, crossing his arms over his body.

"And what is that?"

"From the minute Olly got you involved, this became more than a game, and he clearly never intended to win," I paused. "What makes you think I want anything to do with you? I'm not going to do as you tell me and fall into your arms as you planned. It's not what Olly would want, and you know it. Getting in between you two is the last thing I want, and I certainly don't want to play silly games. Besides, if I did, you would only lose."

Kyle smirked. "I don't expect you to. Olly said specifically to be your friend, but he should have known better. When I'm forbidden to do something, I only want it twice as much."

I smiled and frowned simultaneously, lost for words. As Kyle took my fingers into his hand, I gulped, pulled back, looked around, and then fell back into his gaze.

I hated him. I didn't want to fall for him. He ruined my life, so why did he feel like he was my next wrong decision?

I refused him to be.

"Well, not everyone gets what they want. I should know," I said, turning my back on Kyle as I walked out of the hall.

"I'll take that as my first challenge Ashley Prince," he yelled behind me.

I held tightly onto my breath, denying him to take it from me and my cheeks flushed. Goosepimples then rose, my ears pricked, and I was suddenly looking across the school grounds, following the sound of his wheels tick-tacking against the floor.

I looked at him, and he glanced at me. He winked, and I gasped.

Oh god, I was the villain.

The End

ACKNOWLEDGEMENTS

I am entirely thankful to my husband and my four children. They have adapted to my new passion and allow me to write every morning and evening around work, school and our busy lifestyles.

It may sound crazy, but in some ways, I am thankful for the pandemic. With the craziness around us, I wanted to escape reality, and 2004 is where I ended up. Headphones in, fingers tapping away, mind reliving my teenage years. My first teenage romance, The Boy Next Door, was created, with its sequel, The Skater Boy, soon after.

To the noughties, thank you for the iconic music and fashion trends. After putting a soundtrack to each chapter, my Amazon playlist now lives in this decade.

Avril, you have been and always will be my biggest hero and a true inspiration.

Thanks to my friends and family, who continue to give me their ongoing support. You spur me on, listen to my ideas, read my first copies, and give me the honest feedback I need. You are a part of my writing process and help my dreams come true.

Finally, thank you to those who read this series. I hope it makes you smile and brings back fond memories of high school and your teenage years, which we now consider the best years of our lives.

I'm saying the same thing to my children, who don't believe me, just as I didn't when mine said it. Oh, how times have changed.

ABOUT THE AUTHOR

I'm a romance author whose dreams feel too big to achieve but are my goals regardless. And here I am, completing my second series.

See, you do succeed when you never give up!

You will find me writing or reading; either way, I tend to have a book in my hand. Most likely a raunchy drop-dead gorgeous erotic romance novel that takes me from my busy lifestyle of parenting and work.

When not typing away, I love to spend time with my family and laugh with my friends. I enjoy keeping fit, going to the cinema and love Mexican food and white chocolate. I'm a big fan of the Marvel universe, Netflix, and all things Chris Hemsworth, but let's face it, who isn't?

Over the past few years, I have learnt that everybody has a story to tell. Whether it's based on experiences or something fictional, magical, or an alter ego, you name it, it's worth shouting about. You never know what can happen overnight; why waste time waiting for the inevitable when you have the reigns? Find your dream, your passion, whatever sets your heart on fire and go and get it and don't let anything or anyone get in your way. I didn't.

I've only been writing for three years and will never look back. This dream brought me memories, tears, laughter and courage. I found a passion I never knew I had, and now my stories are coming to life, with plenty more to follow.

Find me on social media for more updates and other published work.

https://linktr.ee/emmaollin

Spontaneous Series
Spontaneously Reckless
Spontaneously Torn

The Boy Next Door Series
The Boy Next Door
The Skater Boy

Coming soon
Drowning in Reckless Lies – Mr Jones' Story

Printed in Great Britain
by Amazon